Ja

CROSSING PATHS

W.H.Wax Publishing, LLC

CROSSING PATHS
New Edition

Written by
Jason Horn
© 2023 Jason R. Horn
jasonhornbooks.com
whwaxpublishing.com/jasonhorn

Published by
W.H.Wax Publishing, LLC.
Jordan, Arkansas 72519
info@whwaxpublishing.com
whwaxpublishing.com

LCCN: 2023946040

ISBN: 9781662944314

Proudly printed in the United States of America

All rights reserved. No part of this publication may be reproduced, distributed, or transmitted in any form or by any means, including photocopying, recording, or other electronic or mechanical methods, without the prior written permission of the Author, except with brief quotations embodied in critical reviews and certain other noncommercial uses permitted by copyright law. For permission requests, contact the author at whwaxpublishing.com/jasonhorn.

DEDICATION

I dedicate this book to my parents, Kenny Horn, and Debbie Webb Horn, who stuck by me through all my mess ups and stupid mistakes in life. Both parents loved to read and did so daily. Diabetes caused my mother to lose her sight, but she never lost her passion to read. She started getting books on tape and that's where you could find her every day, sitting on her sun porch, listening to a good book. I lost my mother on July 2, 2018, but before she left us, my dad had the pleasure of sitting with her for a few hours each night and reading her my book.

My father is my hero and the man I idolize. He set aside his wishes and missed out on things he wanted to do and things he enjoyed in life to take care of my mother. Never faltering, he has supported me and been the patriarch of our family. He has passed along too many books to count and was a driving force behind me to write this book.

I also dedicate this book to the best friend a boy could ever have: Terry Layne Bennett. He was my very first friend, and for the next twenty-six years, we stayed that way. You will not find his name as any character in this book. I couldn't figure out how to make a character to explain how great he was or how much he meant to me in life. Growing up two blocks apart, every day was an adventure for us, and I can guarantee when this adventure ends, our next one will begin.

A very special thanks to author Penny Richards for her guidance, encouragement, and help in finishing my book. Her knowledge is endless, and she taught me that the most important lesson about writing is rewriting.

This book was something I have wanted to write for a long time. In high school, I was the kid who hated to read and fought tooth and nail to avoid it. I loved to write as a young man and did often. I took creative writing in high school where my teacher, Jan Booker, encouraged me to expand my mind and not be afraid to try something new.

During this time, I was taking an Adult Education class under Deb Tackett. One of our assignments for the semester was to go to the Primary school and read to the first, second, and third graders. So once every week, I would read to the little kids and have the best time watching their faces light up as I took them on our adventures from a book.

I would catch myself reading the newspaper or a short story in a magazine. Eventually finding myself holding a book, then another, and another, and so on. As my love for reading grew, I could still hear Jan saying, "Don't be afraid to try something new." With my love for writing and my new love for reading, it made sense to try something different and new. After years of thought and procrastination, I sat down and put pen to paper and created what you are about to read.

I must thank my beautiful wife, Allison Ball Horn, who helped with most of the typing and listened to me gripping that it wasn't fast enough. My little sister, Sydney Horn Wright, who helped with typing and editing, and my aunt, Jana Crank, who helped with editing.

Table of Contents

Chapter 1: Revenge — 1
Chapter 2: Webb — 4
Chapter 3: Andy — 16
Chapter 4: Saying Goodbye — 22
Chapter 5: Moving West — 28
Chapter 6 Hell's Valley — 41
Chapter 7: Making Plans — 59
Chapter 8: The Webb Clan — 67
Chapter 9: The New Place — 76
Chapter 10: New Hands — 84
Chapter 11: Texas Bound — 95
Chapter 12: The China Man — 103
Chapter 13: Hillbillies and Hog Farmers — 116
Chapter 14: The Wolf — 131
Chapter 15: Cowboys and Indians — 142
Chapter 16: The Trail Home — 153
Chapter 17: Miss Dana — 164
Chapter 18: Mexican Banditos — 174
Chapter 19: UAV and Quanah — 183

Chapter 20: Dry Gulched	203
Chapter 21: Cold Trailing	214
Chapter 22: Irish Bob	223
Chapter 23: Boggy Creek	237
Chapter 24: No More War	249
Chapter 25: The Texas Heat	268
Chapter 26: Wagon Train	279
Chapter 27: Chasing Hope	288
Chapter 28: A Hero's Welcome	296
Chapter 29: Plans for the Future	309
Chapter 30: The Race	329
Chapter 31: Lover Boy	348
Chapter 32: Don't Fight Fate	364
Chapter 33: The Surrender	376

Chapter One

1855 Pennsylvania

The weather was still cool for the most part and cold some nights, but the trio kept a steady push and enjoyed the new sights none of them had ever seen. The gray days of winter were giving way to the blue sky of spring. Webb was counting down the days of the two months they had planned for the trip, and each night, he would add up the day's mileage and add to the growing tally.

As the trio stopped for camp at the end of a long day, they all set out to do their own tasks they had each grown accustomed to. Webb was watering the horses and singing a little tune, which is why he never heard the man walk up behind him. A dirty hand covered his mouth, and another held a gun. A familiar voice said, "You make a sound and I kill your Pa first while you watch." Webb knew the voice belonged to Carl Clovis Sr. and knew he meant every word.

"Wakefield! I've got your boy and if you are not out here in five seconds, I'm gonna kill him like you did mine!"

Andy walked out of the brush with an armful of wood he had gathered for the fire. Standing there in dirty clothes and a face that hadn't seen a razor in a couple of weeks was Carl Clovis. He had Webb by the back of the neck with one hand and waving a pistol at Andy with the other.

He had a crazed look in his eyes and was sweating in the cool evening air. Webb was looking at Andy with fright on his face and Andy felt fear and rage boiling inside at the sight of his son being held at gunpoint.

"Where is that no account friend of yours?" asked Clovis.

"Dane, come out here where he can see you!" yelled Andy.

Dane came out from the backside of the wagon, looking straight down the barrel of his rifle.

"You put that gun down or I will kill this kid!" screamed Clovis.

Clovis was pointing the gun from Andy to Dane and back and forth while keeping his other hand on Webb. What he didn't notice was Webb reaching in the waste line of his pants. He was jerking Webb around so much he never noticed the extra movement from Webb. Not until he felt the sharp stinging pain in his side did he realize what was happening. Webb had pulled out a little knife and with one backwards swing, the tip found Clovis' tender side and led the way for the rest of the blade.

Clovis screamed and let go of Webb's neck. When he did, Webb hit the ground, trying to scramble away. Before Webb could even look back, two gun shots sounded and nothing, but a grunt was heard from Clovis as he fell back into the cold, clear water of the creek.

Dane's shot hit him in the right eye and Andy's draw and shoot had been smooth and perfect, which helped place his shot right in the middle of his forehead.

Webb looked back at Clovis as his body's new holes turned the clear mountain water pink.

Webb dropped his knife and ran to Andy with tears already flowing down his cheeks. Andy could do nothing but hold his son as he let out hurt, pain, and fear all at once.

Dane told Andy he would take care of the body so he could stay with Webb. Andy got a fire going, and they just sat there in silence for the rest of the night. Webb didn't even eat a bite of food that night. He just wrapped himself in his blanket and let the stars and wind put him to sleep.

Through the night, Andy and Dane both listened to Webb's moans and watched as he tossed and turned in his sleep as he fought his new demons that came to visit. Andy didn't know how his son would handle all the events that had happened over the last couple of weeks. As he and Dane sat watching his son fight the night and the demons that came with it, they remembered back to how it all started.

Chapter Two

Normalville, Pennsylvania 1855

It was a normal night in Normalville, Pennsylvania. Nothing much ever changed except on the occasion someone new arrived or someone old left, and this was just what sparked the conversation tonight. Randy Scott was at his nightly duty pouring drinks and taking care of customers at his saloon, The Thirsty Pig.

Wes and Glenn, the Grimes brothers, were talking to Randy about Dane Tressler, Andrew Wakefield, and his son Webb leaving Normalville. The Wakefield's had been around since the founding of the town. Andrew's parents owned the hotel, which was left to him when they passed away four months apart. Andy's young wife, Melissa, ran the hotel until the good Lord called her home. With Melissa gone, Andy sold the hotel to do what he always dreamed of, which was owning a cattle ranch.

When Andy was a young man, before marriage, he had asked his father for a loan to buy a few guns to sell out of the hotel, and his father did so without question. He had also given him a room in the back to work on guns. Andy had seen and worked on some of the most beautiful weapons known to man and loved every second. Over the years, he had built quite a collection for himself and his son, Webb. Now, that part of Andy's life was going with the hotel.

"He said it's just time to move on and start a new adventure in life," Randy said, talking about Andy. "It didn't take much to convince ol' Dane, either. He said he's had an itch for traveling and was ready to scratch it. Andy told me he and Dane were heading west. They figured to head west until they got to a spot they both had picked out on a map. After that, they plan on buying a spread and heading on down to Texas where the horses run wild, and the cattle are plenty."

Wes let out a whistle. "Sounds like ol' Dane might get the adventure he's looking for before it's over."

"Yes, but it also sounds like they better have plenty of cash on hand, 'cause depending on where they stop, land ain't always for the taking." Glenn said, "Plus, catching horses, buying cattle, and then driving them to your home range takes hands, and hiring hands takes money."

Randy just gave a chuckle. "You really think after selling the hotel and the gun shop, on top of what his parents left him, that Andy ain't got the money?"

Glenn said, "Now that you say it like that, I guess he can probably make do."

"I guess Dane ain't quite set up in the same fashion, but I bet what he got for this store, plus the bundle his parents left him, will buy him a real nice place," said Wes.

While those three talked at one end of the bar, two men sat by themselves at the other end and listened. One was a weasel of a man (if you wanted to call him a man) named B.K. Moore. He wasn't worth the air wasted to keep him alive. Even worse, he was Normalville's deputy. Sheriff Dull Crinch himself handpicked him.

Dull was worse than B.K. He strutted around like he was God's gift to the world, when in reality he only had the job because of the mayor and the town council. Mayor Carl Clovis led the council to believe he was more than he really was. Clovis had helped get him the job, and then once the council realized what they got, it was too late. Ever since then, the town had been suffering at the hands of Crinch and his understudy, Moore. They did as they pleased when they pleased, holding out money from the town by putting fines and bail money in their pockets. They carried out anything Clovis needed that was underhanded, behind the scenes, and in the dark of night.

The man sitting with Moore was Clovis's son Carl Clovis, Jr. He was good at three things: drinking, being lazy, and spending Daddy's money. So, when

Moore and Jr. heard about all that cash that was to be heading out of town, they naturally decided not to let it leave. Especially since Andrew had refused his father's offer to buy the hotel and gun shop. It was extra insulting when Tressler told Carl Sr., he would burn his store to the ground before he sold it to him.

There were three main reasons Dane and Andrew made their decision to leave Normalville, the Sherriff, his no-good deputy, and Carl Clovis, Sr. They were tired of seeing their town go down the drain because it scared everyone to stand up to Clovis. He owned half the town and was determined to own the other half before it was over.

After hearing all they wanted, Jr. and Moore got up and left the bar. Once outside, and in the saddle, they headed to the south side of town. Wakefield and his son, Webb, were on the south side of town making their last-minute checks, making sure everything was ready for the march west.

Andy and Webb were talking about the upcoming trip while covering the last few pieces of furniture that were being left behind. After talking it over a couple of months before, they left all the furniture in the house for the people who had purchased the home. They knew they could not take it west, and they did not want to have a sale. So, after careful talk, they decided it was just what Melissa would want. They had sold the home to a young man named Christopher Clark. Clark was to be married to Kenzie Grace. Kenzie was the daughter of Daniel and Kate Grace, who had bought the hotel from Andy a year before. Christopher and Kenzie were to be married and live in Normalville, where Chris was to take over the hotel from his new in-laws. Andy and Webb could think of nothing better to give the new couple than a home full of furniture and all the trimmings.

"Pa, do you think Ma is smiling down on us from Heaven for doing this?"

"Son, there is no doubt in my mind as to the answer to that. Your ma would have skinned us both alive when we got to Heaven if we would have done anything different."

Andy looked down at his son and smiled. Every time he looked at Webb, all he could see was his wife. They had named Webb after Melissa's family, the Webbs. He not only had the name, but he had the look. The Webb clan put a mark on you, and it was plain as day to anyone with eyes. Webb was your average ten-year-old, average height, weight, and slim build. What set him apart were his eyes. Ice blue most days with a hint of green and darker blue on others. Even at a young age, his eyes changed with his mood. When he looked at you, no matter what the mood, you forgot you were looking into the eyes of a child. They were piercing.

"I guess that just about does it," said Andy. "How about you go on up and hop in the bed while I go out and check on the horses and wagon team. We will get up in the morning and go have breakfast at Mrs. Bunny's café before we start our last day in town."

Webb gave a smile. "I love Bunny's cooking, Pa, so you can count me in."

While Webb got ready and headed upstairs for bed, Andy went to the barn to check on the stock. All the horses were looking at him when he walked in, plus four big oxen. He had bought the oxen just to pull the wagon. Andy figured to let Webb ride one of the four horses when he wanted and trail the other three along with Dane's two spares. He and Dane would swap out on the wagon, and he might even teach Webb a thing or two about handling a team in the low flat places.

Andy gave all the animals another bait of good grain, plus a little more hay. He wanted them all in top shape for the trip to come. The going was going to be long and hard, and not just on the stock. With that in mind, Andy turned out the lamp and headed back inside.

He walked to the front door and headed for the kitchen to drink him a cup of coffee. As he poured himself a cup of the strong black liquid, he replaced the pot on the stovetop and turned around. Standing there looking at him, guns drawn, were Deputy Moore and Carl Jr.

Andy didn't have to ask why they were here. With two pieces of trash, like the Deputy and Carl Jr., it was plain to see. They wanted all that money he had for their trip.

"Hello boys, nice of you to stop by for a cup of coffee," said Andy.

Carl smiled and said, "We ain't here for coffee and you know it."

Moore chimed in, "Yeah, and you know it."

"Well then, why are you here? It's a little late for a social call and I no longer work on guns, so I guess you two should leave before this gets bad."

Carl chuckled, "In case you haven't noticed, it's already bad."

"Yeah, it's already bad," said the deputy.

Andy looked at the Deputy and smiled. Moore asked, "What's that smile for?"

"I was just wondering if you had ever had a thought of your own," replied Andy.

The look on the deputy's face was answer enough without a reply, but he gave one anyway.

"What does that mean?" Andy let out a sigh and said, "I guess not."

"Shut up, both of you!" yelled Jr. "I ain't here for no talk. I'm here for the money. Now where is it?"

Andy exclaimed, "What money are you talking about?"

"You know what money. I want everything, all of it. I want the money you got for the hotel, the gun shop, the house, and anything else."

Andy said, "Well, then you'll have to talk to Mr. Grey at the bank. He has all my money."

Jr. yelled, "That's a lie and you know it! I'm giving you one more chance to hand it over, or I swear I'll kill you. I might even let the deputy here cut on you and make you suffer a little before I do it."

Moore replied once again, "Yeah, make you suffer a little."

The next thing any of them heard was the hammer being pulled back on a gun, and the words from a small voice, "Mr. Clovis, if you and the deputy don't drop your guns and leave Pa be, then I swear I'll kill you." The look on everyone's face was shock and surprise, even Andy's.

"Ok kid, now listen, you just take it real easy and nothing's gonna happen. Now, I'm gonna lower my gun and turn around real slow, so as I can talk to you, ok?" Jr. lowered his gun and told the deputy, "You keep your gun on Wakefield."

"Yeah, I'm gonna keep my gun on Wakefield." Andy and Jr. both just shook their heads.

When Jr. turned around to look, standing there in the dark shadows was ten-year-old Webb pointing a pistol at him. The pistol didn't really make him nervous. It was the fact the kid was holding it rock steady, pointed right at his chest.

"Hello, kid," said Jr.

"Hello, Mr. Clovis."

"It seems like we have a misunderstanding here, Son. We come by to talk real friendly with your pa, and he got downright mean with us. That's all this is."

"That's a lie and you know it! I heard you tell my pa you wanted our money, or you was gonna kill him." Jr. knew there was nothing else he could say, so the only thing left was to scare the kid.

"Boy, I am gonna give you one chance and one chance only to give me that gun. Now hand it over, right now or I'm gonna let the deputy shoot your pa!"

Right on schedule, the deputy said, "Yeah, shoot your pa, boy."

"Now, are you gonna give me the gun, or do I need to count to three?"

Right then, the deputy asked, "What are you gonna count to three for?"

Jr. snarled, "So you can shoot Wakefield, you idiot!"

"Oh yeah, so I can shoot him."

"Mr. Clovis, I ain't giving you my gun, and I can't let you kill my pa," said Webb.

"Well, boy, it looks like you don't have a choice."

"Deputy?"

"Yeah."

"On the count of three, if the kid has not dropped the gun, shoot his pa."

"Yeah, shoot his pa."

"One..." That was as far as he got. A gun shot roared in the room, and at that split second, the deputy turned to look. Just that split second was all Andy needed. He threw his coffee at Moore's face.

The deputy let out a yell, dropped his gun, and ran for the front door.

There Carl Clovis, Jr. lay on the floor with his hands on his chest, where his life's blood was pumping out with every heartbeat.

Andy picked up Jr.'s gun and pulled Webb to him. "I'm sorry, Pa, but I couldn't let him kill you."

"Son, you did just fine. Don't worry about nothing. The most important thing is, are you ok?"

"I'm ok Pa, but I'm shaking a little."

"Webb, if it was me, I'd be shaking a lot."

As they looked down at Jr., he stared at them and said, "My pa will get you." And that was it. He was still staring at them, but the sight was gone in his eyes, because Jr. was dead.

"What are we gonna do, Pa? His pa will have the sheriff on me, and they may hang me."

"Son, no one is gonna hang a ten-year-old boy, especially when you killed in self-defense. Now, I need you to get dressed and run to Dane's place. Can you do that?"

"You know I can Pa."

"Ok, you tell him what happened and tell him to get here fast. As bad as I hate to, I'm gonna have to fetch the sheriff."

"Ok Pa, we'll be back," said Webb, and upstairs he went to get dressed. Once dressed, he was back downstairs, and out in the dark he went.

Chapter Three

The Tressler place was on the opposite end of Normalville and just about a mile from the town limits. It took Webb about fifteen minutes to make it, and while Dane got dressed, Webb told the story of what happened.

Fifteen minutes later, with Dane dressed and two horses saddled, he and Webb headed south, back to the Wakefield house.

While Webb had been gone, Andy drug Jr.'s body from the kitchen to the front door. He was cleaning up the blood when he heard footsteps on the front porch. The door opened and there stood Deputy Moore, Sheriff Dull Crinch, and Carl Clovis, Sr.

"I told you, Sheriff. Wakefield killed him for nothing," the deputy replied while pointing at Jr.'s body.

"Sheriff, this man killed my son, and I want him arrested, tried, and hung for murder," said Clovis.

"I didn't murder anyone, Mr. Clovis. Your son and your deputy sheriff broke into my home and wanted to rob me."

Clovis yelled, "That's a lie! My son did not have to rob for money." Which was a lie, because just that day Sr. had told Jr. he was done handing over money.

"You can go to work at one of the family businesses, earn a living while learning the business for your own future, or you can starve. Either way, I'm done paying for your drinks and wild nights with women."

Clovis Sr. walked away after that, and Jr. left the house. Sr. could now see where it had led.

"So, these men came to tell you and your boy farewell, and you repaid their kindness with death," stated Crinch.

"They did no such thing, and you know it," replied Andy.

"Are you calling my deputy a liar?"

"I sure am."

"Well, ya see, the thing is, I believe him over you any day."

"You would," said Andy.

"And just what's that supposed to mean?" asked Bill.

"It means liars and cheats run together, and you two are thick as thieves."

With that, Dull's face turned red, and he said, "Well, you see it doesn't really matter what you think or say, 'cause I am the Sheriff, and what I say goes."

"No, what goes is law, and I know what the law says about defending myself, my family, and my property," stated Andy.

"It doesn't matter what you think the laws says, or how it reads, 'cause I change it to fit what I want. The best part is no one can stop me. I can alter the evidence to go in my favor." He laughed and said, "What am I saying? I can alter. Hell, I have done it and on more than one occasion."

Andy looked at him and asked, "Are you proud of that fact, Sheriff?"

"If you would have just been nice and sold me the hotel, along with the gun shop, I could probably overlook this," said Clovis as he waved his hand at his son's dead body. "But since you would not give me a chance, then I see no reason to give you a chance now."

Clovis turned to the sheriff and said, "Kill him and let's be done with it now." The entire time this was going on, no one had a gun drawn, because Andy did not seem to be armed. What they did not know was Andy had Jr.'s gun tucked in his pants, just behind his shirt.

The sheriff smiled and said, "I hate you tried to attack us when we came to arrest you."

As he pulled his pistol from his holster, horse's hooves sounded, and Webb cried, "Pa!"

Dull turned his attention to the door, and with that slight turn, Andy pulled the pistol and fired.

The first shot hit Dull in the breastbone and sent him flying backwards. His next shot aimed at Deputy Moore, who was trying to bring his pistol to bear at Andy.

Andy fired, hitting Moore in the guts, causing him to mess himself; at the same instant, he dropped his second gun of the night.

The next instant, he was staring at Clovis, who had his hands held high.

Then a voice yelled, "Andy! It's me, Dane! Can I come in?"

"Sure thing, Dane. Come on in."

As Dane came through the door, he whistled and said, "This is one heck of a going away celebration."

"It wasn't exactly what I had in mind either, but they didn't give me much of a choice."

Dane looked at Andy, pointed at Clovis, and asked, "What are we gonna do with him?"

Andy said, "Well, just before you rode up, Mr. Clovis here told the sheriff to kill me and be done with it. I wish I could say I could return the favor, but I can't."

Clovis glared at them both. Andy looked at him and said, "The fact that you just lost your son, who you didn't care about one bit, means nothing to you. All your muscle, power, and backing from Dull Crinch, and the town idiot, B.K. Moore, is gone. Leaving you alive will be more punishment than death any day. I'm sure of this because the town council will vote you off the board and the good people of Normalville will elect a new mayor." Andy walked up to him and hit him square in the mouth. Clovis rocked back, hit the wall, and spit out three teeth. As he grabbed his mouth, Webb peeked in the door, and Andy said, "Son, hold the door for Mr. Clovis. He's leaving."

When Clovis was gone, Andy began repeating to Dane what had happened. It was still relatively early in the night, but too late for Webb to be up. So, against his will, Webb was back upstairs and in bed for the second and hopefully last time tonight.

With Webb in bed, Andy sent Dane to the undertakers. Thirty minutes later Dane was back, walking through the door with William Robert Garney, the town's undertaker.

"I hate to bother you this time of night, William Robert, but as you can see, it was urgent. I don't want trash like this in my place."

William Robert smiled and said, "No problem at all. Seeing these three faces, I can understand what you mean about trash."

They loaded the three bodies into the back of William Robert's wagon. Andy said, "It's Clovis's responsibility for burying Jr. Let me know if the town doesn't want to pay for Dull and the Deputy. I'm gonna talk to the council myself and let them know what happened. I'll remind them how much money is going to be saved by getting rid of these two no accounts."

William Robert agreed and said good night. Andy sent Dane home, telling him they would meet in the morning at Mrs. Bunny's Café for breakfast.

With Dane gone and the house cleaned up. It was time to give in to sleep and dreams, which he did. He dreamed of Melissa.

CHAPTER FOUR

The next morning, Webb came down to the kitchen, where his father drank his coffee.

"How'd ya sleep, son? Any bad dreams?" asked Andy.

"Yes sir, I kept seeing Carl Jr. try to shoot you, and then it was like I was watching myself shoot him. Every time I would feel bad in my dreams, Ma was there to tell me how I had done the right thing. But I still feel bad Pa. I feel sick at my stomach, and I don't know if it will ever go away."

"I know you are feeling bad and I'm sure it will last longer than a day or two, but I promise that one day you will be able to handle things that come along a little better because of this. Life ain't cheap and never take it for granite, but just know without you doing what you did last night we would both be dead this morning. And if your Ma says it's ok, then it must be true," replied Andy.

With a big smile, Webb said, "Yep, must be."

Andy finished his coffee, he and Webb saddled up two horses and headed for town and Mrs. Bunny's.

Of course, when they walked in, the town was buzzing. Everyone in the café had already heard from

William Robert and Dane was retelling the events himself.

Andy and Webb seated themselves at the table with Dane and William Robert. The first two councilmen to approach were Darren Adkison and Mike Pennington.

"William Robert, Dane, y'all are 100% right. The town will pay for burial and good riddance to them. We've wanted Dull Crinch out since they hired him. But with Clovis having his hands in it, we just couldn't get it done," said Darren. Mr. Pennington reached over and ruffled Webb's head, and asked, "Are you ok, Son?"

Webb replied, "Yes sir, I am. My ma came to me in my dream last night and told me I did right."

Mr. Pennington looked down and smiled, "Well, if your ma said it, then it must be true, Son."

Everyone agreed, and the conversation turned to finding a new sheriff, one that Carl Clovis, Sr. did not recommend.

Right then, Mrs. Bunny came out to deliver food that Dane had already ordered. She, of course, went straight to Webb to first make sure he was ok and to make sure he got syrup for his pancakes.

Mrs. Bunny had that motherly instinct and gave it to all the boys, from kids to grown men. She would slap a hand for reaching or a head that was wearing a hat at one of her tables. Everyone smiled and treated her with the utmost respect.

Mrs. Bunny was one of the few blacks to live in Normalville. She was the only one to have her own business. Back before Mrs. Bunny's became Mrs. Bunny's it was simply called The City Café. It was owned by the Millers. They were an old couple who had never had children. Mrs. Miller opened the café and ran it for years. Her only cook had been Mrs. Bunny. When Mrs. Miller passed away, Mr. Miller did not want to close the place, but neither did he want to run it.

So, the only smart thing to do was make Bunny his partner and give her free run of it.

His first decision and gesture to show she was his equal was a new sign that read Mrs. Bunny's Café.

The partnership stayed that way for two more years until Mr. Miller passed away. When his last will was read, it was no surprise he had left Mrs. Bunny's free and clear to Mrs. Bunny herself.

After breakfast was over, but before they made it out the door, Mrs. Bunny gave Webb a cloth bag with a wink and pat on the head.

Andy looked at her and asked, "Bunny, what do ya got in the bag?"

Her reply was definite, "If I wanted you grown men to know, I would have given it to y'all instead, but I didn't, so keep your hands off. I made those special for the baby."

No one had to ask because it was the only time Webb allowed himself to be called a baby. She had just given him a sack full of donuts.

With another smile at Webb and another stern look at the men, they all replied, "Yes, Mrs. Bunny."

They spent the remains of the day saying goodbyes and getting last-minute supplies.

Andy dropped the keys to the house at the hotel. He told Daniel, Kate, and Kenzie goodbye and how much he wished he could stay to see the wedding, but they had to be on the way.

He told Kenzie he hoped his and Webb's wedding gift would make up for the fact they could not attend. She assured him a gift was unnecessary but told him whatever it was would be plenty.

Andy gave Daniel a wink, handshake, and promises to drop the last key off in the morning on the way out of town.

Daniel, being the only one who knew about the furniture, just smiled, and told his friends goodbye.

Andy and Webb told Dane they would meet him in the morning for breakfast, then headed home for their last night in the only home Webb had ever known.

The next morning, with the house locked, the keys dropped off, and the last goodbye said, Andy, Webb, and Dane were climbing into the wagon and on their horses.

Mrs. Bunny came out and handed Andy three big sacks. He couldn't resist so he asked, "And just what do you think you are doing?"

Her reply was a pointed finger followed by, "Andrew Wakefield, if you think I won't turn you over my knee, you better think again. You know I can't let my baby get out of here without knowing he will at least eat right and well for another day or two."

The crowd laughed and Andy said, "Mrs. Bunny, there will never be a better woman made. Thank you."

Bunny turned to Webb, handed him a sack for himself and said, "You make sure you keep treating folks nice and always be fair. Say your prayers to the good Lord at night and always know Mrs. Bunny loves you." She leaned down, kissed his head, wiped away a tear, and stepped away.

"Thank you, Mrs. Bunny, I promise I will." He took his sack, wiped away a tear of his own, and climbed in the saddle. "I promise I'll always love you too, Mrs. Bunny."

The morning was young, the sky bright, and the west was waiting.

Chapter Five

On the trail West

Each day brought back a few more smiles and Webb continued to keep up with the miles they put behind them. As they finished for the day, Webb was rubbing his backside and Dane asked him if he was getting a good understanding of what was in store for his new life as a cowboy? "I don't know about a good understanding, but I can bet the trips to the woodshed won't be as bad by the time we reach Arkansas." Webb said with a grin.

As they gathered around the fire, Dane asked, "Webb, where are we by your calculations?"

With a grin and pride, Webb responded, "Well, we are on day twenty-nine and I figure we have come about 550 miles. We are a little behind, but only a day or two."

"Behind?" said Andy with a smile.

"Yes sir. I figure at twenty miles a day we should have been in Nashville, Tennessee by day twenty-nine. Today is day twenty-nine and we are still a couple of days from there, so we are behind."

Dane and Andy looked at each other and smiled, then Dane said, "Well, Andy, I guess we better get it together before the boss here fires us."

Webb shook his head, grinned, and said, "Oh, you ain't got to worry about getting fired. I'll just cut your wages."

The group continued on and, just as Webb said two nights earlier, they approached the lights of Nashville, Tennessee.

It was so late they didn't want to fool with arriving in darkness, so they made camp on a creek a few miles out.

As they pulled their team to a halt, Andy noticed another wagon unhitched with a man and small boy setting up their own camp.

"I figure that's Nashville there in the distance," said Andy.

"Yes sir, that's her alright. Is that where you're headed?"

"It is, but not until the morning. I thought this would be a suitable spot to stop since there ain't enough time to make it before dark sets in."

"Y'all step down and join us. It's just me and my boy and we'd like the company."

"Thank you. I believe we will."

After they unhitched, watered, and fed the team, the three joined the man and young boy.

Andy said with an outstretched hand. "I'm Andy Wakefield. This is my friend Dane Tressler, and my son Webb."

The man took the offered hand of both Andy and Dane as he said, "My name is Calaway Daniels, but I go by Cal to most. This is my son Jasper, but we call him Jack. We are on our way back down to our place in Lynchburg. We got a late start but didn't want to stay in town again, so we thought a few miles away was a suitable spot to hold up for the night."

"Well, since you and Jack here are sharing your fire and camp, how about we share our food and coffee?" said Andy.

"I tell you, that sounds like a real fine offer."

With that settled, the five fell into conversation. The men talked about travels, Andy and Dane talked to Cal about their dreams for a place in Arkansas. While the men drank coffee and talked by the fire, Webb and Jack sat by the creek talking and chunking rocks.

"Where's your ma?" asked Jack.

"She died when I was little,"

"Mine did too. Are you excited about going to Arkansas?"

"Yep, I plan on being a cowboy! What about you? Why are you going to Lynchburg?"

"That's where we live. Me and Pa, and my older brother Robert, come up to buy this new wagon. My brother Robert bought one too, but he is staying in Nashville for a few more days before he comes back."

"Is he your only brother?" asked Webb.

"Nope, I got nine brothers and sisters."

"Nine!"

"Yep, nine," said Jack with a big grin.

"What are you gonna do when you grow up?" asked Webb.

"Well, I don't know, but right now I work for Mr. Dan Call. He owns a store, and he's our local preacher. When I ain't helping him in the store and he ain't preaching, he teaches me how to make whiskey."

"Whiskey?" asked Webb.

"Yep, and that's probably what I will do when I'm grown. It won't be the same as Mr. Dan's 'cause I got my own ideas."

"Like what?"

"Well, I figure I want a square bottle."

"Why?"

"Because I think it will look better and Jack Daniel's whiskey is gonna be known as Old Number 7."

"What does Old Number 7 mean?"

Jack smiled. "It's a secret, but I reckon I can tell you. So, it's like this here..."

Jack proceeded, telling Webb all about his Old Number 7 as the men continued to talk into the night.

The next morning, after a substantial breakfast, the group said their goodbyes and went their separate ways.

The trio spent the day in Nashville restocking supplies and giving the animals a much-deserved day of rest.

After a day's rest, they headed out for Memphis and the great Mississippi. Eleven uneventful days later, the group arrived. Words could not describe their thoughts as they got their first look at the mighty Mississippi. While Andy and Webb went into town for a few supplies, Dane went in search of a captain to ferry them across to their destined state of Arkansas.

When the three met back at the river, Dane had with him a grizzled old man.

"Andy, this here is Hayden Holcombe. He has a barge to take us across the river."

Andy shook hands with Mr. Holcombe. "Nice to meet you, Mr. Holcombe."

"Same here, but call me Billy, if you will."

"Billy it is. So, you think you can get us to the other side?"

"Sure as shootin' I can."

"Well then, I say there is no time like the present."

They all went to work loading the horses and wagon on the barge.

Andy asked as they were crossing the river. "Billy, do you think they'll ever build a bridge across this thing?"

"As a matter of fact, Andy, they already have. On January 23rd of this year, the first bridge across the old girl opened up in Minneapolis."

Dane whistled. "I bet she is a big 'un."

"That's what they say. I figure it's just a matter of time before we have one here. Of course, this one will be a heap bigger than the one up north. It's 1,581 feet long from what I hear, and this one here would have to be the high side of 4,000, I would think."

They reached the riverbanks of Arkansas, relieved to be in their future home state. They still had daylight, and it wasn't wasted as they set out to make a few miles.

Two days later, at the end of a long haul, the men pulled up to a small house with a small boy and a beautiful woman in front.

"How do, ma'am? My name is Andy Wakefield, this is my friend, Dane Tressler, and my son, Webb. We are on our way to Hell's Valley and would like to make our camp for the night somewhere out of your way, if you wouldn't mind."

"Hello, Mr. Wakefield. My name is Barbara Bennett, and this is my son, Brady. We would love for you to camp close by and join us for supper. Unhitch your team. You can water your animals here at the well, then you can all wash up at the basin when I have the food ready."

"Thank you, ma'am, and please call me Andy."

"Fair enough, but only if you call me Barbara. Brady, you help these men with their chores, and I will start on the food."

"Yes, Ma."

As the men got busy with their work, Dane looked at Andy and said, "I bet there ain't many west of the Mississippi who look as beautiful as that one."

Andy smiled and said, "You noticed that, did you?"

"A man would have to be blind or stupid not to. That brown hair and those eyes make it hard to notice that friendly smile, but I noticed it too."

"Would you like for me to leave you here and go on to Hell's Valley without you?"

"Well, I ain't said that, but maybe you ought to think about moving Hell's Valley closer to right here."

"Dane, I think I'm gonna have to work you harder."

"And why would you say a thing like that?"

"Because if I don't, I am scared one of these Arkansas women are gonna hog tie you to make you honest."

"Bite your tongue for even thinking something so vile on me." Dane grinned as they finished ground tying the horses on some good grass.

Barbara called them for supper, and they found out she was more than just a beautiful woman. She could set a fine table as well. They had fried chicken, fried potatoes, cornbread, and, for dessert, a strawberry pie.

"This sure is a fine meal, ma'am," Dane said as everyone chimed their agreements.

"Why thank you. It's been so long since I saw a grown man enjoy my food. I almost forgot how gratifying it was. Since my husband passed, it's been just the two of us."

"Sorry for your loss," said Dane.

"Thank you, but it's been a few years already, so as bad as it sounds, I have grown used to it."

"Ma'am, I tell ya, I saw a few shakes needed replaced on the roof and the fence could use some attention. How bout we let our animals rest a day or two, and we give you a hand in return for these fine vittles?"

"Mr. Wakefield."

"Andy, please."

"Andy, you don't have to do that, but I will admit that I could use a man around for a day or two, and since there are three of you, how could I turn it down?"

"That's settled then. In the morning, Dane, Webb, and I will take Brady, and we'll get to work."

"Thank you, gentlemen, and I will make sure your stomachs are full of a big breakfast."

They thanked her again and started for their camp when Dane said, "We just rested the animals, so I know that ain't the real reason you offered."

Andy smiled and said, "Nope, the real reason is I was hoping to see you hog-tied or at least made half honest before we left."

Dane mumbled as he turned and walked off into the dark. "I think I may need to find a new partner."

"I think Dane may be nervous, Pa."

"You may be right, son."

The next morning, after breakfast, they got started on the roof. By lunch they finished, so the fence was next. Not long into the fence, Andy noticed Webb and Brady were gone.

"Dane, where'd them boys get to?"

"I ain't sure, Andy. It's been a bit since I saw them."

"Webb!" shouted Andy.

"Mr. Wakefield, oops, sorry Andy, I sent the boys down to the creek to catch us a mess of fish. I hope you don't mind."

"Not at all, but if Brady is anything like Webb, I would say they are probably naked as jaybirds and swimming instead of fishing."

"Well, to be honest, I figured the same thing, so I have a fallback plan in case they come home without fish."

It was a good thing too, because at that moment, both boys were in their birthday suits, swimming, jumping, and diving in a deep pool.

"Brady, do you think your ma's gonna be mad when we don't come back with any fish?"

"Nope, she knows what we're doing."

"How do you know?"

"I saw her getting a ham ready earlier."

"I sure hope my pa ain't mad 'cause I run off."

"You don't know nothing, do ya?"

"What are you talking about? I don't know nothing?"

"I'm talking about my ma."

"What does she have to do with my pa getting mad?"

"A pretty woman can make a mad man do just about anything. All she had to do was tell your pa she sent us, and he won't say anything."

"You don't know my pa. He's still liable to take me to the woodshed."

"You don't know my ma, and better yet, we ain't got no woodshed."

Both boys laughed as they kept on swimming.

After their time "fishing," the boys headed home, with Webb worried the entire way.

When they strolled into the yard, Andy looked up and said, "Where you boys been?"

Webb looked ready to run. "We been fishing, Pa."

"Fishing! Well, who said you could go fishing?"

Webb looked at Brady, and just then, Barbara came out. "Boys, where are my fish?"

"Sorry Ma, but they ain't biting today."

"Well, I guess I will make do with something else."

"Pa, Mrs. Bennett sent us to catch some fish."

"She did?"

"Yes sir, she did."

"Well, I guess it's alright, but next time you boys go, maybe y'all might want to put them poles in the water instead of your naked butts."

"Why do you say that, Pa?"

"It looks like you both hooked big ones and got pulled in since you both come back with wet hair."

Webb looked at Brady, and Brady smiled with a wink and a whisper. "Told you, pretty women are the boss."

Barbara called out, "Everybody get cleaned up for supper." True to Brady's words, they all did just as she said.

The next day, daylight found the western travelers on the trail, headed for their new home. Two weeks to the west and two hundred miles away, leaving Brady and Barbara behind.

Chapter Six

As the wagon rolled into the town that Andy and Dane picked out on a map months before, they all knew at once they were home.

The sky was blue, the trees and grass still had plenty of green, and every stream was crystal clear and mighty tasty.

The little town of Hell's Valley, Arkansas, was doing a suitable set of business. People were on the street coming and going from all the stores and shops.

Andy looked over at Dane and Webb. "Well, what do ya boys think?"

They both had grins stretching from ear to ear. "I wonder if the café is as good as Mrs. Bunny's?" said Webb.

Dane and Andy laughed, and Andy said, "Well, if it isn't, don't tell the cook. That may be a hanging offense in the south."

"The first thing we need to do is drop the horses at the livery and we can load the wagon at the general store with everything we are gonna need."

"You folks look like you come a far piece." The newcomers turned, staring at the clean-shaven face of the deputy sheriff.

"Yes sir, we just rolled in, and it has been a haul, I must admit. I'm Andy Wakefield. This is my friend and business partner, Dane Tressler, and my son, Webb."

"I'm Deputy Sheriff Pete Penney. Welcome to our town. Do you plan on staying, or are you just passing through?"

Andy smiled and said, "I guess you could say the good Lord pointed us to your town. We set out here from Normalville, Pennsylvania, with this place circled on our map."

"Normalville, Pennsylvania, huh? That sounds like a far piece. Mr. Wakefield, we are living in our own piece of heaven, so you could not have picked a better place to call home. I'll also say that is a good-looking boy you got there. His name doesn't mean much until you hear it and then look at him."

"And what do you mean by that, Deputy?"

"Well, the look alone was enough for me to ask if you had family here by another name. When you said his name was Webb, well, that just about sealed the deal. We have a family that moved in the area a couple years back from out east by the name of Webb.

Your son could pass for one easy. He has that look, and those eyes cut you."

Andy looked perplexed and said, "Well, my wife's maiden name was Webb, so of course, that's where his name comes from. My wife passed over three years back. Her folks are still alive back east. I'm sure it's possible there could be family members who have drifted west for the same reasons we all do. I guess I may check into it just to satisfy my curiosity."

Well, if you need us, the sheriff's office is right there. I am sure we will see each other again, so take care, and welcome again to Hell's Valley."

"Before you go, could you direct us to the livery?"

"Yes sir, you go two blocks on the right there and ask for Toby Craver. He runs the place."

"Thank you again, Deputy. We'll see ya around."

They found the livery where Pete said it would be. Toby was in a stall mucking out the old hay.

"How are you, folks? What can I do for you?" Toby was a little over six feet of a slim build with an amiable smile and a firm handshake.

"Yes sir, we are planning on being in town overnight and looking to give you a little business."

"I always like business. What have you got?"

"We've got seven horses right now, plus four oxen once the wagon's loaded at the store. I would also ask if you had room for us to park our wagon once it's loaded with supplies? We'll all sleep under it tonight."

"Seven horses, four oxen, and three tired cowboys, with a wagon full of supplies. Yes sir, I think I can take care of you. Bring your wagon around back when you're done and unhitched, then we will take care of your oxen." Toby turned around and called out the back door, "Keith, come here."

In walked a boy who couldn't have been more than seven years old but weighed at least a hundred pounds. The only thing was, it wasn't really fat. He looked like a solid stump of oak. Even more shocking was the plug of chew he had in his mouth. He looked at Toby, gave a spit, and said, "If you call me Keith one more time, I promise you, me and you is goin' to town, and I ain't talking 'bout dancing.

Toby just looked at him, shook his head, and said, "Oh right, I meant Sheriff."

Keith let out a big smile and said, "Now that's better."

Webb looked at his pa and then at Keith and said, "Are you the sheriff, or do you want to be when you grow up?"

"Naw, I just like the sound of it 'cause it sounds important, and I figure, as I'm gonna be somebody mighty important, I might as well get used to the handle."

Andy looked at him and said, "Sheriff, that sounds like some mighty good reasoning."

"Yes sir, I kinda figured that myself. That's how come I come up with it."

"Ok, Sheriff!" Toby let the last word come out strong. "Get these horses took care of, rub 'em down, give 'em grain and hay, and get the back pen ready for four oxen."

The Sheriff spit another stream of brown liquid at a fly on a horse apple, grinned, turned and walked to the horses.

"I bet things could get exciting, pretty fast around here with Keith, oh I mean Sheriff," said Dane with a smile.

"Believe me," said Toby, "you ain't seen or heard nothing yet. The worst part is he believes all the crazy stuff that comes out of his own mouth. The only thing I believe is that he may actually whoop a grown man."

Everyone agreed with a smile. "I guess if the little ones are all like him, then I imagine we won't have trouble finding hands tough enough for what we want," said Andy.

Toby replied, "No sir, if you need hard working, tough hands, you will find plenty here. Keith has some older brothers who fit that bill."

"Now that don't surprise me at all. My name is Andy Wakefield. This is Dane Tressler and my son, Webb."

Toby eyed Webb and said, "Speaking of handles, that's a pretty good one you got there, Webb".

Webb gave a big smile and said, "Thank you. They named me after my ma's family."

"Well then, that settles it," said Toby.

"Settles what?" asked Dane.

"Y'all must have moved here to be by your family, or at least your wife's kin."

"What are you talking about, Toby?" Andy asked.

"I could see it on the boy when you come up. He has the look, same as all the Webbs."

Dane said, "Andy, I think it's time we have us a look see for ourselves."

"I think you're right," said Andy. "Toby, you say my son looks familiar, huh?"

"Yes sir, he looks just like the rest of 'em except his eyes are.... well, his eyes are a little more sure. Does that sound strange?" asked Toby.

Andy smiled and said, "Not strange at all, Toby. Not strange at all. Where exactly can we find the Webb farm?"

"Well, you go straight out of town about four miles south. Follow the top ridge of the hill and keep Mine Creek on your right. You can't miss it. And believe me, you will know them when you see 'em."

They shook hands all around, got things squared away, and left for the store and then some lunch.

As they walked down the main street, they were greeted with smiles from all they met. While living in Normalville, they had gotten used to seeing people not wearing guns. That did not apply here. The only people without were the women. They all felt comfortable with their weapons. Webb didn't like the fact that he had to go without his gun, but Andy figured it was better to let his ten-year-old go unarmed except while on the trail.

They found the store loaded with everything they needed and more. The man behind the counter looked up with a wave and a smile. "Come in, come in, tell me how I can help you gents."

Andy gave the man a handshake and introduced the three of them. "I'm Andrew Wakefield. This is my son, Webb, and my friend, Dane Tressler. We just came from back east looking to settle in the area and we need to restock our supplies." Andy handed the man a long list.

"Yes sir. I'm Joe Buck Jones, and I can sure take care of this. It's a big order. Where would you like me to put it?"

"We are gonna pull the wagon down from the livery. I just didn't know if you wanted it in the front or back."

"You can pull it right to the back door. Give me an hour or so and I'll have it ready."

"Sounds good. We're looking for a bite to eat. Can you point us to a place?"

"Yes sir. Across the street, one block up. You can't miss it. It's called the Pearl Café, and Ms. Wendy sets a real fine table."

"Thank you. I believe we'll try it out."

He told Mr. Jones they would return after lunch for the wagon and to settle up.

It was a little late in the day for lunch, so the Pearl only had a few late comers.

They found an open table and took their seats when the tallest woman they had ever seen approached. She had short dark hair, big dark eyes, and a smile that lit up the room.

She introduced herself as Wendy Haddan, the owner, and cook.

"What can I get you, gentlemen?"

Andy and Dane said, "Coffee to start, and whatever the house special is, we'll take three."

She looked at Webb and said, "You sure are a pretty young thang. How about a glass of milk for you?"

"Yes ma'am, and thank you," replied Webb.

"I'll be right back with your drinks, and your food will be out in a jiffy."

She quickly returned from the kitchen with two coffee cups, a pot of coffee, and one glass of milk. As she returned to the kitchen to prepare the food, Dane couldn't resist saying, "Pretty young thang, huh, Webb?" Andy smiled and Webb blushed.

Dane joked, "I guess being called pretty is better than not being called at all."

Wendy was back with three plates of fried chicken, snap beans, potatoes, some fresh baked bread, and a plate of butter. She gave Webb a pat on the head and a smile as she went to check on the other customers.

All three fell on their food and they didn't speak a word until they finished.

"I'm thinking Mrs. Bunny must've taught her how to cook 'cause if I had to, I don't think I could pick between the two," said Webb.

Dane smiled and said, "He ain't but ten-years-old and already knows how to make a woman happy. I still ain't learned how and I'm a heap older than ten."

No sooner were they done when she arrived with three pieces of fresh peach pie.

"Ma'am, you sure set a fine table, and I think that was the best meal any of us ever ate," said Andy.

She blushed and smiled. "Well, thank you. I hope that means you'll stop in again?"

Dane replied with a smile. "You can be sure of it. We'll be regulars, especially if all the meals taste that good."

She gave her guarantee that all the meals would be just as pleasing.

They paid for lunch and as they were leaving, Wendy stopped Webb and handed him a cloth bag with two pieces of pie. "You eat that after your supper tonight." She looked back at Dane and Andy with a smile and said, "Boy, he sure is pretty!"

Dane chuckled. "If he gets any prettier, he's gonna be big as a house."

Andy laughed and said, "Come on, let's head over to Mr. Jones' store."

They walked across the street and stepped up on the walkway when a voice said, "Excuse me, Mr. Wakefield."

Andy turned and coming towards him was a young man who looked to be about 35 years old. He had dark hair underneath his cowboy hat that showed off his ears and neck, friendly eyes, and a pleasant smile. Andy noticed he also had a star pinned to his shirt.

"Yes, I'm Andrew Wakefield. What can I do for you, Sheriff?"

"I was talking with my deputy, and he told me of your arrival. I just wanted to introduce myself."

The Sheriff stuck out his hand. "I'm Bryan McJunkins, and I guess you already know I'm the Sheriff here. I would just like to welcome you and ask if I can help you with anything."

Andy shakes the sheriff's hand. "I have to say, Sheriff, you sure have a pleasant town. We haven't seen much of it yet, but from all we've seen and all the folks we've met, I can say I believe we're gonna like it here."

McJunkins smiled a proud smile and looked at Dane with his hand stretched out. "Sheriff McJunkins."

Dane gave a nod and replied, "Dane Tressler, Sheriff. It goes double for me everything Andy just said."

The Sheriff looked over at Webb and said, "Well, I don't have to ask who you are, young man. You would be Webb."

Webb looked puzzled and asked, "How did you know my name, Sheriff?"

"My deputy told me there would be no mistaking the look, and he was right as rain. You may not have any idea who they are, but I'm willing to wager that you are blood kin somewhere down the line."

"I don't guess I have to ask if you're talking about the Webbs?" said Andy. "It seems everywhere we turn; we're hearing the same thing. I believe that's gonna settle it. We're gonna have to meet these folks."

The sheriff replied, "I can surely tell you how to get to Zeb's place."

"Zeb?"

"Yes. That's his name, or at least one of their names. Zebidia Webb."

The look on Andy's face was that of sure surprise. "You mean to tell me Zebidia Webb is living here?"

"Yes sir. He also has two cousins and their families. There ain't no mistaking your boy has the mark. Do you know him?"

"My late wife had a brother named Zeb, but as far as I knew, he lived back east with the rest of the family."

"This family has been here going on about two and a half years, I'd say. Good folks, hardworking, honest. They keep a nice place south of town about four miles out on Mine Creek."

Andy replied, "I was thinking of other things we needed to do, but that seals the deal. We've gotta make that trip to the Webb place."

"I guess I'll leave ya to your business. If you need anything, you know where to find me or Deputy Pete."

"Thank you, Sheriff. We'll sure keep that in mind."

The Sheriff walked away, and Andy said, "Now that this has come along, I think I may have jumped the gun on getting supplies."

"I was just thinking the same thing. Plus, while we are out looking for a place, what are we gonna do with the wagon?" asked Dane.

"Good question. I guess since we got ahead of ourselves, we'll just have to figure it out."

They walked into Mr. Jones' store as he came from around the corner, shaking his head. "I'm so sorry, Mr. Wakefield, but as soon as you left, one of my big accounts came in and was in a hurry, so I had to get his first. I hope you don't mind. J.P. McCrary is a good man and would have waited, but I thought since you were at lunch, I would fix him up first."

Andy gave a big smile to Dane and said, "I guess we must be living right."

Mr. Jones looked puzzled and asked, "How's that?"

"Right before we came in, Dane and I were saying we may have jumped the gun on getting supplies filled. We are still looking for some land, and having to leave our supplies in an unguarded camp might be a bad idea."

"I guess that means you ain't upset with me?"

"Mr. Jones, even if we didn't jump the gun, you filling another order was perfectly fine with us."

"So, do you still want your list filled?"

"Yes sir, but not today. You keep that list handy and as soon as we can get a place that's permanent, we'll be back. How's that sound?"

"Fine and dandy. I'll keep your list on my desk until you're ready. Can I help you with anything else today?"

"You sure can. Can you point us towards a hotel or boarding house?"

"They haven't built the hotel yet, but the boarding house is on the same side of the street one block further. It's a big white house with green shutters, ya can't miss it. It's run by a lovely woman, Clair Hutchinson. A real amiable lady. She sets a fine table too if you choose to take your meals there. Her husband is Mr. D.A. Hutchinson. He's a fine man. Oh, and one more thing, Mr. Wakefield, I figure since we'll be friends, how about you call me Joe Buck?"

"Ok, Joe Buck, you can call me Andy. I guess the boarding house is more our speed, so we will pay Mrs. Hutchinson a visit. Thanks for everything, Joe Buck, and I promise we will be back for our supplies as soon as we can."

"You're welcome and don't worry, your list will be waiting. Good luck in your search."

As they walked out of the store, Dane said, "I guess since we're gonna be doing some riding for a few days. I'm gonna take the horses we're not using to the blacksmith for some new shoes all around."

"That sounds like a winner to me if you want to start that. Webb and I will go get us a couple of rooms and then meet you at the blacksmith."

Dane went one way, while Webb and Andy went the other.

Andy and Webb found the house right where Joe Buck said. As they walked up on the porch, the door opened, and a beautiful woman walked out. She was in a green dress with her hair held back by the same color ribbon. She was black headed with dark eyes that radiated all her beauty.

"Can I help you?"

"Yes ma'am. I'm Andrew Wakefield. Mr. Jones told me I may find a couple of rooms to rent here."

"You sure came to the right place. I have two rooms available right now. How long do you need them?"

"Not quite sure just yet, ma'am. My partner and I are looking to buy a place, so until we can find one, I guess we are in need."

"My name is Clair Hutchinson, Mr. Wakefield. It sounds like you have two rooms until you don't need them anymore."

"Thank you, ma'am. Sounds like we do."

"Won't you please come in? You can see the rooms, so you'll know where to bring your things."

She was showing them to their rooms when she looked at Andy and asked, "Who is this handsome young man with you?"

"This is my son, Webb."

"Hello, Webb, and how are you?"

"Just fine, ma'am."

"That is wonderful. You make sure you are here for supper tonight and I will have a special treat for you. How does that sound?"

"Yes ma'am, I will, and it sure sounds real nice."

She looked back at Andy and smiled. "Such a good-looking young man, and those eyes. You must be proud."

"Yes ma'am, I sure am."

Business taken care of, the room paid for, and a time set for supper, the two walked back out into the beautiful Arkansas weather. Andy looked at Webb and said, "At least she didn't call you pretty."

They both laughed and took off for the blacksmith and Dane.

CHAPTER SEVEN

They arrived at the blacksmith. The big smith was finishing the metal band on a wagon wheel and Dane was bent over with a horse's hoof in between his legs, removing a shoe.

Andy looked at the big smith and said with a smile, "I've known Dane his whole life and can't get him to do anything. You've known him for ten minutes and you've got him working. Ya gotta tell me your secret."

The big man let out a hardy laugh and said, "The promise of a discount, my friend. That's all it took."

Andy laughed and said, "That just proves he's not only lazy, but he's also cheap."

Dane smiled. "I ain't lazy or cheap. I'm just pacing myself and saving for my future, sitting in my rocking chair on the front porch."

The big smithy laughed. "Sounds like a well-rehearsed speech to me."

Andy looked at the smithy, who stood about six foot three, bald with a mustache, and weighed at least two hundred eighty pounds. His chest was as thick as it was wide, and his arms looked as hard as red oaks.

Andy offered his hand. The big man took it, "Andy Wakefield and my son, Webb".

"Edward Daniels, but call me Eddie. Most do."

"I will and you can call me Andy." Eddie set aside the wheel and stuck his hand out to Webb.

"It's good to meet you too, son." Eddie's hand swallowed half of Webb's arm.

"Thank you. It's good to meet you as well."

"So, ol' Dane here tells me you're looking for a good place to buy."

"That's right. We're looking for a few thousand acres that will hold cattle and horses."

"I'm sure you'll find land around here for a good price. West and Southwest are prime. There's good graze, but it's also nice timber for building. Plenty of creeks that run year-round, and you have four rivers within thirty-five to forty miles from where we're standing."

Andy replied, "Those rivers and their location to Texas are why we picked this area, but the map didn't show a town. We only found out about it a few days back on the trail, but for us, it seems to be a bonus."

"You're right about that. It's a nice place to call home," said Eddie.

Dane chimed in and said, "And it doesn't hurt with the women folks when you have someone as pretty as Webb."

Webb picked up a dirt clod and threw it at Dane.

Andy said, "Believe me, our new landlord fell right in with the rest. She has something special made for him tonight for supper."

"That just proves we won't ever go hungry having him around," said Dane.

All three men laughed while Webb turned red and grabbed three more dirt clods.

Back at the boarding house, they were all seated around the table, about to enjoy a meal. It was a beautiful meal of pork loin, cabbage, fried potatoes smothered in brown gravy, and fresh baked bread.

"Mrs. Hutchinson, this looks delicious."

"Thank you, Mr. Wakefield. I hope it tastes as good as it looks."

They blessed the meal with a word of grace and assured Mrs. Hutchinson that her hope did not go unanswered. It was a delicious meal.

"Mr. Hutchinson, I understand you are the mayor?" said Andy.

"Please call me D.A. and no, I'm not the mayor. I just do anything I can to help the town thrive."

"Mr. Jones told us you were the mayor."

"Hell's Valley doesn't have a mayor yet or even a town council. I have just kind of overseen any business the town needs and I try to help with any new ventures that come to our town. I will say if, and when, the town gets a mayor, I'm sure hoping for the job."

"What do you do most days when you are not tending to town business?"

"Well, as you know, the boarding house runs itself with help from my wife, but I own a small saddle shop here in town."

"Maybe you can help us, D.A.?" said Andy. "Could you point us in the right direction for land or in the right direction of someone who could help?"

"I sure can. West and southwest, there is a lot of land no one has settled. It starts about two miles east of town. After that, you may find someone every few miles trying to scratch a few rows of dirt for a garden, but it's pretty much wide open."

"Sounds like a spot for us, Andy," said Dane.

"It sure does. I believe first thing in the morning, we're gonna head south for a few miles to see about the Webb family. If we have enough time, we may ride west."

D.A. paused and said, "I've sure been wondering if the Webb's were your kin. The boy has the mark."

"Well, we aren't sure yet. My wife was a Webb from back east, but this is the first I've heard of any out this way."

"If I was a gambling man, I would put money on it. They are kin somehow."

"I guess we'll find out tomorrow."

Mrs. Hutchinson brought out a fresh peach cobbler and the first piece, of course, went to Webb, who was smiling from ear to ear.

"Thank you, Mrs. Hutchinson."

"You're very welcome, young man."

Andy smiled. "I tell you. He ate one piece of peach pie at the Pearl today. Mrs. Wendy gave him two extra pieces to go, and now this. The boy may turn into a peach."

Dane laughed, saying, "Yeah, but he would sure be a pretty peach." Everyone joined in, laughing, except Webb. He just turned red and dug into his cobbler.

The men stayed up, talking for a while, but Webb turned in early. After more talk of land and Hell's Valley's future, Andy and Dane hit the sheets themselves.

The next morning, they found a table set with enough food for a small army. There was leftover pork loin, plenty of bacon, fried eggs, scrambled eggs, flapjacks, and syrup, and biscuits so light you had to hold 'em down with sorghum or syrup.

With the blessing said, everyone dug in.

"Mrs. Hutchinson, you've outdone yourself," said Dane.

"I'm glad y'all enjoyed it. I love watching a man stay healthy with good food. A big appetite shows you're working hard and living right."

As they excused themselves, she gave Andy a sack of food, "leftovers from last night and this morning."

"Thank you, ma'am, but you didn't have to do this."

"There is no way some of it wouldn't go to waste, and I hate waste. Plus," she said, winking at

Webb, "that good-looking young man needs his energy."

"Well, as long as there's no cobbler or pie, I guess it's alright. He has two pieces left from Ms. Wendy. Me and Dane would sure hate to eat all your cobbler in front of him."

"Pa, I'm a growing boy. I'm sure I can handle both." Everyone laughed.

"I'm sure you can, son. Let's go. Daylight's a burnin'."

When they arrived at the livery, they found Toby and Keith, or "Sheriff" as he liked to be called, mucking out stalls.

"Morning, Andy," said Toby.

"Morning, Toby. I see you and Sheriff are hard at it this morning."

"Yeah Andy, If I don't keep him busy, he'll sit around and come up with some of the darndest ideas you've ever heard of. Then I got to listen to 'em all."

Keith grinned with a wad of tobacco showing in his mouth and said, "Mr. Wakefield, I'm just trying to keep him educated, but he is so darn hardheaded, it takes a lot of talking."

"Sheriff, you just keep at him, Son. I'm sure if ya do, you'll finally get through to him."

Toby smiled. "And here I was thinking we was gonna be friends, Andy."

Andy gave him a wink. "We're gonna take a trip this morning, so we came to saddle up some horses."

"Yes sir. Which one ya want?"

"I'll take my bay," said Dane.

"You can give me my big buckskin," said Andy, "and, of course, Webb won't ride nothing but a grulla."

"Smart young man," said Toby. "I like a gray myself." Horses saddled, the three rode out. As they did, they noticed Sheriff was awfully quiet. When Andy looked, he saw why.

Webb had given him a piece of his peach pie and he was eating it, still smiling around tobacco and now peach pie.

CHAPTER EIGHT

They rode south out of town and crossed Mine Creek about a mile later. Winding their way south, following the creek, they stayed on the ridge of the hill. Sure enough, 'bout four miles out, they came to some worked ground and could see three cabins, all with smoke coming from the chimneys.

As they approached the first home, they could see a man coming out of the barn when a kid yelled, "Pa, we got company!"

When the man came out into full view, he and Andy both smiled.

"Andrew Wakefield, what in the world are you doing in Mine Creek, Arkansas? Y'all get down off those horses. Jed, run get your ma." Andy and Zeb shared a firm handshake.

"Zeb, this is my partner, Dane Tressler."

"Glad to know you, Dane," said Zeb as he shook Dane's hand.

"I'll see if you can guess who this is," said Andy.

Zeb looked at Webb and said, "Don't have to guess. I know the look, and from Mellissa's letters, he must be Webb."

"He is indeed," said Andy.

"Son, you definitely got our look."

Webb beamed, "Yes sir, that's what they say."

"Zeb, now tell me what you are doing in Arkansas?"

"I'm wondering the same for you, but I guess I can go first. Come on up and pull up a log under the shade tree."

As they rounded the corner of the house, a woman came out with three young ones in tow.

"Coley Ann, come meet your kinfolks," said Zeb.

The woman was a small beauty. She had brown hair with greenish eyes, and you would never guess she had produced three kids. She was still so tiny.

"Coley, this is your brother-in-law, Andy Wakefield, and your nephew, Webb. And this is their friend, Mr. Tressler."

"It's a pleasure to meet all of you. I've always wondered if I'd ever get to meet you. When we left back east, I thought for sure I would never see family again."

"Well, here we are in the flesh," said Andy.

"These are our children, Jed, John, and Janie Lee."

"I tell you, they could all be Webb's brothers and sisters," said Andy.

"The Webb look is a strong one," said Dane.

"Yes sir, it is," said Zeb.

"Kids, y'all take Webb and run get Jeremia and cousin Zeke. Tell 'em we got family here." The kids took off like a flash.

"Come on. Let's set and talk," said Zeb as walked to the shade tree.

The group each pulled up a log of wood to sit. Coley came out with a coffee pot and plenty of cups. "Can I fix y'all something to eat?"

"No ma'am, we just ate a huge breakfast in town. Thank you, though," said Andy. "So, Zeb, tell me what in the world you're doing here."

"I guess I wanted my own place, somewhere new. The country back home is filling up fast. We just decided we would try to do our part in helping settle the west."

"I had no idea you were even gone from back east," said Andy.

"I don't guess we announced it. The family knew, and I guess that was it. We've been here now about two and a half years."

"I guess the last time I heard anything from you or about y'all was when you wrote to tell us you and Coley had your second boy, John," said Andy.

"Yeah, I guess after Melissa passed, the letters stopped. You know I ain't no good at sitting and trying to write, but Ma and Pa should've kept you up on all of us," replied Zeb.

"I sent them a letter to let them know that Webb and I were heading west but never heard back. I just thought maybe the letter got lost."

"You know Pa don't read and write, and Ma, she is upset we all left. Plus, losing Melissa, I guess she's dealing with it all by ignoring it."

"I understand."

"Now tell us, how'd you end up in Mine Creek?"

"I heard you call it that earlier. Is this Mine Creek?"

"Well, no, this is just the country, but the town you come from is Mine Creek."

"We were told it was Hell's Valley."

"Some call it that, and some call it Pleasant Valley. There was a preacher in these parts around 1835, I believe, named Isaac Cooper. He built Mine Creek Baptist Church back in town on the creek bank. They knew it as Mine Creek until others started calling it Hell's Valley or Pleasant Valley. I guess any name will do. Can't tell, it may change again before you know it."

Just then, a group of folks showed up with a passel of kids.

"Boys, I want y'all to meet my brother-in-law, Andrew Wakefield and Mr. Tressler."

Everyone shook hands as Zeb went along introducing all the group. Jeremia and Zeke were cousins from back home, and both had the look. They both had pretty wives. Jeremia had four kids, and Zeke had five. The brood was no doubt Webbs. The next hour Andy told of their trip and why they were here. He told of their plans, and they talked of land.

"We have a few small communities close. We've got Allbrook a few miles to the southwest. Compton and Doyle are just a few miles northwest of Mine Creek. Then the big city is up ten miles northwest, named Center Point. Now, she is a nice burg."

"Where do you recommend us finding what we want?"

"There ain't nobody holdin' near what you're talking 'bout so there is plenty for the taking. I would say west and southwest of Mine Creek, or Hell's Valley, as you call it."

"That's the spot we've been told about. I think we'll look it all over."

"It'll be a good spot for you and not too far from all of us."

"I see you have a few jersey cows, some chickens, and hogs. I'm sure you didn't bring them with you?"

"No, we didn't. The hogs come from Wayne Harris 'bout two miles due east of here. He has a nice size hog farm, and the Jerseys came from a Mr. Eugene Green over round where you're lookin' to settle. We picked up a few chicks here and there until we started producing our own. We get enough eggs and chickens to keep us in scrambled eggs and fried chicken."

"Do you think we could visit Harris today while we're in the area?"

"Sure can. We can go now."

Everyone said goodbye. Jeremia and Zeke took their families back to their own places. Zeb, Andy, Dane, and Webb rode out for the Harris farm.

Zeb pointed out things along the ride, and they discussed the folks in town. "All fine people. Ain't met a stranger yet."

"You got that right," said Dane.

They arrived at the Harris place and greeted by a lean, dark-haired man with a hawkish face.

"Y'all light and set," said Mr. Harris.

"Wayne, this here is my brother-in-law, Andrew Wakefield, his friend Dane Tressler, and this is my nephew, Webb."

"Hello, gents. How are you?"

"We're doing fine, Mr. Harris. How 'bout yourself?" asked Andy.

"I'm on the right side of the topsoil, so I can't complain."

"No sir, I guess not."

"What can I help you with?"

"Well, we are looking for a place, and hoping when we find it, we can do some business."

"We sure can. As you can see, I've got plenty to choose from."

He had hogs everywhere and corn cribs filled to the rim with corn. As the men talked, Webb had walked over closer to the pens and was trying to call some piglets over to the fence. "Here pig, here pig, come here pig."

Just then a boy about nine years old come out of the barn on the back of a giant sow and jumped off in front of Webb and said, "Just who are you and what are you doing?"

"My name's Webb and I'm trying to call them hogs."

The little boy laughed and said, "that ain't how you call a hog, you turd."

Webb exclaimed, "I ain't no turd!"

"Stand back and let me show you how it's done."

The little brown-headed boy cupped his hands to his mouth and called out,

"Wooooooooooooooooooooooo,"

"Wooooooooooooooooooooooo,"

"Wooooooooooooo, Pig Soooie!"

When the calling started, the hogs came a runnin'. "Now that's how you call a hog, you turd."

"I ain't no turd."

"Yeah, well, you ain't got rid of the Yankee in you yet either and until you do, you won't know nothin' 'bout calling hogs," the boy smiled and extended his hand to Webb.

"Webb, my name is Timmy Harris, and if you stick with me, I'll teach ya all about it."

Webb smiled and said, "I'll stick, but I ain't gonna be called no turd."

The boys shook hands and said, "Deal."

After the men talked, the group left and headed back to the Webb place.

"Zeb, we sure thank you for everything, and I promise we'll come for another visit soon and we'll let you know when we get a place."

"Well, you know where we are, so don't be shy. Webb needs to be around family, and there are plenty of young'uns for him to play with. Matter of fact, after Sunday service, how 'bout we all come back here and have us a Webb family reunion?"

"Sounds good. Then we will see you at Sunday service," said Andy.

With that, they parted ways, and the three land hunters headed north and west.

Chapter Nine

They crossed Mine Creek and headed west. After a few miles' ride, they came to another fast-flowing clear creek and stopped to let the horses drink. The creek headed more or less north, so they decided to follow it.

After a couple of miles, they met a man who had careful eyes and a calm voice. "How do?" the man asked.

Andy replied, "Can't complain none, I don't reckon, and yourself?"

"Right as rain myself."

"Names, Wakefield, Andy Wakefield. This is my friend and business partner, Danc Tressler, and my son Webb."

"Webb? Well, I tell ya I sold a few jerseys to a family with the same name and the boy has sure got the look. Are they kin?"

"If you're talking 'bout Zebidia Webb, then yes sir. He's my brother-in-law."

"That's the one. Your boy has the look. I tell you he has more than their look. He's got eyes that look at ya a sure way."

"Yeah, we've heard that a time or two," replied Andy.

"I guess if you sold Zeb some milk cows, then you'd be Mr. Green."

"I'm him, so say my folks," grinned Mr. Green.

"Looking to take up some land for running cattle and horses," said Dane.

"Plenty for the getting. I'm the only one out here. How much you needing?"

"Looking for a few thousand or close to it."

Mr. Green let out a whistle. "Boy, just how many cattle and horses are you running?"

"I'm not too sure yet, but I'm figuring a thousand to twelve hundred head of cattle and maybe a hundred to hundred fifty horses to start with."

"That's a nice size herd of both. Grass around here will handle it if you don't get much more than that. That's a good two acres to the head, so a few thousand will do you. But since no one's out here but me, I figure they'll roam well over three thousand."

"Yes sir, I figure you're right. I just want to make sure I have three thousand guaranteed." stated Andy.

"Smart thing, probably. This country is filling up. I bet Hell's Valley probably has seventy-five people living in it. Can't see how they move with that many folks."

"Yes sir, I reckon so," replied Andy.

"My place is just three quarters of a mile or so straight west of here. I'm occupying a few hundred acres, but you keep on the way you're heading, and you'll find you a real nice place about two more miles right after the creeks fork."

"Thank you for your time, Mr. Green, and I'm sure we'll see you around," said Andy.

"I'll be around for the seeing. Y'all stop by and the Missus will fix us a might to eat. I'll warn you young'un, I only got one boy, and he's older. But I got a passel of girls that'll sure take a shine to ya, and you may have to fight 'em off."

Webb looked at the man, smiled and got a wink and a smile in return.

Just like he said, they found the creek fork and half a mile later; they found their home. It was the perfect spot, no question. It had one creek a couple hundred yards straight west and another a couple hundred yards straight east.

There was a taller hill across the creek to the east but walking up and down for water would get old fast, so they chose their spot.

They spent the rest of the day riding in a large circle for a couple of miles in every direction, with the hill being the center. They found plenty of clear creeks, rolling hills with good grass and spots of timber for all their building needs.

This was home, so they started making plans. They needed to get the land paid for and start looking for hands to build a cabin, a bunkhouse, barns, and corrals. All that would start tomorrow.

They stabled their horses at the livery. Toby asked. "Did y'all have any luck finding land or the Webbs?"

"We sure did, on both accounts," replied Andy.

"You say little Sheriff has a few brothers who might make some hands?"

"Yes sir. You could get two of them, but you won't have luck with the other two. One lives a day's ride northeast and the other is a preacher down at the church house, Reverend Michael Launius. I reckon he does a good job."

"How about the other two?"

Toby hollered, "Sheriff, get in here!"

"I swear, Toby, you screamin' at me ever' five minutes is startin' to sound like my momma," said Sheriff.

"I'll be sure to tell her you said that."

The look on Sheriff's face was that of worry. "Sheriff, you almost look scared at the thought," said Andy.

"He ought to be. That woman raised five boys, Sheriff's the youngest. The others just keep getting bigger and older. But believe me, when Jeanette speaks, they listen or they know what comes next," Toby said. "Now, Keith... Oh, I mean, Sheriff." Sheriff eyed Toby with a look and spit tobacco juice without taking his eyes off him. "When you get home, you tell Bill and Baccor to be here in the morning to talk to Mr. Wakefield about a job."

"I'll tell 'em but it makes us even, and you don't say nothin' bout nothin' to Momma," replied Sheriff.

Toby smiled and said, "Deal."

"There you go, Andy. Your first two hands will be here in the morning, and I've got a few more in mind for ya too. First, let's see how you like these two, then we'll look at the others."

"Baccor?" said Andy.

Toby grinned and said, "Yes sir, Baccor. I told you from Sheriff, they just get older."

They got cleaned up and made it to supper, just as Mrs. Hutchinson was about to call for them. She had fried chicken, lima beans, mashed potatoes, gravy, biscuits, and white cake with a thick white frosting for dessert.

The blessing was said by D.A., and everyone dug in. "How did it go today, men?" asked D.A.

"Just fine. Come to find out, the Webb family out south of here is my brother-in-law and some of my wife's cousins. We got to spend a couple of hours with them and we're planning to have a get together after church service this Sunday."

"How in the world did the two of you end up all this way from home, just about side by side?"

"The good Lord works that way sometimes," said Andy.

"Indeed, he does," replied Mrs. Hutchinson.

"We also met with a man who is going to keep us supplied in hogs when we get started."

"Was it Mr. Harris?" asked D.A.

"It sure was."

"He does good business in the area," said D.A. "He keeps us, the café, and the store, in cured meat. Plus, he helps anyone who's looking for a pig or two for their own."

"I figure once we get started, we will keep him in business until we can start raising a few for ourselves. When we get our cattle, we'll have our own beef, and we'll get us a few chickens," said Andy.

"That's what we have," said D.A. "My partner and I have a few cattle we use for our own meat supplies with just enough trading to keep us in stock. Like I said, we are small. I came here to run the hotel, and then we opened our home. I like to stay busy and enjoy being around people."

Andy replied, "You seem to be doing well. I hope we're as lucky."

"So, how about a place? Did you find one?" asked D.A.

"We did, and it is more than what we need. Tomorrow we are going to the courthouse to file what's needed and pay for it. Once we get everything squared away and we get a few more hands, we're gonna take off for Texas. Dane and a few others will stay behind to see to building a cabin, a bunkhouse, barns, and everything we need while we are gone."

"Is Webb staying behind?" asked Mrs. Hutchinson.

"No ma'am, I reckon where I go, he goes."

Mrs. Hutchinson asked Webb, "Do you think you're up for it, young man?"

"I reckon I better be, ma'am, 'cause ready or not, it's about time."

"You be careful. It's still running wild with Indians and God only knows what else."

"Yes ma'am, I will."

The rest of the meal passed with small talk. Everyone assured Mrs. Hutchinson the meal was delicious and said good night.

CHAPTER TEN

With a good night's rest, they were back at the table for a hardy breakfast. As soon as breakfast was done, they were off to the livery.

"Mornin', gentlemen."

"Morning, Toby, morning Sheriff, and who do we have here?" Andy was looking at two blond headed boys about fifteen and nineteen. The young one was bigger, six-foot, two hundred pounds. The oldest was six-foot, rail thin, with blue eyes, a beak of a nose, and a jaw with a wad full of tobacco.

Sheriff, as serious as ever, said, "These here are my brothers, Mr. Wakefield. Ain't neither one as smart nor as good lookin' as me, but they'll work."

The young one slapped Sheriff in the back of the head and said, "Yeah, but we're bigger and meaner now, so shut up. I'm Baccor and this here is my little brother, Bill."

"Baccor, huh?" said Andy.

"Yes sir, Baccor. And I can ride anything with hair, rope anything that moves, and I'm what you might call a ladies' man."

"You don't say?"

"I do and it's 'cause I'm so doggone irresistible and good lookin'. The ladies can't help themselves."

Andy grinned and said, "I do believe I see what you're saying, Baccor."

"How 'bout you, Bill?"

"Oh, I'm the smart one, Mr. Wakefield."

"The smart one, you say. Well, tell me how you figure that, Bill?"

"I figure it 'cause I know without a doubt that all my brothers are full of it. By 'it' I mean..."

Andy laughed, "I think I know what you mean. Well, how about a handle or do you just go by Bill?"

"Like I said, I'm the smart one, but you can just call me Bill or Billy Wayne."

"How does twenty-five a month and food sound to you?"

They made plans to have Dane take Bill and Baccor with the wagon to their new place. They needed all their tools for building, so they would just have to figure out something to do with their things at night. Dane took off with the new hands while Andy and Webb left for Center Point.

Center Point was a hopping place, and it had it all. Whatever Hell's Valley didn't have, they would surely find it here. They got all they needed and didn't dally.

They rode back into Hell's Valley about noon, so they went to the Pearl for lunch.

Mrs. Wendy greeted them at the door. "Hello Mr. Wakefield and Webb."

"Ma'am," Andy said as he tipped his hat. "It sure smells good today."

"Well, sit down and we'll see if it tastes as good as it smells. How about two specials?"

"Sounds perfect."

She quickly returned with coffee and milk and a pat on Webb's head. "Pretty thing."

Webb beamed, "Thank you, ma'am."

"You're welcome, darling."

She left for the kitchen and returned a few minutes later with two plates of thick ham, butter beans, fried potatoes, and fresh bread.

"Mrs. Wendy, I think you may have outdone yourself."

"I hope so. I'm trying to give Webb all the strength he can get because I told my little sister about him, and I think she has some plans for him."

Webb looked up, grinning, and Andy said, "You heard the lady. Eat up, Son." They both dug in, and of course, at the end of the meal, she showed up with fresh apple pie.

"Mrs. Wendy, I wonder if you can fix me up three of them lunches with pie to go? I've got three men that are gonna be starved by the time I get back to them."

"I sure can if you give me a few minutes."

Just then, a young girl walked in.

"I was just talking about you. Come here and meet Mr. Wakefield and Webb."

"Hello, Mr. Wakefield. I'm Dana Smith."

"Well, hello Dana. You sure are a beautiful thing."

"Thank you." She looked at Webb and smiled, "I reckon you would be Webb?"

"Yeah. I'm Webb."

"Good, then come on outside with me. You're my boyfriend now, so you gotta do like I say. You gotta hold my hand too." Webb looked lost as he got up and stared at his father.

Andy smiled and said, "Don't look at me, son, you heard the lady. Just don't go too far. We're gonna be leaving here shortly."

"Yes sir," said Webb as he followed in tow behind a girl a head taller than him.

"She's a hoot," said Andy.

"Sure is, and then some."

"How old is she?"

"She's ten."

"Same age as Webb, but she was almost a head taller."

"Our Pa is a big man, so we followed suit."

"You sure did, both of you."

"I'll be back in a few with your food."

She returned ten minutes later with a basket full of food. "This is all I had to put the food in, but I trust you'll bring it back. I also put some plates and bowls in there."

"I promise I'll bring it back to you at breakfast tomorrow."

He paid for the meals and walked outside where Webb and Dana were sitting on the walkway, holding hands.

"Miss Dana, I hate to interrupt your courtin' but we've got to get to work."

"That's ok, Mr. Wakefield," Then she looked at Webb and said, "Now you remember, you're my boyfriend. That means when you come to town, you have to sit with me and hold my hand."

"Yes ma'am," said Webb as he walked off with his pa.

"She made my hand sweat."

Andy grinned. "Sounds like you better get used to it."

"Yes sir. I reckon."

Webb and Andy rode up to find Dane, and the new hands were busy working. They had logs cut and had already started skidding them to the house site.

"Am I glad to see you with that basket. My stomach thinks my throat's been cut," said Dane.

Andy shouted, "You boys take a break and come eat!" Bill and Baccor followed orders and took a load off.

"Webb, what do you say we skid some logs while these men eat?"

"Yes sir."

Andy and Webb took over while the other three ate. The rest of the day went well, and for the next week, Dane drove the wagon into town every evening. It was a little tiresome, but they were just too worried about leaving the wagon and tools alone overnight.

On the third day, as they were hitching the team up, Toby said, "Andy, them other two boys I told you about will be here sometime today. What do you want me to tell 'em?"

"Tell them I'll meet them back here at noon. We'll have lunch and talk. I have to come back to talk to Mr. Johnson over at the sawmill."

They hitched the wagon and saddled the horses. The group was off again.

Just as Andy had said, he was back by noon, and waiting for him at the livery was Toby and the two new hands. "Andy, this here is Bryan Clifton and Josh Butler."

Josh was a small fella, 'bout five eight, one fifty, sandy hair with a mustache. Clifton was just the opposite. He was five inches over six foot, two hundred forty pounds and had a slow southern drawl when he talked. His shoulders were an axe handle wide, and his young hands were hard from work.

"Hello boys. I hear you're looking for work?"

"Yes sir. I reckon we could use it," said Josh.

"I'm paying twenty-five a month plus found. Right now, there ain't much found to offer other than food. The boys I got working for me head for home every night until we get the bunkhouse finished, which should be in another three or four days. How far are you boys coming from?"

"I come from bout twelve miles out," said Clifton.

"And I come from four miles farther on," said Josh.

"Well, that's too far for you boys going and coming. How 'bout I get y'all a room over at the boarding house with us? You mind sharing a room?"

"No sir, that sounds fine."

"Let's get a bite to eat, then we'll get situated."

The three went to the Pearl for a meal, Andy got a room at the boarding house for the boys, and they went to the sawmill on Mine Creek to talk to Mr. Johnson. John Johnson built his sawmill back in '25 and did fair business.

"Mr. Johnson, I was hoping to buy a little lumber from you. I figure it will end up being a lot before it's over, but right now, I need to finish out the inside of the bunkhouse. So, I'm gonna need a couple wagon loads of boards."

"Well, I got plenty, Son. Business has been slow. I figured to let my help go until things got busy again. I sure don't want to. He's a good worker."

"Yes sir, I understand. Maybe I can help you. I'm needing another hay cutter for a while, and when the hay's cut, if you're still slow, I can probably find him something else to do."

"Son, you are a God send I tell ya. I've been worried over it, but I reckon it sounds like you've took the worry away."

Mr. Johnson walked over to the back door and called out, "Tem, come in here."

A young man came through the door. He was about five foot seven, with a red tint to his head and beard, and light eyes.

"Yes sir?"

"Tem, this is Andy Wakefield, and he may have saved our bacon, boy. He's needin' a hand for a while. I'm hopin' by the time the work's done over there, business will have picked up here. Then you can come back to work with me. How do you feel about that?"

"Sounds fine, but I gotta be honest, Mr. Wakefield. I've heard you're planning a cattle ranch, and, well, sir... I don't know a thing about no cows."

"That's alright, Tem. I don't even have cattle yet. Right now, we are doing some building and getting settled in."

"I can sure help build. I know a bit 'bout such things."

"Good. How about using a scythe? I've also got a lot of hay to put up."

Tem smiled. "I'm pretty low to the ground, so I can cut hay with the best."

"Do you live close, or do you need a place?"

"I'm close to town. Me and my ma live up at the Gunter place. I'm Tem Gunter, sir, Tem, with an E."

"Well, Tem with and E, I'm paying twenty-five plus found. You can stay at our place when the bunkhouse is ready, and I would rather you do that so there won't be no worry 'bout coming and going so early and late."

"I reckon it's a deal. When do I start?"

Andy looked at Mr. Johnson and asked, "When can you turn him loose?"

"How 'bout he starts for you Monday? Let him finish the week here?"

"Sounds like a plan," said Andy.

Sunday rolled around and, as planned, Andy, Webb and Dane rode out to the Webb farm for a family get together. They spent the day with delicious food, grand stories, and kids having a good time.

CHAPTER ELEVEN

They spent Monday morning moving out of town and into the bunkhouse. With a roof over their heads at night, they were finally happy to be in their own place.

They built a barn with a good size crib for corn and filled the loft full of hay. A deep well was also dug to supply cold, clear, sweet water.

A few springs had been dug out for extra water, but with two creeks flowing year-round, it was only a precaution.

It was coming on fall and Andy heard southwest Texas would be a good place to be for the winter. The cattle were a little cheaper down there and the work wasn't nearly as hot.

Andy and Dane talked it over and decided that Bill and Dane would stay behind to start work on the main house. Andy would take Webb, Baccor, Josh and Clifton to Texas with him.

Andy had been over on the Little River to the Sykes trading post a few times, talking to John Sykes about some business with horses and cattle.

He had two hands lined up through Big John and figured to hire a few more hands, but would wait until he got to Texas.

With the summer dying fast, the trip to Texas arrived. Gone before the sun was up, they crossed the Saline, the Cossatot, and were coming up on the Little River. They could hear voices over the horse's hooves. When they topped the riverbank, they could see why.

There at the Rocky Shoals River crossing were three boys, none over ten years old and all three as naked as the day they were born. They were taking advantage of the cool water in a waist deep pool on a sultry morning. As they rode down the riverbank, all the boys stopped to turn and look.

The oldest boy asked, "Hey, mister, where y'all headed?"

"Son, we are on our way to Texas," said Andy.

"Texas! Whatcha gonna do in Texas?"

"We're going to get some cattle and catch some wild horses."

The oldest boy shouted, "Woooo weeee! I'd sure like to catch me a wild horse!"

"Are you gonna fight Injuns?" said the youngest boy.

"I sure hope not. Injuns can sure be some fierce fighters," replied Andy.

"I want to kill me a buffalo," said the middle boy.

"And I want to fight me an injun," said the youngest.

The oldest boy laughed. "I've seen you shoot with Papaw's gun, Bubba. You couldn't hit water if you fell in the creek."

"How far is Texas, mister?" asked Bubba.

"Texas ain't far. It's only about twenty miles from here to the border. But we are going to the other side of Texas and south. So, I figure it's about seven hundred miles."

The youngest boys hollered, "Seven hundred miles! Boy, I bet that's almost all the way around the world."

"Shut up. I swear you two are dumber than horse turds. It's like two thousand miles around the world," said the oldest. "Ain't that right, mister?"

"Something like that," smiled Andy.

"Do you need any hands? I can ride and shoot."

The littlest one laughed. "You can't ride. Our old milk cow, Bell, bucked you off."

"Boys, not this trip, but you give it a few years, and I bet I could use you then. How's that sound?"

"As long as you don't catch all them horses before we get to."

"Or kill the Injuns."

"And don't forget about my buffalo."

"What's your names, boys? I need to know who my future top hands are."

"I'm Brandon Adams. This is my little brother, Bubba, and our little cousin, Russell."

"Brandon, Bubba, and Russell. I promise I won't forget you boys."

"Thanks, Mister."

Brandon turned around, dunked Russell in the water, and Bubba started peeing in the pool.

The riders rode up the south bank to Sykes Trading Post. The building sat on the high bank, away from flooding.

Sykes had a huge horse pen out back with two more large corrals sitting farther back. There were three horses tied to the hitch rail out front.

"Relax, boys, while I talk to Big John," said Andy.

He stepped into a large room that was filled with anything a man needed. Big John sold everything. From the smallest items like needle, thread, and buttons to the biggest things like cattle and horses. He would buy, sell, or trade just about anything.

Two men were sitting at a table drinking coffee. Andy knew they were his new hands.

"Ringold and Harrington, I'm guessing," said Andy as he approached the table with an outstretched hand.

"Yes sir. That's us. I'm Lynn Ringold and this is Dwayne Harrington."

"Heavy on the D and light on the wayne," said Dwayne.

"I'm Andy Wakefield. If you boys are ready, you can go on outside and introduce yourself to everybody. I'll be out after I talk to Big John."

"Yes sir. Will do."

Andy stepped over to the counter where John was talking to another man.

"Morning, Andy."

"Morning, John."

"Andy, this is Ronnie Smith. Ronnie, Andy Wakefield."

"Pleasure, Mister Smith."

"Yes sir, but you can call me Shorty."

"Ok, Shorty, and I'm Andy."

"Them three down in the river belong to you?"

"Only the youngest one is mine, but I lay claim to all three."

"I'll be honest with you. If they were a little older, I think they'd try to hire on with me. It seems one wants to fight Injuns, one wants to catch wild broncs, and the other wants to kill a buffalo."

Shorty laughed, "Hell, I can't keep 'em in clothes longer than five minutes at a time. Every water hole we pass, they think they gotta strip and get in. Can't you just see three bare butts going across the plains after Indians, buffalo, and wild horses? The Indians would die laughing."

The men gave a hardy laugh.

"Well, I got to go. The wife's promising fried chicken for lunch. Nice to meet you, Andy, and you boys be careful down there. They say old Chief Peta Nocona is a terror."

"Who's Peta Nocona?"

"He's the war chief for the Comanche. And the Comanche are pure poison."

"I'll keep that in mind," said Andy.

Shorty walked out and you could hear him holler, "Good Lord boys, cover them thangs up 'fore the fish nibble 'em off!"

Big John Sykes was six foot one, sandy-haired, two hundred forty pounds, with a hard and firm shake.

"I see you're ready," said Big John.

"Ready as I'll ever be, I reckon," replied Andy.

"Them two boys are hands, and I'll put my name on it."

"Good, 'cause you recommended them, remember?"

"You'll get your money's worth and then some."

"Lynn looks like a handful," said Andy.

"Believe me, he's more. He's pure poison with them huge hands, and all muscle, bone wrapped in sun-dried leather. He has a wild-eyed grin, a taste for whiskey, and a natural dare for anyone who wants to try him."

"How 'bout young Dwayne?" He said as he stressed the D.

"Dwayne can rope anything, including the wind. He's easygoing and there is never a dull moment with him. His only downfall is women. He loves 'em all."

Andy grinned, "Don't we all, Big John, don't we all?"

"Indeed, we do. Remember, Andy, I'll buy any horses or cattle you want to drop off here when you get back. I know you're going after your ranch seed, but I'll pay goin' price for all."

"If we catch more horses than we need, I promise ya they're all yours, and under the going price. I know you need to make a dollar."

The men shook hands and walked outside. The boys were ready, climbing in the saddle, when Andy stepped off the porch.

As they rode away, you could hear a holler in the distance, "Boys, put them clothes on! Y'all can't walk home necked!"

Chapter Twelve

Not long after noon, they arrived in Texas. They crossed over the Red River, moving steady.

"Webb, since your pony ain't a cow pony, you're gonna want to get him used to the most important thing. He's got to get used to a rope swinging over and around his head. Every day, while you're riding, I want you swinging a rope," said Josh.

"What will I rope?" asked Webb.

"Nothing, for now. You're gonna learn to swing your rope the right way, and your horse is gonna learn to get used to it."

Josh gave him his rope, showed him how to swing it, and told him to fall to the back, away from everyone. Every day a different cowboy fell back to ride with him, giving their own thoughts and helpful hints on how to swing a rope.

Webb's gray never gave notice to the rope, although he did turn to look at Webb the first few times it swung by his head.

Each day found them further west, and the trees were getting fewer and smaller. On the fifth night, they stopped just as the sun headed over the horizon to hide.

They found a clear, flowing stream and good grass for the horses. Baccor walked out fifty yards from camp to keep watch. To be on the safe side, they kept lookouts through the night.

The coffee was brewing, biscuits, bacon, and beans were on the fire when suddenly a whistle from Baccor sounded. Everyone put a hand on a gun and all eyes looked to the west.

"Hello to the camp," came a voice from the dark.

"Hello yourself! Come in if you're friendly," shouted Andy.

"We are friendly and pleasant to boot," proclaimed the voice.

"Now that's a boldfaced lie," came a second voice.

As the two voices moved closer to the fire and into the light. Everyone could see it was two grizzly looking men leading mountain bred horses.

One was in a coonskin hat with a red beard, only five foot seven and built like a small bear. The other had long brown hair under a flop hat, five foot ten and slim. He had a patch over one eye and his beard was the same color as the hair on his chest. Both men were in greasy buckskins.

"Don't let him tell you no yarn, mister. He is about as pleasant as a grizzly with a bullet in his hind parts," said the short one with a grin.

"Well, as long as you can control him, I guess we will all be safe," said Andy.

"Good luck with that," said the one with the beard.

"Seen your fire, smelled your coffee, and hoped we might enjoy a night with you?"

"Y'all are sure welcome to the coffee, the food, and the camp."

"Thank you kindly. I see ya got yourself a nice size group here. Are you heading west?" said the short one.

"We sure are. We're headed to locate us a herd of cattle and some horses to drive home."

"Sounds like a job."

"How 'bout you two? I'd say you look like you came right out of the mountains."

"That we did, sir. Me, I been more than thirty years in the wilds, and this varmint here, he's been about twenty-five years."

Andy whistled with fascination, "Boy, I reckon you have sure seen a few things in that time."

"That we have," said the long-haired one.

"Us two fought near ever' injun known from the Blackfeet up north to the Apache and Comanche down south. We been back and forth from north to south more times than you could count. We decided last year to do her one more time and call it quits. The beaver is running thin, the markets drying up, and them greenhorns is filling the mountains. So home is where we're headed," said the short one.

"I thought you lived in the mountains?" said Webb.

"Well, Son, that's right. We lived in them mountains for so long it seems it's home. But before the mountains I was a youngster just like yourself with a Ma and a Pa and even a little sister. I'm hoping I still got all them things, although it's been so long, I just don't know."

"Where's home, if ya don't mind me asking?" asked Andy.

"My partner here," he said as he motioned towards the man with the eye patch, "he was raised by a puma. That's how come he got the name Wild Cat Kendricks and it's how he lost that eye. He got out of line and his puma pa took that eye with a swipe."

Webb asked in amazement, "Did a puma really take your eye?"

"Sure did, boy. Knocked me right off my horse and took my eye all in one swipe... I kilt him, though. I stumbled around long enough trying to catch my horse that run off on me and that's how I come to meet this here ugly feller I been traveling with."

The short one laughed and said, "I been trying to shake his trail ever since."

"I ain't got no home to speak of," said Wildcat. "That's why I figured on giving Arkansas a try."

"My folks been back east so long I'm 'fraid of trying to make the trip without knowing if they're still there. I'm gonna send me a letter first before I go. I had me a feller last winter to write it for me. He even learned me to write my own name. I figure my ma will be proud to see me write Layne in a letter. I ain't used my Christian name in so long it felt like I was telling a lie."

"If your home is back east and you're going to Arkansas, that must mean you're from there?" said Andy.

"That's what it means alright. I left home back in '27. 'Bout the only thing around were Caddos and Choctaws. They weren't ten white families within sixty miles. Nobody was settling there 'cause of the great raft."

"What's the great raft?" asked Webb.

"It was a big ol' raft of wood that'd been piling up for years down the Red River. Come from trees uprooted, vines, dead logs, and anything else you can imagine. The Red was stopped up for over a hundred miles."

"What happened to it?"

"Well, the last word I got was back in '40. I hear say that folks went to workin' on gettin' it gone and around '38 the Red was flowing. Before that, ya couldn't travel the river, so ya had to drive a long way for supplies. People just didn't want to settle in the area. There was one trader, 'bout three miles west of us on the Little River. He done some trading, but he didn't have much more than the rest of us. Good man, though, name of Sykes."

Andy asked, "Are you talking about Big John Sykes at Sykes Trading up on the Little River?"

"Yes sir, though he wasn't named Big John. If I remember right, he did have him a boy running round with that handle."

"Yeah, his daddy passed and now that little boy is called Big John 'cause he ain't so little no more. The store's a good one," said Andy.

"If you say you're from a few miles east of Sykes, then you must be talking 'bout Bush Hill," said Lynn.

The man eyed Lynn. "Now what do you know 'bout Bush Hill, boy?"

"I know enough. I also know the folks that live there. If you're one of 'em, then that means your name is Phillip Bush."

The man just stared for a minute and said, "I tell ya, that is a name I ain't heard in a while. But I'll also tell ya, I'm one and the same, only I go by Flip. Now you mind telling me how you seem to know so much about me and mine?"

"I'm from downriver, 'bout ten or twelve miles, in Peytonville. I know your family because I saw your ma and sister up at the trading post a few times. They sell Big John fresh eggs and vegetables from their garden."

"So, they're still there after all these years?"

"Yes sir, I mean, at least the women are. My folks have been in the area since they cleared the Red and I know your pa's been gone since then. I even seen his marker once when I stopped by your place to drop off a letter for your ma."

"I been afraid of what I might find for so long. Guess I don't know what to say."

"You'll figure it out when you see your ma."

"Yeah, I reckon you're right."

Everyone ate as the old mountain men told one story after another. It was getting late, so Andy told Webb to climb into his bedroll.

The next morning there was breakfast and coffee, and soon after, they said their goodbyes.

Andy shook hands with the mountain men and said, "If you two ever find your way Northeast of Bush Hill, y'all be sure to stop by the T2W for a meal and a visit."

"Young feller, you watch out for them Comanche. They are sure enough poison."

"Yes sir. I will," said Webb. Wildcat gave a big smile and one last wave goodbye.

Andy and the group rode on for another seven days when they came to the town of Waco to stop for supplies. Andy knew he needed a wagon and a cook, but he was trying to wait until he made it to his destination. That's when he saw the drummer's wagon sitting there with a sign that read...

For Sale

See the Marshall

He thought it might be worth asking. He stepped into the jail, and there was the Marshall, kicked back with his feet on the desk and eyes closed.

When Andy walked in, the Marshall turned his head, opened one eye, and said, "Yes sir, what can I help ya with?"

"I saw your sign on the wagon out there. I thought I might check on it."

"You sure don't look like much of a drummer."

"No sir. I'm actually needing a wagon with extras. I figure with a little work I can make do with that one."

The Marshall gave a smile and offered his hand, "I'm Dan Russell and I'll sure make you a deal. I even got the mules down at the livery to pull it."

Andy grinned as he shook the Marshall's hand. "Sounds like the only thing I need now is a cook. I don't suppose you got one of them lying around?"

"Son, this must be your lucky day. It just so happens I got me a Chinaman and I'll throw him in for two dollars. That's how much his fine is to get him out of jail."

"Two dollars don't sound like much of a fine. What did he do?"

"Well, ya see, they's two ol' boys in town who I reckon like to pick at folks and, well, sometimes they go a little farther than they should. They was just having some fun with the Chinaman, they told him they was gonna shave his head and shave off... well, something else. They went to grab that little feller and all hell broke loose. He come off that ground a spinnin' and kickin' and hittin' so fast them boys didn't know come here from sic 'em. One of 'em was even hollerin' make 'em stop, make 'em stop! He actually thought they was more than one."

"Marshall, I don't know if I'm looking for a brawler, especially a Chinaman brawler. Is the Chinaman the one that owned that wagon?"

"No, the owner was a drummer. He had a heart attack and died while givin' a sales pitch. There was nobody to claim it, so the town was selling it to pay for his planting up at the cemetery. The Chinaman ain't really a brawler. I ain't never had the first minute of a problem out of him. I'm just hopin' to be rid of him before those two he whooped come back for blood and cause me more headaches."

"Can I talk to the Chinaman first?"

"Sure, come on back here."

They walked through an open door down a narrow hallway into a dark area of steel doors and bars. There in the middle of the floor, under a dusty beam of broken light, sat a little, squinty eyed, black-haired man. With a disciplined posture, and legs crossed under him, he appeared to be studyin' on something.

"Chinaman, I got ya a visitor."

"I no Chinaman, I Laotian."

Andy said, "So you're from Laos?"

The little man smiled. "You very smart man. I from Laos."

"What in the world are you two talking about?" said the Marshall.

"He isn't from China." said Andy "He's from Laos, which makes him Laotian."

"And just where is Laos?"

"Well, it's in Asia, Marshall."

"Sounds like you've been there Mr... I don't think I even caught your name."

"It's Wakefield, my name's Andy Wakefield."

"Well, Mr. Wakefield, since you two seem to be good friends and all, how 'bout that two dollars?"

Andy looked at the little man and said, "I hear you whooped two men pretty good?"

"Yes." He said as he looked down. "They say they shave off my..."

Andy interrupted. "That sounds like a good reason to fight. Can ya cook?"

"I good cook."

"What can you cook?"

"I cook any food you want and cook very good."

"Do you cook as good as you fight?"

"Better." He said with a grin.

"Would you like a job cooking for a bunch of cowboys on a roundup and a drive back to Arkansas?"

"What happen when trip over?"

"I need a cook at home, so you can hire on for good."

"I go." He said with a bow.

"How 'bout a handshake?" said Andy. He held out his hand. "I'm Andy Wakefield."

"My name Meko Ketkeorsmy."

"Meko?"

"Ketkeorsmy?"

Andy grinned and said. "I reckon we'll stick with Meko."

As the Marshall opened the door to the cell, he said. "Y'all can walk down to the livery and get the mules."

Andy had the wagon dropped off to be fitted for his needs before he set out to introduce Meko to the group.

Somewhat awkward introductions were complete, and Andy announced, "We're gonna camp out here on the edge of town tonight. Probably the next too, while we wait on the wagon being fitted. If you boys wanna go to town tonight, y'all go 'head."

Baccor, Josh, and Dwayne wasted no time. They hit their saddles and off to town they went.

"Clifton, you and Lynn might as well join 'em."

"We will later, Andy. We're gonna work with Webb on his roping skills while we got some time," said Clifton.

Chapter Thirteen

The next few hours of daylight, Clifton and Lynn ran along the ground in front of Webb and his horse, taking turns letting him rope them.

After a delightful meal cooked by Meko, Andy and Webb got comfy as Meko started talking about life across the sea.

Clifton and Lynn told Andy they figured to go have a few drinks and would see him later.

Meanwhile, at the saloon, three big men sat at a table glaring across at Baccor, Josh, and Dwayne while they conversed with three bar girls. Eventually, the big men approached the table.

The biggest man named Burns stood over Baccor and said, "I guess you three think you're something special hogging all the women?" Baccor turned and looked up. He quickly realized that Josh and Dwayne put together barely made up the size of one of Burns.

Josh grinned and said, "No sir, we sure don't, but the women do."

"Since you boys ain't from here, let me explain the rules to you. You see, them's our girls you got, and we don't like you. So, I reckon we is gonna have to whoop you a little, so as we can get our point across to you."

"We ain't your girls, Burns." said a brown-haired dove named Cassy.

"You hear that, boys? They ain't our girls."

The three men grinned.

"Where you boys from?" asked Burns.

"We are from Arkansas." said Dwayne.

"Arkansas! Well hell, they ain't nothing but hillbillies and hog farmers from Arkansas. You see, boys, we are from Texas, and that means this here is our place."

Baccor wrinkled his nose, "Is that what that smell is?"

"You smart mouth little turd. On your feet all of you. We are gonna have to teach you and any other Arkansas boys a lesson."

Just then, Lynn and Clifton came through the doors, and Josh gave a big smile when he saw the two come strolling in.

About the only difference between the two were their looks. They were both well over six feet, with shoulders wide as an axe handle. They were both lean in the hips with hands the size of hams and harder than ten-pound sledgehammers.

"You say you're gonna teach us Arkansas hillbillies a lesson, huh?" said Dwayne.

"That's right, you runt. Now step forward and take your medicine."

Lynn tapped Burns on the shoulder, and when he turned around, Lynn smashed him with a straight jab. The free for all began. Lynn stayed on Burns. Clifton was giving a man named Thompson what for, and out of the corner of the room, a man came barreling in on the third man.

Baccor, Josh, and Dwayne were cheering on their friends and the man no one knew.

When the dust cleared, Burns and the other two Texans were all on the floor, unconscious from the butt whooping's received. That's when Lynn said, "I don't believe I know you, but I sure do appreciate the help with the third one." He looked at Josh, Baccor and Dwayne and said, "It don't look like we was gonna get no help nowhere else."

Dwayne said, "We was protectin' the ladies."

"Well, thank you for that, Dwayne," said Lynn.

Lynn stuck out his hand. "Lynn Ringold, and again, you didn't have to get in the ruckus, but thank you."

"Names Mike Lee Jones, Jr. and I had to. He said he was teaching all the folks from Arkansas a lesson. I'm from up Ft. Smith, so I hated to miss out on my lesson, Bub," he said, smiling.

Mike Jones, Jr. was six four, two hundred ninety pounds, and he called everybody Bub.

The Marshall came in and wanted to know what the problem was, and the bartender told him.

"It was these three troublemakers again, Marshall, but as you can see, it didn't go their way."

He looked at the group; "You boys must be with Wakefield."

"Yes sir, we are."

"I tell you what, since your boss spent so much money with me today, I reckon all I will ask is that you help drag them three over to my jail, and we will call it square."

"We'll help you, Marshall," said Clifton.

Lynn looked at the other three, and while he, Clifton and Mike Jones picked up the three Texans, he said, "You three protect the woman while we're gone."

Baccor smiled and said, "Finally you understand we are lovers, not fighters."

Lynn looked at Clifton and said, "I thought my side of the Little River had all the igits, but after meeting Baccor, I realize you have your fair share as well."

"Just wait till Josh gets cranked up. You ain't seen nothing yet."

The rest of the night, the boys bought Mike Jones drinks, and they all enjoyed stories of Arkansas. Mike rode back to camp with them and shared their place under the stars.

The next morning, they introduced Mike to Andy, and right off, Andy offered him a job.

"I reckon I'm just driftin', but when it's over and we're back in God's country, I probably won't stay on. I ain't seen my ma in a while, and her and my grandma sure mean the world to me, so I figure to head back to Ft. Smith, Bub."

"That sounds fair enough. You work until we're back in Arkansas, or God's country, as you say, and then you're free to go."

They shook hands and made the deal.

All the hands spent the rest of the day taking turns roping with Webb and lying around, resting.

They turned the wagon into what would one day be called a chuck wagon. Andy had it fitted with everything needed at the general store before they left. They stayed one more night on the edge of town. Then, with the rising sun, they were again heading southwest.

Two days later, they rode into Austin a little after dinnertime. They headed straight for the livery. They found the liveryman sitting inside the door, whistling a tune, and enjoying the shade.

"You boys lookin' to give me some business?"

"Sure thinkin' on it," said Andy.

"You've come to the right place. Name's Jason Reed." The man, with auburn hair and a big smile, stuck out his hand.

Andy accepted and said, "Andrew Wakefield."

"How long you boys gonna need my place?"

"At least tonight, and probably a few more. I'll pay every day if it's all right with you?"

"Yes sir, whatever tickles your fancy."

"You know of any big outfits around who might sell some cattle?"

"Plenty of places with cattle. I figure some may sell you a few head. How many you lookin' for?"

"Thousand head." said Andy.

"I figure you can split it up between several places and get that many. You need to go down to the feed store and talk to Chuck. He can point you in the right direction."

"Can I park my wagon out back?"

"Sure can. Plenty of room."

"How 'bout a blacksmith? Can you point me towards him?"

"One block over can't miss it."

"Thank you, Mr. Reed."

Andy took care of his bill and told the boys to go to the saloon and have a beer. He flipped Lynn a half eagle and told them he had business at the blacksmith, then he'd get them all some rooms at the hotel.

"Webb, Meko, you two come with me."

"Thinking I stay here. I no think they let me in hotel. I sleep in loft."

"Mr. Reed, do you mind if my man stays in your loft?"

"No sir, don't mind at all. He's right, they won't rent no room to a Chinaman."

"Meko, sounds like you're not gonna be as comfortable as the rest of us. I am sorry."

"You no worry, I be fine. I tired of Mike Jones' snore. I finally get rest."

"Mr. Reed, sounds like you got a guest."

"You play Chinese checkers, I reckon, since you're a Chinaman."

"I no Chinaman. I'm Laotian."

"You what?"

Meko looked at Andy, then Reed. Andy gave a big smile.

"Yes, I play," said Meko.

Andy and Webb grinned and walked out. They found the blacksmith right where the liveryman said it would be, and they were both in for a shock. Standing there, working on shaping a shoe, was the biggest man either had ever seen. He stood six foot six, three hundred and thirty pounds, with light red hair, a red beard, and arms the size of most men's legs. He looked up and smiled, then with a deep voice that boomed he said, "Hello my friends! What can Big Al do for you?"

Andy shook the man's hand. It was twice the size of a shovel.

"Andy Wakefield. I was hoping to do some business with you."

"Name's Alan Glover. If it's business you want, then business we'll do. Now who's is this young man with you? The boss, no doubt."

Webb smiled as Andy replied, "I tell you, Mr. Glover, if he gets any better at his roping, he very well may be the boss before long."

"A cowboy, is he?"

"Live and in the making."

Webb, still grinning, offered his hand. "My name is Webb, sir."

Webb's hand wouldn't even wrap around two of Alan's fingers.

"Glad to know you, Webb."

"You too, sir."

"So, what can I do for you men?"

"I was hoping you can build me three branding irons for my ranch in Arkansas."

"You came a long way for three irons, Mr. Wakefield."

"Well, I heard you were the best," Andy said, smiling.

"You heard right."

"Me and my men just rode into town. We're hoping to buy us a herd of cattle and be back at my place in Arkansas before anyone misses us."

"I tell you what, since you came so far, how about I make four? Three for full price, one extra for half."

"You got yourself a deal, Mr. Glover."

"Please, call me Alan."

"Will do, and I'm Andy."

"You can pick them up in two days. How's that sound?"

"Sounds fine. I reckon we'll leave you to it."

Andy left the blacksmith and went to the hotel where he got four rooms. The hands were gonna have to double up for the few days in town.

From the hotel, Andy and Webb went to the feed store, where they found Chuck Davis.

"Yes sir, can I help you?"

Andy offered his hand, and Chuck took it.

"Andy Wakefield, and if you're Chuck, then I think you can."

"I am, I'm Chuck Davis."

"Good to meet ya. Mr. Reed, down at the livery, said you may be able to point me in the right direction. I'm wanting to buy some cattle."

"I'm sure I can. How many you looking to buy?"

"I'm figuring a thousand. But all I want is two hundred steers and the rest, two-year-old heifers."

"I figure I know enough places to send you to so you can get what you need. Do you have cowboys of your own?"

"I have six men and myself."

Webb interrupted and with a grin he said, "that'd be eight men.".

Andy looked down as he laughed and then looked back at Chuck and said, "Well then, let's call it seven and a half men. But I was hoping to get a few more hands who'd like to make the drive back to Arkansas."

"Arkansas you say. I figure I can point you towards a pretty fair hand. My oldest boy sets a horse real good and throws a good rope. He'd sure make you a hand."

"When could I meet him?"

"Right now." Chuck yelled out the back, "Bubba! Come in here." A minute later, a young man, about six-foot, with light hair, a crooked smile, and wearing glasses, walked in.

"Yes sir?"

"Bub, this here is Andy Wakefield, and he is looking for a few hands for a cattle drive."

Bubba shook hands with Andy.

"Your father tells me you can ride and rope. He says you may be interested in a drive."

"Yes sir, I sure am. Where ya headed?"

"Up into Arkansas, just across the Red River."

"Yes sir, if Pa don't mind, I sure would like to do it. Do you need any other hands, or just me?"

"I would like you and two or three more if I can get 'em."

"I know two who would jump at the chance. They're both cow savvy and hard workers."

"Are either one good at breaking horses? I plan on catching our remuda wild before we start on cattle. Everyone is gonna be on horse duty first."

"Yes sir. Chuck Gill rides like he's sewed to the saddle and Ward Cobb is tough as they come."

"Do you think you can get them here tomorrow so I can meet 'em?"

"Yes sir, I reckon I can."

"I'm staying in the hotel, room 203 upstairs."

"I'll have 'em here tomorrow."

Andy and Chuck talked of ranches to call on for cattle. Andy then started picking Chuck's knowledge of wild horses and where he might find some.

"Your best bet is to call on Red Wolf. He's a breed that lives about five miles out on a little creek just to the West. He's half Comanche and is friendly with Peta Nocona."

"I've heard of Peta," said Andy.

"If you want wild horses, you better make a deal with Red Wolf. He can help you deal with Peta to keep him and his warriors offen your backside."

"Do you know where Peta is now?"

"Nope, the Llano Estacado is a big place and he and his warriors run it all. They keep their own horse herds in Blanco Canyon, but they know the Palo Duro like you know your own hand."

"Do you think Red Wolf can find them?"

"That breed can track a bird through the sky."

"Sounds like he is my kind of man."

Andy thanked Chuck, and he and Webb took off for the saloon.

Andy left Webb outside the saloon and found some of his men at the bar. "Where are the other three?" he asked, looking for Baccor, Josh, and Dwayne.

Lynn shook his head and pointed upstairs. Andy laughed and said, "Heck, it ain't even supper time yet."

"I told Josh the same thing, Andy, but he said he needed some fun before supper so he could work an appetite."

"Well, when the three ladies' men get back, y'all's rooms are 204, 205, and 206. We are sleeping double while in town. If you want your supper, be at the café across the way at five o'clock."

"We'll be there, but those other three may be dead from overworking themselves. Cause I swear two of those gals gotta be a good two seventy-five," said Lynn.

"Whoever shows up eats, I guess. See ya boys."

A little later, everyone showed up on time for supper. The conversation centered on the upcoming days and things to do. Andy told them of Red Wolf and his plans to have a parlay with Peta Nocona.

He ordered dinner to go for Meko. He and Webb went to check on the little Laotian. When they walked in the livery, Jason Reed looked up and said.

"You sure he ain't a Chinaman? I ain't won a game at them Chinese checkers yet." Meko smiled and said, "I beat six times. He no good."

"Well, I brought you a plate of food from the café if you think you can take yourself away long enough to eat it."

"I eat and play. Still beat him."

"You ornery little joker. I'm gonna whoop you this time for sure!"

"Mr. Reed, I'm sorry, but I didn't think to bring you anything. Would you like me to go back and get you a plate?"

"Thank you, but I get a plate delivered by the wife every night around this time."

"Ok, I figure I'll leave you two to your game."

"Believe me, it ain't a game no more. It's war!" said Reed.

Andy and Webb turned away and called it a night.

Chapter Fourteen

The next morning, after breakfast, Andy took Lynn and Webb with him to find Red Wolf.

They found his place right where Mr. Davis said it would be. When they rode into the yard, they saw a dark-haired, dark-skinned man standing in the doorway.

"Hello. My name's Andy Wakefield. I'm looking for Red Wolf."

"You found him. Climb on down and sit a spell."

Andy shook hands with the man they came to find and said, "I understand you may be able to help me find Peta Nocona?"

"Who told you that?"

"Chuck Davis, up at the feed store."

"Chuck Davis, yes, a good man! I can help you, but do you mind me asking why? I'm not trying to get in your business, but I have a relationship with Peta that's built on trust. If you have plans for ill will against him or any other Comanche, then the answer is no."

"Understood, and I give you my word. I've got no ill intentions. I need to buy some cattle for a drive back to Arkansas. But first I need to catch a large group of wild horses for working cattle. I am hoping to take at least forty head for me and my hands, then another sixty or so for seed and sale."

Red Wolf nodded his head in understanding, "And what do you want with Peta?"

"I want to get his permission, I guess. I figure it would be better to talk with him and hope to let him understand I am not after his great herds, nor do I plan to stay. Maybe then I won't have to worry about a fight or horses being stolen every time I turn around."

"Sounds like you're a smart man, Mr. Wakefield. Give me a week, and I'll have an answer for you. When I find him, I will come get you. You ride on to Ft. Lancaster and just wait. I'll be there sometime next week and then we'll go."

"Where is the fort and how far?"

"It's just about due west. If you stay four long days in the saddle, you can make it by the fourth night."

"Sounds like a plan."

"Lynn, I want you to go back to Austin and tell the men to enjoy some time off, but stay close and ready. I don't want to lose any more time when we get back to town."

"What do you want me to do?" asked Lynn.

"I want you to find us some men who are looking to sell cattle. You know what I want, and you know beef. I trust you to make a fair deal. If you need help, you get the men to do what you need."

"Andy, I will do what you say, but are you sure it's safe for you and Webb out there by yourselves?"

Red Wolf said, "I'll be with them for the next two days. I'm sure they will be ok after that."

Andy looked at Lynn and shook his head, indicating all would be ok.

"Ok. We will have everything ready when you are back," said Lynn, before he rode away.

Andy waited for Red Wolf to get his things together and the trio headed west into the Llano Estacado.

They rode hard and made almost 30 miles before making camp.

"Red Wolf, if you want to take the first watch, I'll put us some grub on and get the coffee going."

"Fine with me. Just send the boy with my cup and plate when it's ready."

Webb and Andy went about the task of building a fire and getting some food on the fire. The food was simple, with biscuits, slabs of bacon, and strong black coffee to wash it down. Webb had his normal drink of water.

It was halfway through the night when Red Wolf woke Andy and whispered, "Someone is watching us."

"Who is it?"

"Not sure, but the horses are restless. I've heard him twice now."

"Doesn't sound like a very good horse thief," said Andy. "Could it be an animal?"

"Could be, but I don't think so. You and the boy be ready. I'm going out to see what I can find."

As Andy got up, Red Wolf melted into the dark.

"Webb, get up and grab a rifle."

"What is it, Pa?"

"Not sure, but Red Wolf thinks someone is out there watching us."

Webb got up and grabbed his rifle and looked out into the dark.

After a few tense minutes, a voice from the dark said, "Andy, feed the fire and give us some light."

Andy threw on some twigs and small sticks and got the fire going. When he could see well enough in the shadows, out came two figures. One was Red Wolf, and in front of him and his pistol was an Indian who was bleeding from cuts on his face, arms, and chest.

As they walked into the light, Andy looked into obsidian eyes that never wavered.

"Looks like you came out on the winning side of the fight, Wolf."

"None of this is from me. I walked up on him from behind while he was trying to get up close to our horses. He didn't even put up a fight."

Those black eyes found Webb and never looked away as those eyes bore into his thoughts.

Red Wolf came around and pointed to the ground. "Sit." The Indian just looked back at Webb. "Sit!" Wolf said, a little louder.

"Maybe he don't understand," said Webb.

"I think he does."

The Indian looked at Andy and sat down cross-legged.

"I speak your tongue."

"Speak it pretty good too," said Andy. "What's your name?"

"I am Black Spotted Horse."

Andy looked at Red Wolf and Wolf said, "Sioux."

"Sioux? What in the world is a Sioux doing on the staked plains?" asked Andy.

"I am Lakota Sioux. I am here for my wife."

"What's your wife doing here?" asked Andy.

"The Arapaho took my wife. They traded her to the Apache. Before I could find her, they killed her. I killed all of them before they killed my horse. I fought another one and killed him, but not before he gave me these." He pointed towards the cuts and scrapes. "I have been moving at night and coming east for three days. They gave up when a band of Comanche warriors gave chase."

"Why are you headed east instead of north?" said Andy.

"I need a horse."

"I'm sure there are horses in the north too."

Black Spotted Horse smiled and said, "Yes, but the white man is east, and it's easier to take a horse from a white man."

Red Wolf chuckled, and Andy smiled.

"Black Spotted Horse, how is it you can speak so good?" asked Webb.

"When I was a boy about your age, a white man came to live in our village during the winters. He was a French trapper. He taught me both English and French."

Andy looked at Red Wolf and said, "What do you think we need to do with our new Sioux friend?"

"I think we should tie him up until we leave in the morning."

Andy looked at Webb. "What do you think, son?"

Webb looked into the black eyes of Black Spotted Horse. "I don't think he'll hurt us, Pa."

"The young warrior is smarter than most men twice his size. I give you my word as a warrior. I will not harm you. Nor will I steal your horse," he added with a big grin.

"Mr. Horse," said Andy, "there's some biscuits and bacon left, and coffee too if you want some. I believe it's my watch, so everybody turn in."

Black Spotted Horse looked at Webb with a grin and a wink.

Instead of going back to sleep, Webb stayed up and talked to Black Spotted Horse. He listened to the story of White Buffalo Calf Woman.

"Long ago the Lakota were in a famine. They were starving, so the chief sent out two scouts to hunt. While hunting, they saw a figure in the distance. When they got close, they noticed it was a young Indian woman in white buckskin. She had dark hair, her skin and eyes caused one man to be filled with lust. He told his companion he would claim her as his wife. His companion told him the woman looks to be sacred. To do anything sacrilegious would be dangerous and disrespectful. The man ignored the friend's advice. He watched as his companion embraced the woman. Just then, a white cloud enveloped the pair. When it disappeared, it left only the woman with a pile of bones. The bones were the remains of the man. Scared, he drew his bow. The woman beckoned him forward, telling him no harm would come to him as she could see into his heart and knew he did not have the same motives as his companion. The woman spoke Lakota, so he moved forward, believing she was one of his people.

She explained she was the Wakan, which means holy. She promised if he would do as instructed, his people would rise again. He was told to return to his village, call the Council together, and prepare a feast for her arrival. Upon her arrival, she taught the Lakota seven sacred ceremonies and gave them the Chanunpa."

Webb asked, "What is that?"

"The Chanunpa is the sacred ceremonial pipe. She gave us these gifts and promised one day she would return. She made Lakota a strong people. We are still waiting for the return of Pte Ska Win."

"Do you think she will ever come back?"

"Yes. She will return when needed the most." Black Spotted Horse looked at Webb and said, "Now it is time for all young warriors to rest."

Webb smiled and lay back against his saddle and listened to the night as it sang him to sleep. The next morning, as his father was loading things on the packhorse, Webb walked up and asked, "What are you doing, Pa?"

"Sending Mr. Black Spotted Horse back to Lakota country, son."

"You giving him our pack horse, Pa?"

"Well, son, I figured either that or give him your horse."

Webb grinned and said, "You made a good choice, Pa."

Red Wolf and Black Spotted Horse walked up. "If you ever find yourself in the land of the Sioux, all you have to do is speak the name of Sapa Gleska Sunkmanitu. I will tell my people of the name Wakefield and how you are a friend and of the Wolf who is red. I will tell of the young warrior named Webb, who is called Iktomi, in my tongue and how he is wise like an old warrior and of his eyes that see the truth."

Webb smiled and they all shook hands. Andy handed Black Spotted Horse a knife and sheath, along with a few biscuits and some bacon. "I wish it was more, but we still have a few days ahead of us."

"You have done enough, and I hope one day I can repay you."

With that said, he rode away as they watched him go. "If Webb can eat in the saddle, I reckon we can go," said Andy. Webb said he could, so they loaded up and headed towards Ft. Lancaster.

After one more night, Red Wolf left them to themselves. Andy and Webb made camp about a half a day ride from the fort on the fourth day.

A few hours after dark, while Webb lay asleep, the familiar voice of Red Wolf called out, "Andy, it's me, Red Wolf. I'm coming in."

"Come on in, Wolf." Out of the dark he came in leading his horse.

"Take care of your horse, and I will have you some food when you are done." When Wolf came to the fire, he squatted down with the cup and plate offered by Andy.

"He is waiting for us. We can be there in a half day's ride."

"Sounds good. You finish eating and get some sleep. I'll wake you when it's your time for watch."

"Deal, I am ready for some sleep. It's been a long day."

Chapter Fifteen

Halfway through the night, Wolf took over the watch and rode it out for the rest of the night.

The next morning, Andy said to Wolf, "I want to go ahead to the fort. I have a few things I want to get."

They loaded up and headed out. It was just after lunch when the fort came into sight. "Wolf, you can spend the rest of the day relaxing while I get the things I need, and we'll pull out in the morning at first light."

Andy rented three pack saddles and mules to carry everything. He loaded all his supplies and was ready when Red Wolf came.

"Looks like you're planning on staying a while," said Wolf.

"I figure a few gifts would be a friendly gesture."

"It sure wouldn't hurt," replied Wolf.

Wolf looked at Webb, then back at Andy, and asked, "Are you nervous about taking the boy?"

"Nope. I figure that shows trust, and where I go, Webb goes."

"Smart man, Mr. Wakefield, smart man."

They rode steady all day, stopping only to rest and water the horses. They chewed on jerky and drank from their canteens.

The first night's camp Red Wolf told of his life. His mother was a Mexican, and his father a Comanche warrior. When his father was killed, his mother left the village and took Wolf back to the border to be raised in her village. He was three years old when his father died and his mother went to work on a large ranch as a cook. There, he learned his mother's tongue of Spanish, and she taught him his father's native tongue of Comanche. The cowboys at the ranch taught him English, and he spoke all languages flawlessly. That's also where Red Wolf learned to cowboy and other valuable life lessons he would need later on.

The next day, around noon, Webb was opening his sack of rock candy his father had bought him the day before. Suddenly, Webb looked shocked to see thirty Comanche warriors in front of them. They were the fiercest looking men he had ever seen. The hair on the back of his neck jumped out at the sight of them.

Red Wolf looked at Webb and said, "Just sit steady and don't worry, they're just here to escort us in."

"Nervous, son?"

"Little bit, Pa"

"The son may be as smart as the father," said Red Wolf.

Red Wolf spoke to the warriors, and they split up. Half riding in front of Andy's group and the other half behind. They rode about five miles until they made their way into a canyon. When they got to the deepest and coolest part of the canyon, they came upon the village. As they drew closer, the entire village came to see their arrival.

"That is Peta in front, his wife, Na Ura, and their young son beside him."

Red Wolf spoke to Peta, who in turn motioned for the group to get down. They followed Peta and a group of warriors to a wickiup where a pipe was brought out. Andy gave Wolf a bag of tobacco, who passed it to Peta, who then took the bag and smiled as he filled the pipe. They passed the pipe around before the first word was spoken.

Peta began to speak, and Wolf translated.

"He wants to know why you want this talk?"

"Tell him I have heard of the great chief Peta Nocona and his fierce warriors. I wanted my son to see this great nation of people and meet the great chief."

Peta looked at all the other warriors with swelled pride and nodded his head.

"We also came to ask if I can catch some of the wild horses that roam the Comancheria. I do not want any of the horses from the great Comanche horse herd. I only want to catch those that still run wild."

Wolf spoke the words, then Peta did in return. "He wants to know how one man, one boy, and the Wolf will catch so many great horses?"

Tell him I have ten more men in town. We are planning a cattle drive to the northeast, to the old land of the Caddo and Choctaw."

Peta listened to the words spoken, then gave a reply. "He says he likes the fact that you have honor, that you came to speak with him, and ask for his guidance, not like most whites who just come and take. He also likes the fact that you brought your son to show you have no fear of him and his people, but respect and believe they can be a peaceful people."

"I do believe that. I hope that someday our sons will be men of honor and good friends. We have also brought gifts to the people to show we are a friend to the Comanche."

Peta looked at Andy as Red Wolf spoke. He shook his head and spoke, "He says you and your men can catch horses and he wishes you well. He says the

Comanche will not bother or harm you. You are always welcome in his village. He will accept your gifts."

They all walked outside and back to the pack mules. Andy gave out twenty-five blankets, fifty pounds of flour, sugar, and coffee. He also gave Peta five pouches of tobacco. While the exchange was going on, Webb was watching and listening. He kept looking at the woman Wolf said was Peta's wife. She was dressed like an Indian woman, but she wasn't as dark as the other women. She also had light eyes, he noticed. He could have sworn she was a white woman. He also kept looking at the little boy standing behind her and hiding behind her legs.

Webb reached into his pocket and took out a piece of the rock candy and walked towards the woman, then offered the candy to the boy. The little boy turned and ran away. The woman smiled, took the candy, and said something Webb didn't understand. "She said thank you," said Wolf.

After Andy had the mules unloaded, he and his group climbed in the saddle, and he had Wolf tell Peta thank you again. As the group rode away, the woman Na Ura called to the little boy, "Quanah, come get your gift."

The ride back was uneventful but filled with conversation.

A few days later, they rode back into town. Andy gathered the hands, plus Chuck Gill and Ward Cobb, the new men Bubba had mentioned. He had also hired Red Wolf for the gather of both horses and cattle. Supplies were bought and loaded into the newly converted wagon. Plans were made and discussed. Everyone got their orders.

The next morning, they all set out with the rising of the morning sun. They rode for three and a half days when they finally came to the spot Red Wolf said they would need to make their camp. It would be their central working spot. Meko set up the cookfire and started on supper while the boys scouted around the area.

As the daylight faded, after a good meal, the hands were all gathered around.

Andy broke out Webb's pistol and handed it to him. "After our talk with Peta, I don't think we will have any problems with him, but Apache's may come this way from time to time."

Webb took the pistol and immediately checked it, cleaned it, and loaded it.

"Webb, now you being a youngster, you need some pointers with that thing," said Baccor.

"Thanks Baccor, but my pa has been teaching me since I was old enough to hold a gun."

"Well, I figured that, but shootin' at a man is gonna be some different than shootin' at a target is all I'm saying. If a feller is coming to do you harm, you can't hesitate."

"Baccor, just how many men you kilt?" asked Josh.

"Well, none, but I'm a growed man and if it comes to it, I know I got it in me. I just want the kid to know he can't hesitate none."

Webb just looked at his father and never said a word. Everybody took turns on guard duty, except Meko and Webb. During the last watch, Andy told Baccor about what happened back in Normalville. He told him he could be assured that if trouble came, eleven-year-old Webb would stand.

"Sorry Andy, I didn't know. I was just trying to reassure the youngster."

"Don't worry, Baccor. He knows."

The next morning, they split groups up, and the search began.

"Meet back at lunch," said Andy, "and we'll talk it over. If you run into trouble, fire three shots and we'll try to come if we're close enough to hear."

Andy, Lynn, and Webb took off to the west.

"What do you think about our new hands?" asked Andy.

"They all seem like good fellers. Chuck's kinda quiet. Bubba seems to have some knowledge, and Ward looks like a small bull. Once the work starts, ask me again," Lynn said.

They scouted around for hours and found nothing fresh. There were plenty of tracks and sign but all of it was weeks old.

When they got back, they found everyone but Red Wolf and Mike Jones had made it in. Everyone ate their lunch and Andy discovered everyone else found about the same thing, which was nothing. About the time Andy started to worry, Webb said, "Look! Somebody is coming." As they turned to look, a lone rider was approaching. It was Mike Jones. As he got close, they could see a big smile on the man's face.

"Mike, you're missing someone, ain't you?"

"Yeah, I reckon I am, Bub, but you see one of us had to stay behind and hold all the horses." He said with a big smile.

"Are you telling me you and Red Wolf caught some horses?" asked Andy.

"Only about a hundred, Bub, but I figure that's enough."

Everyone looked at each other and Mike said, "You better get the wagon loaded and ready to move, Bub. We need to get back so we can start building a big corral."

Mike just sat on his horse grinning and not offering any other explanation.

Andy said, "I reckon we better do what he says, boys; daylight is burning."

Andy, along with everyone else, tried to get the lowdown from Big Mike on the way back, but it did little good.

"Look, boys, just 'cause all y'all are sitting around bleeding Mr. Wakefield dry of money, don't mean me and the wolf ain't making him some hands."

"Mike Jones, you're eating him out of house and home, you big ox," said Josh.

"Yeah, but when you're working hard as me and the wolf, you work up an appetite." And he just smiled.

Two hours later, they rounded a bend. There was Red Wolf and ten Comanche warriors sitting in front of the opening to a canyon that was lined in brush. Andy looked at Big Mike, who was still grinning.

"You and Red Wolf, huh?"

"Well, Bub, I didn't want to spoil it."

As they approached, Wolf said, "Well, it seems like you made a friend."

"How do you figure?" asked Andy.

"You see this brush? Well behind it is a box canyon that is about one hundred acres. It's got a good source of water and plenty of good graze."

"So how do I have a friend because of brush, water, a box canyon, and graze?"

"Because also behind this brush wall are one hundred wild horses, give or take."

"You're kidding me!"

"Not at all. These gentlemen right here have been holding them for us since yesterday. They came and found me and Mike this morning. When we got here, we couldn't hardly believe it."

"They did this for us?"

"Seems you made an impression with Peta, and these boys said they seen the horses enter the canyon on their own, so all they had to do was close it up with brush and guard it."

"Meko, I want you to get out twenty pounds of coffee and two big bags of tobacco. I know it may short you fellows, but seeing as how those boys saved us all that work, I figured they deserve that and more."

"Are you kidding me? You dang right they deserve it! I say we give them Dwayne too, just so they can have a fresh scalp," Lynn said, smiling.

Clifton spoke up and said, "I cast my vote for giving them Baccor or Josh. Or better yet, how about all three?"

Josh looked at Baccor and Dwayne and said, "It's tough being this good looking, boys, 'cause the ugly ones are always gunning for you."

Andy laughed along with everyone else and said, "I reckon the coffee and tobacco will be enough, but keep them three in sight in case I change my mind."

Red Wolf told the Indians they were thankful and gave them the coffee and tobacco, and the warriors rode away.

CHAPTER SIXTEEN

"Boys, I want those post hole diggers to start eating at that dirt right now. I want four of you in the timber cutting poles. I know the pickings may be slim, but find what you can. The rest of you start snaking out the poles they cut. Webb, me, you, and the Wolf are gonna set and guard the entrance. Meko, let's celebrate the easiest hard day of work yet. Fix us something good!"

Meko made a meal fit for a king, then over the next two days, they built a big corral and a pen for breaking the horses. The third day started with bucking and snorting. Josh, Clifton, Ward, and Bubba were catching horses with Webb helping, doing his best at throwing his rope at something other than other cowboys. Baccor, Lynn and Chuck were giving every horse the what for. Baccor and Lynn were good. They were better than good, but Bubba was right about Chuck Gill. It was like he was sewed in the saddle. Dwayne and Mike Jones kept them in new horses for the breaking. After four days they were out of room in the corral, so Andy, Wolf and Webb took twenty-five head into town that had took to the saddle pretty good. Without the wagon to slow them down, the trip only took two days. Andy made a deal with Jason Reed at the livery and told him they would be back.

The four day turn around was just right. They made the trip three more times, and all made the last trip. There had been one hundred and seven head. After they culled the old ones and a stallion that was too crazy even for Chuck, they ended up with eighty-eight pieces of horseflesh. Andy figured to let everyone pick out four head to work cattle from and the rest he would keep at the livery. They enjoyed one day of rest in town, and then it was time to gather cattle.

They headed south and gathered from south to north. The first man he met was one of the two Andy had spoken to at the feed store. His name was E.A. Branch III. Edgar Almond Branch was a tall, slender cowboy with a big grin and a firm shake. He had agreed to sell Andy two hundred and fifty heifers and fifty steers. He also sold him three bulls to go along with the herd. Branch's cowboys were driving the cattle to a spot for the T2W cowboys to work the cattle. The work was hard on their horses, but the new mounts were learning fast. The cowboys were roping, and Webb found his calling, branding hides.

Though the work was tiresome on animal and man alike, it went steady and smooth.

The next ranch was about ten miles northeast and belonged to one of two brothers who ranched in the area. Michael Paul Tollett and his hands had Andy three hundred heifers, one hundred steers and two bulls. Michael Paul was a short blonde headed cowboy with blue eyes and an easygoing manner.

The final stop was another twelve miles away and was owned by the second of the brothers. Mathew Tollett was the same height as his brother, but was twice as thick in the chest. He had the same blonde hair and the same blue eyes. He oversaw the work as they gathered their last three hundred head of heifers, one hundred steers, and three bulls.

After two weeks of long days, short nights, and hard work, they were pointed northeast. They had with them eight hundred fifty heifers, two hundred fifty steers, eight bulls, and eighty-seven horses. Andy left one horse for Red Wolf, who waved goodbye as the herd drove away.

Andy and Lynn took turns riding point and scouting ahead. Dwayne, Baccor and Josh rode flank on one side. Bubba, Chuck, and Ward on the other side. Clifton and Big Mike swapped out on drag and helping Webb with the remuda. After a few days, Clifton and Mike swapped to flank, and two others rode drag. They made the swap every few days, so everyone got a good taste and bad view.

They followed the same trail, more or less, as they drove their new herd home. The first few days were a fight to keep the cattle bunched and a fight for the cattle to find their own leader. Finally, a big brindle steer fought his way to the front and stayed there.

With every mile they made to the northeast, the temp dropped, and so did the grass. It was winter, and the only thing saving them from being cut in half by the icy wind were the pine thickets of east Texas. Water was plentiful. Every creek and river was flowing. The grass was sparse, but longhorns could live off a lot less. After the first week of slow going, they were now putting twenty miles a day behind them.

They made the trip back to Arkansas with no stampedes or problems of any kind. Webb even got to ride flank, swing, and drag a time or two.

Just as Andy promised, he stopped by Big John's on his way in. He cut out one hundred steers and twenty horses. They forded the river that day and camped at the trading post.

"Heard you ran into a couple of old mountain goats on your way to Texas," said Big John.

Andy thought for a second, then smiled, "I reckon Ol' Flip and Wild Cat made it home then."

"They did, and you never seen such a smile on two women's faces. The ladies were in early one morning selling their eggs when in walked two buckskin clad fellers. And as soon as Flip opened his mouth, his ma flew across the room a huggin' and kissin', and his sister fell right in behind."

"That's good. I'm glad they made it."

Andy and Big John pulled a snort or two from the jug before John closed up shop. Andy told him they would pull out first thing in the morning so they could make it home the next day.

When the sun was rising the next morning, the cattle were already heading into it. They crossed the Cossatot and then the Saline Rivers, and just at dark, they hit home range. "Dane, you might want to come listen," Bill said. As Dane stepped out onto the porch, they both smiled. He could hear the bawl of cattle, and he knew his friends were home.

A minute later, Andy rode into sight. "I see you still got your hair, so I guess that's a good sign," said Dane.

"Got my hair, got horses, cattle and a few new hands. Texas was a success."

"Glad to hear it. Me and Billy Wayne here was wondering if you would make it before ol' Santy Clause came."

"Santy Clause? What's today?"

"December 22nd."

"I tell you, Dane, I don't guess any of us thought about that. We been so busy with everything, I guess it just slipped all our minds."

"Well, as you can see, we got a new house and a chimney he can come down if he shows."

Andy looked at the new home with approval. "It looks good from the outside."

"It's warm and dry inside too."

"Then it sounds like it will do."

As the two men talked, the hands started to trickle into the yard.

"Boys, let's take care of our horses, and it will give Meko time to fix us some grub."

"Dane said, "Meko?"

"You'll see."

The wagon came rolling up, and Dane got his first view of Meko.

"It's a Chinaman."

"Laotian," said Andy.

"What's a lotion?"

"Not lotion. Laotian. He is from Laos, not China."

"Looks like a Chinaman to me," said Billy Wayne.

"You two are hopeless. Meko, unload what you need and carry it into the cook shack and bunkhouse; fix up something simple, and we will worry with the rest tomorrow."

Meko did as he was told while Andy went inside with Dane and told about the trip.

The next day Dane was introduced to all the new hands and jobs were given. Mike Jones figured since it was so close to Christmas, he would high tale it for Fort Smith. He figured he would surprise his ma and grandma.

"Bub, I sure thank you for the work, and I won't never forget y'all," Mike told Andy.

"You ever need work, you know you can always come back," said Andy.

"Thank you, Bub. I'll keep that in mind."

He collected his wages, said his goodbyes, and rode out.

"Boys, today is December 23rd, and I guess we all forgot it was close to Christmas. I figure the cattle and horses will be all right for a day. So tomorrow we will stop work at lunch, and any of you want to go home can do so. Any of you who want to stay are welcome. I plan on inviting my wife's kin from over southeast, and hopefully, we'll have a good Christmas. Bubba, Ward, Chuck, and I know we ain't family, but you know you're welcome to stay. Or if you just want the day off, you can go into town to do as you wish."

"No sir, I reckon since leaving Texas behind, you and Webb is the closest thing we got to family so we'll spend it with you," Ward said with Bubba and Chuck agreeing.

"I figure me and Lynn will stay too," said Dwayne.

"Me and Billy Wayne are close enough to home. I figure we better go slap Sheriff around," said Baccor.

"Same thing for me and Clifton, I reckon. We're close enough to go home."

"Fair enough boys. Y'all just ride back in sometime on the 26th, and we will start to work."

Andy told Dane he was gonna make a quick trip over to the Webb's and invite them all over for a feast.

"Meko, I figure we'll kill a beeve and I'm sure the Webb women will bring some things. So, you figure whatever you want to cook, but figure it to be thirty people. Can you handle it?"

"I handle," said Meko.

"Good. I'll see you boys this afternoon. I figure the cattle are here to stay, but make sure we turn our horses in the corral or back lot so we don't have to worry about them running off."

"We're gonna gather up twenty head and start rotating them every week. That way, it will keep them worked and get them used to staying around," said Lynn.

"Good. You boys know your jobs. I'll be back this afternoon."

Andy rode away, and the hands went to work. Webb followed Josh and Clifton that morning.

"We get out here around the cattle and we'll practice on your roping, Webb," said Josh.

"I'll swap ponies with you, and you can ride Popcorn here. He knows cattle better than most folks, so he will be good for you to start learning on."

"Sounds good to me, but how will my horse ever learn?"

"While you're learning how to rope off Popcorn, I'll be beside you teaching your gray."

"And me and Millie here will supervise," Clifton said, indicating him and his horse.

"That's all he's good for, Webb, 'cause he sure can't rope," said Josh.

The boys put in a good, hard day. The cattle were still bunched close from the night before, and the horses had actually stayed close to the barn with the other horses. Lynn and the others didn't have to go far in the lot to pick out twenty mounts.

After the horses were caught and penned, Baccor took Lynn and Dwayne and set out taking them around the ranch, since they had joined the drive from Sykes' place and had never seen it.

Billy Wayne did the same thing with Bubba, Ward, and Chuck, except he started in the other direction.

Andy was back that night and told Meko the Webbs would be coming on Christmas Day, so be ready. He also announced to Webb that he had gone to town and run into Miss Dana Smith, and she was wondering when he would be back around. All the boys whistled and cat called until Webb turned red.

"Boys, I want you all to get up in the morning, make a quick ride around the place, then you get gone. Just remember, don't be in a hurry on the 26th. Just make sure you're back sometime that day or night for work on the 27th."

He undid a big bag and told them all to come up one at a time, and he gave them all a brand-new Arkansas tooth pick he had picked up that day in town.

"These are your Christmas gifts boys, and I'm sorry, but it was the best I could do on short notice."

All the hands thanked him. The knives were beautiful. They had all been made in Washington, Arkansas, at the same blacksmith shop where the famous Bowie Knife was forged.

The first Christmas went well. The Webb clan showed up, and there was enough food for an army. Webb got to tell how he had met Peta Nocona and rode into the Comanche village.

The women were amazed at some of the dishes Meko prepared, so they spent some time asking questions for their own personal benefit. The men played music on their fiddles, banjos and harmonicas and enjoyed all the stories Andy told of Texas.

When it was over, the Webb's climbed into their saddles and wagons and said goodbye.

CHAPTER SEVENTEEN

The hands settled into life on the T2W, and things went well for the next few years. The hands stayed the same for the next two years until Bubba, Chuck and Ward figured to head back down to Texas.

"You boys come back if you ever want to. I can't praise you enough, and I thank you all," Andy told them.

"We hate to ride on you, Andy. It's just we ain't been home in two years," said Bubba.

"You boys are free to ride; you always have been and don't worry. A man knows when it's time to ride."

It was 1858, and folks were drifting in and out of Arkansas. Andy hired a couple of drifting cowboys in time for the spring roundup. Steve Rhodes and Keith Couch were looking for a place to light for a spell, so Andy hired them.

"You boys showed up just in time. I was needing a couple hands."

"Well, we can't promise to stay long, but we will stay for the roundup," said Steve.

"Fair enough. If you want to ride after that, it's fine. If you want to stay, that's ok too." Steve was a bearded six-footer with a raspy voice and a quick smile. Keith was a little different cowboy. Instead of riding a horse, he rode a big Missouri mule. He was a few inches over six feet and weighed close to 300 pounds. He always wore a smile and was always ready to work.

Andy, Steve, and Keith were out on the range one morning when a lone rider appeared. He never changed pace and never changed direction. They watched him for fifteen minutes until he rode right up to them. He had dirty blond hair sticking from under his hat, spectacles on his eyes, and a wad of chewing tobacco in his mouth. He gave the three men a once over as they did the same to him. Then he spoke. "Names Spigner and I'm looking for Mr. Wakefield."

"Spigner your last name or first?" Andy asked.

"Does it really matter?"

"No sir, I can't say as it does; I guess I was just a little curious. No harm intended. I'm Andrew Wakefield, Mr. Spigner. What can I help you with?"

"Looking for some work, and I heard you may be looking for hands."

"I may be. Do you know cattle?"

Just then, Keith spoke up. "I don't know if he knows cattle, but I have seen him use that iron on his hip."

Spigner just looked at Keith with a blank face.

"I seen you last fall down in Texarkana. You killed Pink Barnes over a card game."

"Did you see Pink trying to slick deal me from the bottom?"

"No sir, I can't say as I did."

"Too bad 'cause you won't ever get to see him try it again."

Andy looked at Spigner and asked, "Are you as good at working cattle as you are with that pistol?"

Spigner grinned and said, "Nope."

Andy smiled a big smile and said, "I think I like the way you tell the truth Spigner, so I think you just found a new job. Only requirement is I'm gonna need to know your first name or last, whichever I don't know as of now."

"Names Steve Spigner, since you ask so nice," he said with a grin.

"Now we have two Steves," he said as he introduced the hands, "so I guess I'll just start calling you Rhodes and Spigner, so we don't get you confused."

Keith shook his head and said, "I hope you work harder than this Steve. If not, then Andy is gonna have to give me a raise." Andy laughed as they all rode away towards the house.

The new hands stayed on for a year, or close to it, until after the spring roundup of '59. Andy promised them jobs if they ever drifted back his way, and that was the way it usually went for cowboys.

Andy and Webb got up and rode into town one morning in the wagon to get some things Meko needed. As they pulled up to the store, Webb was climbing down when a voice yelled, "Webb Wakefield, I been waiting for you all week to come to town." It was Dana Smith standing in front of the café. "You know the church social is in two weeks, so I expect you to be sitting with me."

Webb looked at Andy, who was grinning.

"Dana, now you know I can't come to town ever' single day," said Webb.

"Don't try to give me that excuse. You act like you may try to sit with another girl, and I have told you already, you are mine, so you will be sitting with me. Now come hold my hand and walk me over to meet Ma."

"Be right back, Pa."

"Take your time, son. No hurry," Andy said, smiling. As they started walking away, Dana looked at

Andy and gave a big wink and a smile. Andy did the same in return.

Andy walked into the store to Joe Buck's greeting, "Hello Andy. Come on in."

"Hello Joe Buck, how's business?"

"Can't complain as long as you keep having to feed all those hands."

"That's something that ain't changing 'cause they sure like to eat. Only thing is, I lost a few hands a few days back. Steve Rhodes and Keith Couch decided to move on, and Spigner got a better offer and better pay as a gun slick for an outfit on the other side of the Red River."

"Have you hired you any replacements?"

"Nope, but I figure I need to."

"They was two boys just in here buying a few supplies and said they was driftin' and may be looking for work. They was headed over to the Pearl, so I'm sure you can catch them there."

"Do you know their names?"

"No, but one was wearing spectacles, and the other is the size of a white oak stump that's been sawed off."

"I'll leave my order with you and come back." Andy took off to the Pearl where he found who he was looking for.

"Andy, I sure hope you brought Webb with you because my sister is about to have a fit," said Wendy.

"She has already latched on to him Mrs. Wendy. She informed him where he would be sitting at the church social."

"And let me guess, he smiled and agreed."

"Is there anything else a man can do?" asked Andy.

"I reckon not."

"Wendy, I'm gonna just have some coffee while I talk to these two men," Andy said as he indicated the two men at the table.

"You men mind if I sit?"

"No sir, have a seat."

"My name's Andy Wakefield and I have a spread out west of town, and I'm looking for a couple hands. You boys interested?"

"Yes sir, we sure are. I'm Douglas Lovewell."

"And I'm Cary Ashbrooke. When can we start?"

"Boys, don't you want to hear what I'm paying first?"

"I reckon so, but I don't figure it matters cause if you're paying more than nothing, then it's more than we're making right now," said Doug.

"I'm paying more than nothing, so I guess you're hired. Finish your meals and we'll go."

The door opened and in walked Webb.

"I see you're still alive," said Wendy.

"I swear, Mrs. Wendy, there are times she scares me."

"Then she has you right where she wants you. You got to stand up to her."

"No thank you. I figure just to do like she says."

"Oh, don't fret, son. I figure she will ease up in sixty or seventy years."

Webb just shook his head.

Andy introduced the new hands and paid for their meal when it was over. On the ride back to the ranch, Andy found out Doug was from over around Big John's place. He knew the old mountain man, Flip Bush, that Andy had met on his first trip to Texas.

"Yes sir, he's still around. Him and that other fellow with the eye patch have a place down on Bush

Hill, and I tell you Flip's ma and sister ain't never been happier."

"That's sounds like a good ending for good folks. Cary, how about you?"

"Not really much to tell, I don't reckon. My folks live over about forty miles east, and I been wanting to get away from home since I was about twelve. When I hit seventeen a few months back, I just left out and kind of been riding in a circle ever since."

Andy looked at Cary, who was six foot five inches and weighed at least three hundred pounds. "Are you telling me you are only seventeen years old?"

"Yes sir, that's what I'm saying."

"Well, I'll try to keep you and my son, Webb, together, since you're both close in age."

"I thank you for that, Mr. Wakefield, but don't give me any special treatment. I don't want the hands to treat me different."

"You will be just fine, and believe me, the hands are gonna give you just as much grief as they do each other."

When it came time for heavy lifting or something that needed brute strength, everyone forgot Cary was a kid. He was so strong, and he didn't know his own strength. Doug was a different story. He fit right in with Dwayne and the rest of the jokers. Life on the ranch was normal and not much changed until the year 1861.

The south decided it would no longer be ruled or told how to live by the people of the north. The country was being divided by what each thought was right and wrong, and war was coming. Some of the boys decided to head for the action. Billy Wayne was already on his own place and Cary and Doug decided to join up for the Southern cause. Webb, at sixteen, had made a man and top hand.

"Lynn, what about you and Dwayne? What are y'all figuring to do?"

"We both figure to stay right here. We work here. We ain't got no land and ain't holding no slaves, so I figure you're our boss. If you need us, then here we are. If you want us to leave and fight, then you tell us."

"No, boys. I don't want to lose any of you, but I am just trying to make plans, so if you boys want to stay, then stay."

That was that. The T2W was now down to six hands, and a war was starting. How long would it last, and what was to come?

For the next year, Andy put three boys he met years before over on the Little River to work. Brandon and Bubba Adams and their little cousin Russell had made good on a promise that one day they would make top hands. They were fourteen, thirteen and twelve, but they worked as hard as their young bodies would allow, and that was all Andy could ask or hope for. With the three boys, Webb, Lynn, and Dwayne, the place held on.

Chapter Eighteen

1862

"Boys, we need some horses. I know we don't have the manpower to do what we done six years ago, but I need you in Texas. I need you rounding up horses. With the war, I don't know what hands you will find, if any, but with the horses we have sold and lost, we need new seed. The few we have left are too young or too old to do much, and our remuda has to stay strong. We've lost cattle and horses both to the war and folks starving. What cattle we have are still multiplying, and I ain't much worried none, but we need to start back raising our horse numbers."

Lynn, Dwayne, and Webb all agreed.

What little cowboying there was to do could be done by Dane, Andy, and a few of the young boys who had been helping since the war. They were all under fifteen, but were all good hands and hard workers.

Two days later, Lynn, Dwayne, and Webb climbed in their saddles and headed down a trail they had traveled six years before.

It was the same trail, the same miles. New homes built and old homes gone. New towns, old towns, a few faces they knew, and most they did not.

Three faces they did see and recognize were Chuck Davis, Jason Reed, and Red Wolf.

Chuck told of all three of the boys coming home from Arkansas. Now all were off in the war. "What brings you boys back?"

"Horses."

"You and everyone else. They is still plenty running wild, but your friend Peta Nocona was killed a couple years back, and right now, the Comanche are raising nine kinds of it."

"Is Red Wolf still around?"

"Sure is. He is still in the same spot. Do you remember how to get to his place?"

Lynn said, "I do."

They thanked Chuck and made their way to Red Wolf's. He was standing in the door like six years back.

"Climb down, light, and set," said Wolf.

The three got down and tied their horses.

"Lynn, I see you're still being followed."

"You ain't a foolin' none. I can't shake him. I been trying for six years, and he is like a fly on a turd."

Dwayne smiled. "You said that right." Lynn just shook his head.

"I tell you boy, them eyes are a dead giveaway. How are you, Webb?"

Webb shook Wolf's hand. "Good, Wolf. How about you?"

"Can't complain. If I did, it wouldn't do any good nohow."

He turned and walked inside.

"You boys come in and have some coffee. Webb, you still drinking water and milk, or are you finally drinking with the men?"

"Wolf, if coffee makes a man, I'll be a boy forever."

"What are you boys doing back in Texas?"

"Come for horses and hoping you can help."

"I was afraid you were gonna say that. Boys, right now is a bad time to be on the Llano Estacado. Two years ago, when Peta was killed at the Battle of Pease River, and his wife Na Ura was taken, it caused the Comanche to go on a warpath that has not ended."

"You say they took his wife? Why?"

"Come to find out, she was a white captive."

"You know what, that day we were at their village, I thought she looked like a white woman. Her skin was lighter than the other women and so were her eyes," said Webb.

"She was white alright. Her name was Cynthia Ann Parker. They took her back in May of 1836 from Fort Parker, Texas. She was eleven years old, and for the next twenty-four years she lived the life of a Comanche. She became Chief Peta's wife and had two sons and one daughter."

"Where is she now?"

"With family somewhere here in Texas is all I know."

"So what you're saying is it probably ain't safe for us to be on the plains catching horses."

"Boys, it ain't even safe for me to be on the plains anymore."

"Well, we come for horses. Do you have any suggestions?"

Wolf grinned a big grin and Lynn said, "Now that is my kind of smile, so I'm in no matter what it is."

"Come back in three days. I will have someone for you to meet."

That was it. The boys left and went back to town. For two days, they rode the country, went to the saloon, café, and lounged around their rooms. Then, on the third day, they were back at Wolf's.

Wolf had a guest. He was a young Mexican in a Texan's outfit. He was five nine and lighter than most Mexicans.

"This is my friend, Caesar Monarrez."

"Hello, Mr. Monarrez. Nice to meet you," said Webb.

"Please, I am Caesar."

"Ok. I'm Webb. This is Lynn and Dwayne. Wolf says you may have some horses for us."

"He tells you the true word. I can get you horses."

"How many can you get?"

"How many do you want, señor?"

"Well, I guess that depends on the price and the horseflesh you're selling."

"The horses are the best, and the price will be very cheap."

They talked for five minutes, settled on a price, and Webb said, "How about thirty to start, and if they are what you say, then we may want more."

"It is a deal, my friend. My friends and I have to travel across the border..."

"Woah Now! I don't think I'm interested in stolen horses."

" Señor, we will take these horses from the banditos who come across the border into Texas to rob and kill. These banditos killed my wife and child, now I do everything I can to hurt them in return."

"Yeah, but stolen horses, I don't know."

"These horses all come from Mexico. They will not have Americano brands. I assure you I will give you papers for each."

Webb looked at Lynn, who was grinning; "You would love this, wouldn't you?"

"Dang right. Pay back for all the bad those boys have been doing."

Webb looked at Wolf. "What do you think about this?"

"Where do you think my last two horses come from?"

"I want a bill of sale for all thirty."

"Deal, Señor."

Plans were made, and Caesar told them where they were to meet in five days. When they got back into town, Webb went to the café, while Lynn and Dwayne went to the saloon. When he walked in, Chuck Davis waved him over.

"Have a seat, son."

"Thank you, sir."

"Did Wolf help you out?"

"Uh, yes sir, I think so."

"Did he introduce you to Caesar?"

Webb looked shocked. "You know about Caesar?"

"Are you kidding, son? Caesar is paying those sorry brown banditos back ever' chance he gets for all the hell they cause on our side of the border. Those dang Federales on the other side of the border don't do anything. So, I say like the Romans do, Hail Caesar!"

Webb laughed. "Then I reckon if you agree, my pa shouldn't say much."

"I promise, son. He won't."

They talked on for twenty or thirty more minutes, and Chuck finally said he had to get back. His youngest boy, Ty, might have the feed store burned down if he stayed away too much longer.

Finally, four days passed, and the three men set off for the eighty-mile trip. The Texas sun was alive and hot, and the wind was dead.

As they traveled, they spotted several unshod pony tracks. Some were pretty fresh. That night, they took turns on watch. The night passed without a problem, and by mid-day, they were at the spot where they were to meet Caesar.

Within two hours, he was there. When he showed up, he was with four men, all of which were Mexicans.

"Hello, my friends."

"Hello to you, Caesar. Well, you were sure right. They all look good."

"I told you."

"I don't hear any gunshots, so I guess we don't have a war coming."

"No, señor. They kept these horses at one of their many holding pens. When they come across the border to steal, they leave horses at different spots on the Mexican side, just in case they have to run hard from pursuit."

The cowboys looked the horses over and all agreed they were well worth the price.

"Caesar, do you think you can get fifty more?"

"Si, señor. It may take a couple of weeks, but I know I can do it."

"Would you and your men be interested in driving them to Arkansas?"

Caesar turned and spoke in Spanish to the others. They all nodded yes.

"Si, señor, we can do this. Once we get there, will that be it, or will there be work for us?"

"My father and his partner have a few thousand acres of cattle and a few horses left. The war has taken most of our hands, and our horses are all but gone. I don't know if he will have room for all of you, but maybe for a couple."

"Three will not stay. They will come back home. But myself and two men may stay if we can. It is a deal then. Fifty more horses, same price, plus you pay us all for the trip."

"Deal." Webb stuck out his hand. He took out a pencil and paper from his saddlebag. He drew a map for Caesar to follow and paid the money owed. They shook hands again, and the three Arkansas cowboys took their thirty new horses and headed north.

CHAPTER NINETEEN

The three cowboys had been riding for a few hours when they rode through a small group of trees. As they exited the trees, gunshots sounded in the distance. Across the opening, about three hundred yards away, a horse raced out of a small group of trees with two riders. The horse vanished behind an outcropping of rocks. As they waited to see the horse and its double burden show itself from the other side of the upthrust of rocks, another group of riders emerged from the trees. The second group was just two horses with a single rider each. Just as fast as the first horse, these two horses disappeared behind the rocks. Webb looked at the others and said, "Stay here. I'm going to check that out."

He rode out of the trees and turned the grulla toward the rocks. As he approached the rocks, he jumped down out of the saddle and let the reins fall, knowing the horse would not stray far.

As he peeked around the edge of the rocks, he could see two men with guns drawn laughing at something he could not yet see. Just then, he saw the biggest one raise his pistol and fire towards something on the ground.

"Zeke, you couldn't hit the broad side of a barn if you was in it."

"I ain't trying to and you know it. I'm just having some fun with the little buck, so's I can scare him a bit. Now stand back so's I can do what I'm aiming to do."

Zeke pulled up his pistol and fired as he and his partner both laughed. Webb decided to take a look. As he rounded the corner, he could see what the two were laughing and shooting at. There on the ground were two boys, both Indians. One was knocked out from what looked like a hit on the head from falling off the horse and striking a rock.

The other Indian, who looked to be a bit older than the first by a couple of years, was around eleven or twelve. A good age for fighting. He was wide awake and stuck, trapped under his dead horse.

The two toughs were seeing how close they could kick up dirt around the boy trapped under the horse by shooting at him. Webb walked to within twenty feet before the boy saw him, and Webb finally said, "Now that don't seem to be too much of a sport."

Zeke and his partner turned to see Webb standing there as calm as a tree in a windless plain.

"Fred, it looks like we got us an injun lover," said Zeke.

"Yeah, I think you are right. But what I don't understand is where did he come from, why is he putting his nose in our business, and where you think he left his sugar tit? 'Cause he ain't nothing but a pup," replied Fred.

Webb laughed and shook his head. Then said, "It's better for all involved if you two just mount up and ride on out."

"Dang, Fred, but ain't he funny? Boy, I tell you if you weren't so funny, I would kill you right now. But, seeing as how you're just busting me up inside making me laugh and all, I think I'll just pull your britches down, bend you over my knee and spank your little bottom."

Both men let out another roar of laughter, but the expression on Webb's face never changed. He simply said, "If you ain't gonna leave, then I guess you got it to do. But seeing as how you're both shooting at an unarmed kid, I don't know if you would want to take on one with a gun of his own."

"Boy, are you trying to tell us you think you're gonna down both of us and us facing you and me with my gun in my hand?"

"If that's the choice you make. But I would rather see you mount up and ride out."

"Zeke, I think we might want to just ride out," said Fred with a nervous look.

"Are you telling me you're scared of this snot-nosed brat?"

"It ain't that I'm scared, and you know it. But he is way too calm. I'm looking into eyes that could smile bright as the gold at the end of a rainbow or send the devil himself to knock on your door, and I don't like it."

"Boy, this is your last chance. You turn around and walk back to where you come from, or I'm gonna kill you just like I'm gonna do to this injun and his little friend," said Zeke.

"Yes sir, I understand, and I am sorry, but I can't let you kill those boys, and I can't leave."

"Well then, I'm gonna count to three, then I'm gonna shoot you, whether your gun's holstered or in your hand."

Webb still looked calm because Zeke still had his gun pointed halfway between the Indian and him. With the count of one, Zeke started to swing his gun around on Webb.

"One." Boom! The stillness was shattered by the voice of Webb's gun.

Zeke was on his knees peeing his pants as blood from his chest was mixing with the liquid coming from his bladder.

Fred had never moved a muscle. He just stood still with his hands frozen above his pistol grips.

"Do you want to back your partner's play, mister?" asked Webb.

"You heard me tell him we should ride, and if you let me, I will do it now, kid."

"Yes sir, you can leave, but you leave your rifle and go. I don't want anybody getting any idea to shoot at me from a distance."

"Now wait a minute. That there is my new rifle and..."

Webb gave him a look that could freeze the Brazos River.

"I don't know who you are, kid, but life is gonna be hard for you with an attitude like that."

"Hard attitude for hard life. I guess I got a head start then, don't I."

Fred turned and rode away without even looking or asking about his friend.

Webb turned, walked back to the edge of the upthrust, and waved his hat.

He turned around and walked back to the trapped Indian, who was looking at him with big eyes. Webb stared at the eyes because they were not black, but almost the same color as his own.

The boy didn't move or ever show worry. He just watched every move Webb made.

At the sound of horses, the Indian turned and looked as the others rode into view.

Lynn jumped down and looked at the dead body of Zeke, which was staring at a cloudless sky with lifeless eyes.

"I don't guess I need to ask who did this," Lynn said with a grin. "And seeing these two bucks, I don't have to ask why neither. But I will ask who is riding off the other way?"

"Fred is all the handle I got or care to have," said Webb.

"Dwayne, get your rope and drag this horse off the kid so I can see about his leg."

Dwayne did as Webb said and pulled the paint pony off the kid's leg. As he did, the boy winced with pain.

Webb could see the boy's leg was broken by the way it looked.

He sent Dwayne off to get some straight sticks for braces, and Lynn was checking on the younger boy, who was still unconscious.

Webb felt around on the leg as the boy made faces from the pain. Webb told him, "You probably don't understand this, but this is gonna hurt."

He grabbed a small stick and acted like he was biting it and gave it to the boy.

The Indian understood and bit down. Webb made a pull and released. The boy made a grunt, but that was all. "Tough hombre, ain't he," said Lynn.

"I'd say so, but I bet he's tougher than anything we are thinking."

Webb took out some leather strings from his saddlebag and had Dwayne hold the sticks in place while he tied them tight.

By this time, the younger boy was coming around. He saw the white men and tried to scramble away, but the voice and words of the older boy calmed him and stopped him.

Webb pointed to himself, "Webb".... "Webb". The boy just stared at him. Webb looked in the crevice of the rocks and saw a spider web. He walked over, pointed to the web, and said, "web" then at himself "Webb". The boy nodded and said, "UAV". He then put his fist to his open chest and said, "Quanah."

Webb replied, "Quanah," and smiled.

Dwayne stripped the saddle off Zeke's horse and went through his things. He found some papers that said he was Zeke Boone. He also found a wanted poster for $1000 for Boone.

Dwayne asked what they were going to do to the body and the belongings.

"We're gonna take the body with us. He will last for the rest of today, and we can turn him in for the reward tomorrow when we hit town. As for his horse, well, we are gonna give it to these two young men right here. We will take the pistol, but the knife is going to the young one, and that rifle is going to my new friend, Quanah."

Lynn smiled that wild-eyed smile and said, "Somehow, I knew you were gonna say that."

"Do you think that's smart, amigo? I mean, arming an Indian is one thing, but a Comanche is even worse."

"Something says this one is different," said Webb.

"And just what makes you say that?"

"His eyes. I can tell by his eyes. This one is a true warrior, but he ain't a ruthless killer. I can see it."

"I'll remind you of that when he shoots one of us in the derriere when we leave."

Webb laughed and said, "Oh ye of little faith."

"There he goes, Lynn, spoutin' off them words nobody understands from them books he is always a reading."

"Yeah, but don't they sound nice?"

Dwayne said with a smile, "I take it back. I hope he shoots both of you."

They got the boys on the horse, gave them their new gun and knife, and Webb stuck out his hand. Quanah took it and said, "UAV friend."

Webb smiled and said, "Quanah friend," and with that, the boys rode away.

When they rode into town the next day, a crowd gathered as they stopped at the Sheriff's office. The Sheriff stepped out on the walk, and Webb got his first look at him. He was six foot even, with light eyes and a chest like a rain barrel.

"Looks like you're carrying extra weight," he said, nodding towards the body of Zeke Boone.

"Yes sir, we are and hoping you can take him off our hands," said Webb.

The Sheriff had walked down to have a look.

"This is Zeke Boone."

"Yes sir, we found this in his saddlebags," Webb showed him the wanted dodger.

"Was he breathing when you found it, or was he like this?"

"Like this."

"And who was the cause, may I ask?"

He was eyeing Lynn when he asked that. Lynn just grinned.

"I was, sir."

"You? How old are you, son?"

"Seventeen, sir."

"So, you're telling me you at seventeen bested Zeke Boone."

"Yes sir."

"Get down and come in. Little Ron!" He yelled.

"Yes, Sheriff."

"Run down to the undertakers." He flipped the boy a coin. Tell Bran Arnold to get down here and get this body before it gets riper than it is."

"Yes sir, Sheriff."

The boy took off at a dead run.

The Sheriff stuck out his hand. "Mike Mathews"

"Webb Wakefield, and this is Lynn Ringold, and Dwayne Harrington. They work for my father over in Arkansas."

"Arkansas? You're a little off your home range, I'd say."

"Yes sir, and as you can see by our string of horses, we're headed home. Would you mind if these men took our string to the livery while we take care of this?"

"Well, I would like to hear from all of you what happened."

"These men were not there to witness it. The only witness was Boone's friend. A man named Fred. I never got his last name."

"That would be Fred McGrew. He and Boone were lawmen together once."

"Lawmen!"

"Yes, ONCE and only once. Neither one was ever any 'count. The only thing they were even good at was bullying people. They bullied the wrong person, a stranger in town. Come to find out he had connections, and they knew their time was up, so they had to make a move. Next thing you know, they were robbing the bank. They killed two people in the process of the robbery. In the end, they didn't even get the money. The teller filled the bag with paper clippings he kept in his drawer. Just in case he was ever robbed, he had the plan to give the robber simple paper. Mr. Bell, over at the bank, he always thought it was crazy that Mr. Wright would keep paper clippings in his drawer. That is until he got robbed, and they got nothing for their trouble. After that, Mr. Bell was giving Mr. Wright all kind of praise. I swear the whole town thought Heath Wright was the savior of our town. I guess, in a way, he was."

"Was McGrew in on the robbery?"

"Somebody held the horses in the alley behind the bank and Boone was seen leaving town with a man, but despite knowing it was Fred; nobody could say they seen his face."

"I didn't even know who he was when I shot him. I was making sure he didn't shoot me like he promised."

"And your men didn't see anything?"

"No sir, we didn't," said Lynn.

"All we seen was the Fred fellow riding off, and Boone was already dead," said Dwayne.

"You boys go on up to the livery. It's on the other end of town. You can't miss it. Man named Jones runs it."

"I'll be right behind you," said Webb.

Webb went over the details for the Sheriff and filled out a statement.

"I'll have to send a letter with the stage to get authorization for payment. It will take a few days."

"That's fine Sheriff. We could use a rest anyway." With that taken care of, Webb left for the livery. It was a big place with a big sign that said Jones Brothers Livery.

Webb walked in to find all the horses turned in a big pen, and Lynn and Dwayne were pulling on a jug of who-hit-John, with a man Webb figured to be one of the Jones brothers.

Webb walked in as the three looked around to see him. "Help you, son?" said the man.

"This is our friend, Webb."

"Mighty fine string of horses you boys brought in."

"Thank you, sir. We're proud of 'em. Are you one of the Jones brothers?"

"Nope! I am THE Jones brother." He said "the" with effect.

"Was my daddy's place. I kept everything the same, even the name. Folks get used to things and expect no change, so that's why it's been the same since my pa passed."

"Yes sir, reckon you are right about change. It looks like we're gonna be here for a few days waiting on the money. I guess we need three stalls for personal horses and the use of your pen."

"I'll treat 'em like they was my own."

"Fair enough. Figure me a bill for three days, and if it's more, I'll be back."

"I'll do 'er." He held out the jug. "Snort?"

"No sir, but thank you just the same."

"She'll put hair on your chest."

Dwayne said, "And burn it off your tongue."

Webb shook his head and grinned.

With the horses taken care of, they headed for the hotel. Webb paid for three rooms for three days and then they headed for the café.

As they crossed the street, a man was watching from the saloon, but no one noticed.

The sign on the café said Nessa's. It was nice and clean, and the food smelled good.

They sat down, and instantly a beautiful woman approached the table. She was as pretty as sunshine on a rainy day. She had light brown hair, big brown eyes and one heck of a shape.

"Hello men. You must be new to town."

"Yes ma'am," said all the cowboys.

"You chose the best place in town. What can I get you?"

Webb said, "Are you Nessa?"

"Vanessa, actually, but I go by Nessa. Vanessa Walker at your service."

"What would you recommend, ma'am?"

"Are you not just the most polite young man?!"

Dwayne smiled and said, "Ain't he, though?"

"Ain't hard to be so polite when you hang with heathens like us, ma'am," Lynn said, smiling brightly.

"Three jokesters I see," said Nessa. "Well, boys, everything here is great, and my pie is the best west of the Mississippi."

"How about three specials? One pot of coffee for these two, and milk for me."

"Yes, coffee for us men folk and milk for the young'un," said Dwayne.

Nessa looked at Webb blushing and told Dwayne, "I promise you boys, with eyes like that, there is a man inside there."

She turned away to get their orders.

"Well, that settles it, Lynnard. After dinner, we are gonna take him outside and black both his eyes or we ain't never gonna get us a woman for ourselves."

"Yeah, but if we did that, then we would lose our jobs and the women 'cause his daddy would fire us. The women would love him even more 'cause they felt sorry for him," said Lynn.

Webb just grinned and Dwayne said, "You're probably right."

The Sheriff came in and sat down with the three cowboys.

"I got Bran Arnold to come over and get the body. I swear, that little knot head I sent to get him can tell some sure enough whoppers. Half the town says little Ron has told it all over. He seen the whole thing. Swears Boone took on all three of you and in the process, you had to gun him down."

Webb grinned and said, "Well, thank goodness us three came out on top. Tell Little Ron thank you for making that possible."

The Sheriff just laughed. "You boys like it here in Texas?"

"It's a nice place, but nothing like home. It's two different beauties. Like apples and oranges. It just depends on what you like. We live in the Red River Valley, or just out of it in my case. These two live in between the Red and the Little River. I live just north of the Little River, south of the Little Missouri River and east of the Saline and Cossatot."

"Sounds like there is plenty of water."

"Yes sir, there is. Our own little paradise."

"Are you having problems with the war?"

"Not yet, but who's to say if it will stay that way. We live twenty miles from the capitol of the confederacy. So, we have soldiers come by pretty regular and we have lost some cattle and horses both to the cause. My father lost some hands to the war, but so far we have kept our nose out of it and tried to continue on with our business of cattle and horses. My father, his partner and I have only been there seven years. We came from Pennsylvania, so some people expect us to be sympathizers to the North. At the same time, our neighbors think we should follow the South.

While we believe it ain't right to hold slaves, we also believe it's more than that. My father believes people put their nose where it don't belong. Most folks think it's just about slaves, but it's about one group having control over the other, and that's what my father is against."

"Very well put, son. If everyone could see things so clear we wouldn't be in this mess."

Nessa brought out fried chicken, black-eyed peas, fried squash, and homemade biscuits with fresh butter. "Here you go, boys. Sheriff, what can I get for you?"

"Just coffee, Nessa. Thank you."

"Coming right up."

Even though the food smelled and looked great, they all turned to watch the beautiful woman leave. The lady at the next table looked at the table and said, "Well, Sheriff, I never."

Dwayne said under his breath, "With an attitude and looks like that, I know why she ain't never." Everyone chuckled and finished eating.

When the plates were cleaned, Nessa brought out four plates of chocolate cake and another glass of milk for Webb. "Enjoy, boys. It's fresh out of the oven."

"Nessa, darling, I didn't need this," said the Sheriff.

"Please, Sheriff, you hardly cast a shadow," she said with a wink.

He smiled and said, "Flirt."

When she walked away, everyone looked except the Sheriff. He simply turned to look at the lady at the next table. He tipped his hat, smiled real big and said, "Mrs. Young."

She gave him a "harrumph" and turned away.

Dwayne said, "You just got her eating out of your hand, don't you, Sheriff?"

The Sherriff looked at Webb and Lynn, and Lynn said, "Why you looking at us? We got to listen to him another five hundred miles."

Dwayne just giggled.

Lunch over and the bill paid, they walked out but not before Webb took one more look at Nessa, who smiled and winked, "Ma'am."

Outside, the Sheriff said, "I've got the papers filled out, and I will send them on the morning stage. Take a day to get there. Get approved that day, but won't leave until the next morning stage. So, three full days before I have your money."

"That's fine, Sheriff. We will just let Dwayne stay with you for those three days," said Lynn.

"If he stays with me, it'll be as a guest of the crossbar hotel."

"Rest, relaxation, free meals, and friendly conversation with the Sheriff here. Now that sounds like a vacation."

Lynn looked at Sheriff Mathews and said, "Five hundred miles."

The Sheriff just turned and walked away.

Lynn said, "I'm starting to see why you never stay in jail long."

Chapter Twenty

With a three-day rest, the boys decided to wash up, change shirts, and have a drink. Nighttime found them in the town's only saloon, the Dew Drop Inn. Dwayne said, "I ain't no schoolmarm by no means, but I think they got that spelt wrong."

"It's right. It's just a different type of dew," said Webb.

"How many dos is there?"

"Three, the kind you're thinking of is do, as in do something. The next is due, as in something is due, like the stage is due in at eight o'clock. Then there's this dew, which is like the dew of the mountain or dew on the grass."

"I don't know about you two, but all this education do make me thirsty," Dwayne drew out do.

"Five hundred miles," Lynn said with a grin.

It was early, so the bar was empty and only four tables occupied.

"Hello gents, seen you come in town today with a string of horses. Just passing through?"

"Yes sir. On our way back to Arkansas."

"Arkansas, huh? It's a long way, so first beers on me. Paddy O'Shea's the name." He spoke with an Irish brogue.

"Thank you much. I'm Webb Wakefield, and these are my trail partners, Dwayne Harrington and Lynn Ringold."

Paddy looked at Lynn and said, "You helping break the young ones in right?"

"Sir, the youngest one there, Webb, is my boss and as for this one here," he pointed to Dwayne, "he is beyond help."

"Boss?" Webb said. "He's full of it, Mr. O'Shea. We all work for my pa."

Lynn gave Paddy a wink and said, "Future boss then."

Paddy gave a nod and said, "Yep, sounds like boss to me. I guess that means you're buying this one, boss."

"Seeing as my limit's one, then yes sir, I'm buying theirs if they're having milk with me."

Dwayne threw a ten-dollar gold piece on the bar and said, "I'll be drinking doubles, Paddy."

Webb looked at Lynn and smiled. "Yep, five hundred miles." After his one beer limit, Webb walked over and was watching the poker game going on, when a lady come down the stairs and headed right to him.

She was wearing a red dress that hung off the shoulders to the point other things were almost hanging out. She was dark headed with dark eyes and a ton of paint on her face.

"Hello, handsome. Buy me and you a drink."

"Yes ma'am," he looked at Paddy, "Mr. O'Shea, two milks please."

"Milk? Honey, you do know you're in a saloon, don't you?"

Dwayne walked over and said, "Yes, you dooo know you're in the Dew Drop Inn and you're overdue with hogging all the pretty ladies."

Webb shook his head and Dwayne walked to the bar with the woman in tow. "Paddy, two cervezas," Dwayne announced.

Webb told Lynn he was turning in and he would see them in the morning.

Webb walked out onto the walkway and turned towards the hotel. As he stepped off the walk, he started across the street. Out of the corner of his eye, he saw a bright flash. It felt a blow to the side and his knees buckled. He tried to get up, but the wind was gone from his lungs. He laid on his back, still trying to move, when he saw Lynn and Dwayne standing over him. Then the lights went out and darkness took him.

The next thing he remembered was a girl's face looking at him, wiping his face. Then he was gone again. He opened his eyes again to darkness. When he tried to move, pain shot through his side and back. He knew he was still alive, but just didn't know where he was or what had happened. He tried to speak to the darkness, but his voice was weak. A light came from a crack just then. He heard footsteps and then a door opened. The light approached and with it came beauty.

Sandy colored hair with blue-green eyes and a look of concern. It was the same face he had seen before. "Please lay still, Mr. Wakefield. You're safe."

He croaked out, "Where am I?"

"You're in Doctor Reid's recovery room at his office."

"Recovery? I don't feel recovered."

"And you won't for a while. Now be still and go to sleep." With that, she turned to leave.

"Wait. Who are you?"

"Toni, now sleep."

He laid back and closed his eyes as the darkness came back, and so did the black of sleep. He faded away with one thing on his mind... Toni.

The next time he opened his eyes, light was coming through the window, and it filled the room. The room was bright, not just with light, but decorations too. There were even fresh flowers in a vase on a table.

"Well, look who decided to come back from the dead to the living."

Webb couldn't see him but knew it was Dwayne. Webb's eyes hurt so he was squinting from the light. Dwayne walked over and leaned next to Webb as he was squinting. "Yes, I am such a bright sight. I know it's hard to look at me," Dwayne said, grinning.

"It ain't the brightness. It's the pain of looking at you, making me squint. Where am I?"

"You're at Doc's."

Then it hit him. Doc Reid and the girl, Toni.

"You was shot three days ago."

"Three days ago?"

"It was only two nights ago, but three days. You was shot walking across the street when you left the saloon. We brought you here. Doc cut on you and got the bullet out. Then you was out all day yesterday and last night, and now the third day here you are."

"Who shot me?"

"Me!"

"That's a lie. You can't shoot that good."

"Says you."

Just then, the door opened. "I thought I heard voices."

In walked a man over middle-aged, light auburn hair around his ears with a touch of gray and not much on top. He wore glasses and had a healthy stomach on him.

"I was just fixing to tell him the news, Doc."

"Oh, and what news is that, Mr. Harrington?"

"That he was dying."

Doc looked from Dwayne to Webb and grinned.

"Well, that's a fact. We all are, only I'd say he has a long time before that happens. Assuming he stops getting shot."

"So, if I ain't dying, why do I feel like it?"

"Young man, you lost a lot of blood, plus you have two broken ribs and two fractured ribs. May as well say four broke because they all hurt like Hades."

"I figured out the hurt part already, Doc."

"Believe me, son, you ain't seen nothing yet. I had to cut you open on your back. The bullet entered between your bottom two ribs on the front side of your left side. It broke those two ribs, then traveled straight up and back to the next two ribs, where it lodged itself and fractured the next two ribs up. I cut you in the back so as I could retrieve the bullet."

"So, what's next?"

"Lots and lots of rest, son."

"How much is a lot?"

"You don't need to sit a horse for at least two weeks. Then you need to do it in short intervals."

"Two weeks! Doc, I can't be here for two weeks. The three days we've been here is all we can spare. My pa is waiting for a string of horses that are already promised to a buyer."

"Well, even if I told you to go, you wouldn't make it. You couldn't climb in a saddle to save your life. Now the young heal faster than the old, so that's why I told you two weeks instead of a month. I know you young cowboys got to be tough, so I knew you would push the two weeks. I assure you, son, two full weeks and then it's gonna be a rough, rough ride."

Webb just lay there, staring at the ceiling.

There was a knock at the door. "Come in."

Lynn walked in, followed by Toni. "I knew he would wake up when a pretty woman walked through the door," Lynn said with a smile.

Webb couldn't even blush. He was so mad at the situation.

"Has something happened I don't know about? You don't look so happy for a man just been shot," Lynn asked.

"Being shot, I can handle. Being stuck here for two weeks, I can't."

"The Doc has already told us about the situation with you. We've decided to wait. Your pa will understand."

"We can't wait. I know Pa would understand, but those horses are to be delivered on or before a certain date, and if we stay two weeks, we won't ever make it. It's the buyer that I'm worried about. Maybe you two should go on ahead with the horses. You two can handle 'em by yourselves."

"If you think you're leaving me to ride five hundred miles with him by myself, you're crazy," said Lynn.

Webb started laughing, "Ohooo... that hurts. Don't make me laugh."

"Here he goes, playing the sympathy card in front of the pretty lady," said Dwayne.

Lynn looked at Webb and said, "Need I say more?"

"Well, we are gonna let you boys talk. If you start hurting too awful, call for Toni. She will give you something for pain, but go easy on it."

Webb was looking at the girl. She was even more beautiful than he first thought. She had big, long eyelashes, and the prettiest part was she had a light touch of freckles around her nose and top cheeks just barely visible.

"I'll just be in the next room, Mr. Wakefield."

"Thank you, ma'am, and it's just Webb."

"Thank you, ma'am. It's just Webb," Dwayne repeated. "Good Lord, give it a rest. Can't you leave just one for us?"

"Have you told him?" asked Lynn.

"No. I was about to when the Doc came in."

"Told me what?"

"We know who shot you. It was Fred McGrew."

"How do you know, and where did he come from?"

"Apparently, he was in the saloon when we came into town. The man at the bar said he noticed him watching us but didn't think much about it. Then, after the shooting, the horse that rode out of the alley was a red roan and it was the same red roan McGrew was seen riding."

"Who was the man at the saloon and who seen the horse?"

"The man at the saloon was Wilcher. He's a buffalo hunter. He was the short man playing poker. They call him Little Larry. The person that saw the roan tied at the end of the alley was your little nurse friend's brother, Cody. He had seen McGrew on the horse earlier that day when he talked to him. Not only that, he told Cody where he was headed."

"Where?"

"New Orleans."

Webb lay there thinking and getting madder by the minute. He finally looked at Lynn. "That settles it. You and Dwayne are taking the horses on home."

"And what about you?"

"You heard Doc Reid. Two weeks of nothing but rest."

"So, after two weeks, you're coming home alone?"

"Nope. After two weeks, I'm going to New Orleans to kill ex-deputy Fred McGrew."

After planning and discussing the rest of the day, they decided to hire a hand to help drive the horses home. Lynn brought in Cody Tackett, the young man who saw the horse and nurse Toni's brother. He said he was hankering for a trip somewhere, and Arkansas sounded good.

Webb put Lynn in charge despite Dwayne's objection that he should be boss since he was the best looking. Webb gave him all the papers, money they would need, and a note to Andy saying he was sorry, but he had to do this.

Dwayne swore he was faking just to stay behind with the pretty nurse.

Goodbyes were said at daylight the following morning, and the three men and string of thirty horses left town, headed for the Red River and the Arkansas border.

CHAPTER TWENTY-ONE

The next two weeks felt as though they drug by while lying in bed. Of course, the moments his nurse was with him sure made a difference. When he could get up and move around, he and Toni would walk together and enjoy their talks. She took care of his every need. When Doc Reid said two full weeks, he was right. After week number two, he was in the saddle, but it hurt. After two weeks and two days, he said his goodbyes, paid his bill, and headed east to New Orleans.

He didn't make very good time those first few days. Still in pain, he stopped often. The third night, he came upon a large wagon being pulled by a team of huge draft horses. There was a wooden sign painted on the side that said G.C. Cooley Tools. The man standing beside the wagon was maybe five eight with light hair and a friendly wave.

"How do, young feller?"

"Hello, sir," said Webb.

"Are you stopping for the night, young man?"

"Yes sir, I am."

"Well good. Get down and pitch your camp with me. You can share my food, fire, and conversation."

"Thank you, sir. I think I will."

Webb eased out of the saddle and took care of his horse and staked him on good grass after a long drink from the creek. After that, he helped the man with his team.

The man stuck out his hand. "Gene C. Cooley."

"Webb Wakefield, Mr. Cooley. Nice to meet you."

"You look like you're moving a little slow, son."

"Yes sir, I got shot and got some busted ribs."

"Shot! You're just a kid. No offense. Why would someone shoot you?"

Webb told him the story as they worked. Afterward Gene told his story.

"I travel from town to town, zigzagging back and forth, north, south, east, west, selling tools. I sell to farms, ranches, homes in town, hardware stores, blacksmiths, and anyone else you can think of. Big tools, little tools, and all in between."

"Sounds like it keeps you busy."

"It does, and I sure enjoy it."

They talked for a while longer about Arkansas and Webb's travels from one place to another, then turned in and welcomed their sleep.

The next morning, they ate a small breakfast and said their goodbyes.

Webb rode on, getting a little stronger with each rise of the sun. He wasn't even in a hurry anymore. If McGrew was there, he would find him. He knew he was almost three weeks behind him, so he was driven by hope and faith now anyway. It was coming on dark one evening, when he came to a little farm that looked pleasing. As he rode up to the well and started to say hello a little voice said, "Please step down and get a cool drink."

Webb turned and saw a beautiful woman not much older than himself. She was a looker. She had auburn hair and the most beautiful green eyes Webb had ever seen.

"Hello, ma'am. Would you mind if I got down and watered myself and my horse?"

"Not at all. Help yourself, Mr.?"

"No Mr., just Webb, ma'am."

"Then that goes double for me. My name is Tish Burke, and it's a pleasure to meet you, Webb."

"I promise, Tish Burke, the pleasure is all mine."

"Who do we have here?" a voice called from the house.

"Hello ma'am. My name is Webb Wakefield, and I am just passing by on my way to New Orleans."

"You are awfully young to be riding to New Orleans by your lonesome."

"Yes ma'am. I'm young, but not as young as I look."

"Well, take care of your horse and clean up here at the wash pan while my daughter and I fix you up some food."

"No need to do that, ma'am. I don't want to be any trouble."

"Nonsense. We haven't had a man at the table since my husband left for the war."

Webb looked at Tish, and those green eyes told him he was staying right where he was.

"Thank you, ma'am, I'd be honored."

Webb finished watering his horse then put him in the barn where he forked over some hay and gave him a good rubdown. He washed up and knocked on the door.

"Come in, young man."

Webb walked in to a clean and tidy home. The smell of coffee and food filled the home. "Smells real good, ladies."

Tish turned and smiled, and he thought he may melt.

"I hope you like chicken and dumplings," Mrs. Burke said.

"Yes ma'am, I do."

"Well, coffee is on if you would like to get a cup."

"Thank you, ma'am, but I don't have a taste for it. I am a simple youngin' with a taste for cool water or milk." He said with a smile.

Mrs. Burke smiled. "I'm sure that will change the older you get, but I reckon we can take care of that problem. Tish go down to the root cellar and bring up the fresh milk."

"Yes ma'am."

"Have a seat, young man."

"Yes ma'am."

Tish came back with the milk and helped her mother set the table and fix Webb a plate of food.

"Hope you like it, Webb," said Tish.

"It looks beautiful! I mean wonderful! I mean delicious!"

Mrs. Burke turned around, grinning. "Let the boy eat, child."

"Yes ma'am."

Over dinner, the group talked of the war and how Tish's pa was off fighting for the south.

"I told him he was too old to go off a fighting, but he was determined to go, so off he went," said Mrs. Burke.

"My pa told me I was too young, and he was too old, so as of right now we have stayed out of it, but we lost some of our top ranch hands."

"What takes you from Arkansas to New Orleans, Webb?" Tish asked.

"To be honest, I am looking for a man."

"A friend of yours?" Mrs. Burke asked.

Webb hesitated and Mrs. Burke could see it.

"Not a friend, I take it?"

"No ma'am. I'm looking for the man who dry gulched me in the dark."

Both women just stared until Mrs. Burke said, "And I guess you're not looking to talk?"

"No ma'am. I guess I ain't. I plan on giving him a chance, which is more than he gave me."

Webb decided to tell the whole story, so over the rest of the meal, that's what he did.

"I can't stop you from what you have in mind, but I can sure pray the outcome goes in your favor. I can also tell you my Tish here is about marrying age, and as you can see, the pickings for a good man are slim."

"Ma!" Tish was turning almost as red as Webb.

"Oh shush, girl. I can see it on both your faces, and I can't blame you. Those eyes he has draws you in."

"Ma'am, don't think I ain't real interested or even flattered, but me and settling down ain't exactly on speaking terms."

"You're not the first to think that way, but I sure wish we could change your mind. We could sure use a good man around the place."

Webb didn't know what he was supposed to say, so he let his pa bail him out.

"I'm already overdue at home, and I'm sure my pa is ready to take me to the woodshed. I figure, since I'm so far behind the man I'm after, and you ladies have done so right by me. I can stay a day or two and pile up your firewood and fix a few things before I leave."

Tish looked pleased and Mrs. Burke said, "Now that was said like a true man."

So, for the next three days, Webb stayed at the Burke place and fixed a couple of leaky spots on the roof at the house and barn. He fixed the corral gate and set up enough wood to last the women several weeks.

After long days of working, he and Tish spent the nights talking about life and things they each wanted out of it.

The morning of the fourth day found him in the saddle with the sun. Mrs. Burke handed him a cloth sack.

"Young man, you always have a place to come to if needed. This will feed you for a couple of days, and the only other thing I can say is you be careful."

"Thank you, ma'am. I promise if I'm ever back this way, I will stop."

Tish was wiping tears and could do nothing else but say, "I'm gonna miss you."

They had said their goodbyes the night before because she knew this morning would be too hard.

Webb tipped his hat. "Ladies."

He felt a little tug at his heart as he rode away towards New Orleans and what lay ahead.

Chapter Twenty-Two

New Orleans

Webb rode into New Orleans, and even with a war going on, it was jumping. People were everywhere, coming and going. He rode into town for a couple of blocks and stepped out of the saddle in front of a saloon. He tied his gray to the hitch and slapped the dust from his clothes. He walked through the doors and let his eyes fall from face to face in search of McGrew. As he made his way to the bar, a bar girl approached him.

"Hello, honey. You're a new look for these old eyes. Buy me a drink."

"Sorry, ma'am. I'm only having one beer. Then I'm on my way."

"Sugar, don't you want to have a good time with me?"

"Ma'am, I would love to, but I got some pressing business to tend to first. When I'm done, then maybe we can have a drink."

"I'm gonna hold you to that, honey. You just ask for Candy."

"Yes ma'am."

Candy turned and walked away as Webb stepped to the bar. "Beer, please, sir."

The bartender placed a beer in front of Webb, took payment, and continued cleaning glasses.

"I guess plenty of strangers come through town, don't they?" Webb asked the bartender.

"Not as much as before the war, but still quite a few."

"You seen a man couple inches over six feet, brown hair, mustache, Texas drawl?"

"Can't say as I have, but there are lots of saloons in town, so he could frequent one of the others."

"Thank you."

Webb finished his beer and stepped back out into the sunlight. As he was watching the crowds move up and down the street, he could not help but hear an Irish voice booming and could not help but see the man it was coming from. Six two, two forty, black hair, blue eyes and enough of the Irish brogue to know he was from across the ocean. The man stood out even without the big black eyes.

"Miss Gail, I would love to treat you to a nice dinner, and I promise to be the perfect gentleman," the man was saying.

"Sir, I have no desire to be associated with a brute who hurts people for a living," she said.

"Lass, I'm not for hurting people other than the ones trying to hurt me. I'm a fighter. It's what I do."

"Yes, and when you're not fighting, you are one of Mr. Allen Brown's hired men of muscle, are you not?"

"Ma'am, have you seen Mr. Brown? He is quite capable of taking care of himself. I just run his warehouse for him."

"Still, you fight for money. Look at you, sir. As you try to speak to me, you have the marks on your face and those two big black eyes."

"So, you won't have dinner with me?"

"No sir, not until you have a respectable job and stop fighting."

"So, no fighting, but I can continue to work for Mr. Brown?"

"That's a start. Now good day, sir."

The lady was beautiful. Blond hair, fair skin, and pretty light eyes.

The man saw Webb looking at him with a smile and said, "I see you are enjoying this, lad."

"No sir, just couldn't help but enjoy your persistence."

"That it is, and I am wearing her down, laddy." The big man stuck out his hand. "Robert McGill, but they call me Irish Bob."

"Webb Wakefield, and you can just call me, Webb."

'I see you're new to New Orleans, lad. You just rode in, did ya?"

"Yes, I did, and how did you know that?"

"Irish Bob knows everyone, laddy, and I don't know you. You must be new."

"Well, Irish Bob, since you seem to know everyone, then maybe you could help me. I'm looking for a man. He may have been in town for the last two weeks. Riding a red roan, six two, mustache, Texas drawl when he talks."

"Friend of yours, lad?"

"No. He dry gulched me in the night back in Texas several weeks back. I've tracked him here to kill him."

"I see. I may know someone that fits that description, but I don't know where he is staying, only where he favors to drink come the night."

"Would you tell me?"

"I will. You come to the warehouse at nine tonight. He will be there."

"The warehouse where you work?"

"Well, laddy, it's only part of a warehouse. You see, lad, I am head over heels for the lass you just saw. Until I can find honest work, I keep the peace at a bar called The Warehouse, while working at a true warehouse for Mr. Brown. So, it was only a wee bit of a shine."

"So, The Warehouse is a saloon?"

"Not so much, no. It's a place where men fight for money and drinks are also served. Since the war, the big money fights are no more, so we sporting men have to do what we can."

"That's where your nice shiners came from?"

"Oh no, laddy. 'Twas a kiss from me dear old ma," Irish Bob smiled.

He gave Webb directions and told him again to be there at nine that night and he would meet him there.

Webb found a livery for his horse. He was given directions to a boardinghouse and stored his gear. He found a café and had, for the first time, alligator tail, a big bowl of red beans and rice and of course a glass of milk.

He walked around the town and wasted time by enjoying some music from a saloon, but at nine o'clock, he was in front of The Warehouse and hoping the trail ended here.

As soon as he stepped in, Irish Bob was there. "He's here, lad. Back corner, the table by the wall."

Webb turned and there was no mistaking it. There by himself was Fred McGrew. Webb turned and walked directly to his table. As he approached, McGrew looked up and their eyes met.

"Knew you'd come. Been waiting for you."

A gun sounded. Webb felt a tug at his shirt as the table McGrew was sitting at exploded. Webb was drawing his gun and firing as McGrew was bringing his gun up from under the table. McGrew never got a second shot. Webb's first shot hit him in the right shoulder. His second in the chin and third in the left eye. McGrew's body never fell from the chair.

Webb was staggering. He felt his side and pulled away a bloody hand. Then Irish Bob was there beside him. "Easy, lad. You're leaking like a mug of spilt Guinness." Webb could feel himself starting to fall in the well. As hard as he tried to fight it, he could not; darkness consumed him.

He woke to voices. Voices he had heard before but could not place. He tried to focus when he heard a woman's voice. "This is why I will have nothing to do with you. This boy is a child and look what you have done."

"'Twas not me, lass. I only met the lad today. He was after the man who did this."

"So, you say. And I guess The Warehouse is just a warehouse."

"No, lass. It's more and I see you already know it, but I swear on all the love I have for you, I did no harm to the boy. I sent for you because he deserves a good hand to help, and you are the only person I would trust to give such care. All of my work has been to hurt with my hands. But if you will just help the lad, I promise to quit the ring and The Warehouse. I will live right even if you don't give me the chance I'm hoping for."

"I'll help, but only for him, not for you."

"Thank you, lass."

"Young man, you've been shot through the side and have lost a lot of blood. I will do what I can for you."

"Thank you, ma'am. My name is Webb and I want you to know..."

He was out again.

The next time he woke, it was to a small stream of light trying to peek through the curtains. As he tried to move his head, there came the shuffling of feet.

"Lay still, Mr. Webb. We don't want your side to bust open."

He was looking up into the face of the lady from the street.

"Where am I, ma'am?"

"You're in Mr. McGill's room. You've been here all night."

"Where is Irish Bob?"

"I sent him away. I don't want him around. He seems to be a man of trouble."

Webb remembered their conversation last night.

"No ma'am. He's not a man of trouble. He may be a little rough around the edges, but given the chance, I believe he would make a fine husband."

"Please, Mr. Webb. He says you're new to New Orleans, so how would you possibly know him?"

"He helped me find the man who dry gulched me and brought me here. He sent for you to look after me, and like you said, we don't even know each other, but he still did this."

She didn't know what to say.

Then there was a knock, and the door cracked open. "Can I come in, lass?"

"Yes, Mr. McGill, you may."

"Well now, laddy, there you are alive and well. Now, did I get the right person to nurse you or not?"

"Yes, you did, and I thank you."

"Glad to be of service to you. Now, if you will excuse me, I am off in search of work," he said, looking at Gail with a smile.

"Work?" she replied.

"Yes, lass. I promised you, did I not?"

"Mr. McGill, are you expecting me to believe you're done with fighting for sport and money?"

"I do, and I am telling all who will listen that the reason is for my friend Webb and the lass I intend to marry."

"And just who is this lass you are going to marry?" asked Gail.

"Why you, of course."

"I've agreed to no such thing!"

"No, not yet. But since I have half of the town after me for canceling the big fight, I was hoping you would agree, so we could marry and be gone for a new land and new lives to live."

"What are you talking about, a fight and half the town?"

"Just that, lass. I canceled a fight between Bulldog Shaw and myself, and now half the town is in a frenzy."

"And you did that for me?"

"I did. I told you I would. So how about it, lass?"

"Mr. McGill, it will take more than one day to convince me, but you do your job hunting while I watch over my patient, and we will see how things go."

"I'm off, lad. Wish me luck," he said, smiling.

"I told you, ma'am. He's a good one."

"I guess we will see, Mr. Webb."

"It's just Webb, ma'am."

"Fine. I am Gail Hartsfield, but you can call me Gail. Now tell me your story, Webb. How did you end up here during the war?"

Over the next few hours, Webb told Gail of Texas and home in Hell's Valley. He assured her Hell's

Valley was just one name it went by. It also went by others, but it was a lot closer to Heaven's Valley than Hell's.

Irish Bob came back disgusted at the poor pickings for work. Especially now that the town was mad at him. Webb and Miss Gail assured him if he wanted it bad enough, then something would come along. The three sat and talked about Webb's home and just enjoying each other's company.

Webb stayed in bed for two more days while Gail came and went, escorted by Irish Bob. When it came time for him to go back to his own room, Gail checked on him once a day for four days to change his bandage. After that, it was time to say his goodbyes.

"I can't thank you enough, both of you. I hope and pray the best for you both and hope I may see you again."

"You can never tell, lad. I may talk her into a life in Arkansas before it's over."

"Miss Gail, you keep him in line and out of trouble."

"I will, Webb. You be careful and, of course, you're in our prayers."

Webb tipped his hat and rode away.

For the next month, Irish Bob and Gail were seen together in the mornings and afternoons as he escorted her to and from her home and work. One afternoon, as they strolled along enjoying their conversation, three men stepped out of an alley. "Last chance, Irish. You either fight Shaw or else."

"Or else what?"

"Or else you will deal with us every day until you do," the man sneered.

"Come now, lads. I've told you. I'm fighting no more. Tis a promise I've made to me lass here."

"Well, I hate to hear that because your lass here is fixin' to watch us whoop you, and since you won't fight back, it ain't gonna be pretty."

The three men spread out in a half-moon.

"Ma'am, you better back up. We don't want you to get in the mix of this," the man said. Gail stepped to the back of the half-moon behind the three men.

"Please, lads. I've made a promise to me lass. I am not gonna break that promise."

"Good. That will just make it easier," the man said. Then there came a sound everyone knew. It was the cocking of a gun as the hammer was pulled back.

As the three toughs turned, they all saw Gail holding a pistol pointed at the speaker.

"You know, Bobby, I've been thinking. How would you like to fight three more fights?" she asked, smiling.

"Three more, lass? I believe only with your permission I would do it. But where do you suppose we could find three lads to fight?" Bob said as he took off his coat.

"Well, it seems we have three volunteers right here, Bobby."

"I believe you're right, love. Then three and no more you say?"

"I sure do. Now you two back away and stand with your hands on your heads," she said to the two who had said nothing.

"Make it quick, Bobby. The preacher and Hell's Valley are waiting."

"Indeed, they are, lass."

For the next twenty minutes, Irish Bob dismantled the three wannabe toughs. He broke noses and jaws, knocked out teeth, broke arms, and fingers, and ruptured one ear drum.

As they walked off, she said, "How many children will we have, Bobby?"

"Lass, I'm thinking two, a girl and a boy, maybe."

"How about names?"

"How about Marcus for the lad?" he said.

"And I love the name Michelle," she told him.

"Michelle and Marcus McGill. It sounds like a wonderful family!" declared Irish Bob. They strolled arm in arm as they made their way home.

Chapter Twenty-Three

Webb had ridden easy on his way from New Orleans. He was back in Arkansas now, looking for a place to camp, when he found a nice creek not too far past the Sulphur River and laid out his bedroll. He made himself a few biscuits, fried some bacon, and replaced his water in his canteen with fresh water from the creek.

He sat up for a couple hours after dark, feeding his fire and talking to his horse. Sleep came easily when he finally laid down. He felt he was only asleep a short time when the gray snorted.

He woke in an instant. The fire had burned down to coals, but he could see the horse. It was standing head up, ears forward, and looking straight across the fire in front of Webb.

"What is it, boy? You hear something?" Webb took a handful of dried leaves and twigs and threw them on the fire. The leaves caught, and the twigs ignited. When Webb's eyes looked up across the fire, he was looking into the eyes of a creature he had never seen or even dreamed of seeing. The creature, whether man or beast, was well over seven feet tall and completely covered in hair.

Webb froze. He didn't know if he should draw his gun or not. He did not know what he was looking at, but so far, it had not tried to do him any harm. After what seemed like hours, but was only fifteen to twenty seconds, the creature turned and simply walked back into the shadows and disappeared.

"Gray, one thing I know for sure is nobody can blame what we just seen on the who-hit-John 'cause I don't drink it. I will say if I had a jug right now, I would take a pull or two."

Webb didn't even attempt any more sleep that night. He was wide awake and made sure he fed the fire. He wanted to saddle up Gray and hightail it for home, but he decided he wasn't moving until full daylight. As the sky changed from gray to blue, he started moving around. He finally got up and made his way to the other side of the fire and was looking at a footprint. He squatted down, looking at the footprint that was bigger than both of his feet put together. The depth of the print told him the weight of the creature was at least four hundred pounds.

As he was looking at the print, a voice said, "Nice size foot he's got, ain't it?" Webb looked up to see a man fifty years old with dark hair and eyes and a round face.

"So, you've seen this before?" asked Webb.

"Well, you know, I ain't never seen it, but I've seen its track. I've smelt it, and I've heard it."

"Well, I've seen it, and I think what I smelt was my drawers 'cause I'm sure I messed myself."

The man smiled big and offered his hand, "Ed Burgess, and this is my place you're on here. It's called Boggy Creek."

Webb shook his hand. "Webb Wakefield and I didn't mean to be trespassing."

Ed waved his hand. "Ain't worried about that. You're more than welcome anytime. So, tell me, what did he look like?"

"He was huge, seven plus feet, four hundred pounds, hairy, and, well, I guess I would say he was quiet."

Ed laughed, "Ain't he though? Everybody that seen him up close said he walks like a cat. Quiet as a mouse."

"What is it?"

"I ain't real sure, but I think it's some kind of man. I call him the Boggy Creek monster, but I think he is some form of man. If I can ever get lucky like you, I plan on asking him."

"Lucky? I tell you, Ed, if that's luck, then I hope the rest of my life is bad luck from here on out."

"Son, you just seen something only a handful of folks on God's green earth have seen, and you say that ain't luck?"

"Maybe I spoke before thinking about that, but in the middle of the night staring across the fire at that thing with no warning, luck wasn't the word I would have used at the time."

"Well, you know I figure you may be right."

"Ed, I hate to leave good company, but it's good and light and your Boggy Creek is a place I want to put in the south end of my north bound horse. I figure I will leave you with happy hunting."

"I'm gonna tell folks about you, boy. Tell 'em you've seen it," yelled Ed.

But Webb never turned around. He just waved and kept riding.

He rode hard all day and made it back into the yard of the T2W. The door to the bunkhouse opened and out came Lynn.

"You're still alive. Your pa will be happy."

"I am, but not from the lack of trying on Fred McGrew's part."

"He come after you again?"

"More like I went after him, and he was waiting."

Webb raised his shirt to show the second bullet wound from McGrew.

"You seem to be collecting those things."

"It ain't by choice, believe me."

"Is it over?"

"It's over."

"Good. Turn in and welcome home."

Webb took care of his horse before going into the main house. Once he was climbing onto the porch, the door opened, and Andy was there. "Son, you sure had me worried."

"Sorry, Pa, but I had to go."

"I know you did, but it still worried me. Come on in and get some rest. We can talk tomorrow." Webb climbed in bed and was asleep as soon as his eyes closed.

The next day, he related what happened after Lynn and Dwayne left him in Texas. Andy and Dane listened with approval until he got to the part about Boggy Creek. Dane looked at Andy and said, "Well, it was only a matter of time before he got on the sauce."

Webb just shook his head and said, "I don't know why I even bother." Then he walked out to the bunkhouse.

Andy followed him outside. "Son, I forgot to tell you those horses you got from Mexico were some fine horses and you did good."

"Glad you're happy, Pa. Did a Mexican named Caesar show up with fifty more?"

"Nope."

Webb shook his head. "Dang. I thought for sure he would show up."

"Oh, I didn't say he did not show. I said he didn't show with fifty horses."

"I wonder why he came without bringing the fifty horses."

"Oh, I'd say it was to deliver the seventy-seven horses," Andy said, smiling.

"Seventy-seven?"

"Seventy-seven and all of them are fine animals."

"Did he go back?'

"Are you crazy? I tried to hire all of them. Him and his five friends, but I could only talk him and his friend Jose Mendez into staying. The rest said it was too far from the senoritas."

"Where are they at?'

"I imagine in the bunkhouse eating breakfast."

Webb walked to the bunkhouse, and sure enough, there was Caesar and Jose.

"Hello, Señor," said Caesar.

"Hello, Caesar, Jose, I see you made it."

"Si, Señor. Your map was perfecto, and when we got here, the jefe say you all have jobs, but only me and Jose stay."

"I'm glad y'all did."

"Come sit down, eat a bite and tell us about your trip," Dwayne said.

"Yes, sit, eat. I cook good food for you," said Meko. Webb sat down and told of the trip as he ate. After he told the story about Boggy Creek, Lynn reached over and slapped Dwayne in the back of the head.

"Ow. What did you do that for?"

"I told you to keep those corn squeezins' away from the boy. Now see what you've caused." Webb got up, walked out without a word. Everyone in the bunkhouse laughed as he left.

As Webb walked outside, he met his father, who started to grin when he saw Webb's expression. "I guess you told 'em about your hairy man."

"Don't know why I waste my time with any of you," stated Webb.

"Cause we're family, Boy," Andy said, smiling.

"Where are the rest of the boys, Pa?"

"I sent them home when Jose and Caesar showed up. Shorty and the women needed them back at home, so I sent them on. Despite their reluctance, they left because Shorty needed more help at home. I told them they could come back when things settled down at home."

"What do we got planned for today, Pa?

"Well, I'm thinking me and you need to ride into town. Ed Stavely at the land office sent his two boys out, Robert and Mark, or as you like to call him, Spanky. They talked to us about filing on some land for you and Dane. Said there is two good tracts that join us and would improve us some. Give us some more hay meadows and grazing."

"Has Dane already filed?"

"Yeah. He filed a few weeks ago. I figure we could get you took care of today. Plus, I got a new hand in town getting some lumber. I sent him in bout dark yesterday before you got home. He is gonna get loaded up this morning and head back. I figure we can meet him and load the wagon."

"Where did he come from?"

"Just drifting. Name's JD Dickinson. Pretty good hand. Sits a horse well and knows his way around cattle."

"Well then, what are we waiting for? Sounds like town is where we're headed."

Father and son rode into town and headed straight to the sawmill. They found Tem Gunter, who had bought the place from Mr. Johnson a few years before, already hard at it sawing lumber. JD was busy loading the wagon.

"JD, looks like you could use a little help."

"Ain't never turned down good help."

"This here is my son, Webb."

"Hello, Webb. Heard a bunch about you and glad you made it home safe."

"Well, if all the things you heard come from Lynn and Dwayne, you can be sure they're all lies."

JD laughed and said, "Figured as much."

The three men fell on the lumber and had the wagon loaded in no time. Afterward, Andy sent JD back to the T2W, and he and Webb went to Stavely's land office.

"Good morning, Andy, Webb," Ed said, looking up as the men came into the office.

"Morning, Ed."

"Morning, Mr. Stavely."

"Webb, I been waiting on you. All I need is your signature a few times and you will be an official landowner in Arkansas." Just then, Robbie and Spanky Stavely came walking in, both grinning like cats who ate the canary.

"Hello, Mr. Wakefield, Webb." Said Robbie.

"Morning, boys. Looks like those two grinning faces is up to something."

"No sir, but we figure to get a front-row seat for what Webb's got coming," said Spanky.

"And just what do I got coming?"

"You got someone trailing you."

The door opened and everyone turned to see Dana Smith standing in the doorway.

"Webb Wakefield, you get over here right now! I been sick with worry. All I hear is you was shot down in Texas, and you've gone off to New Orleans on a manhunt."

Webb was red faced and embarrassed.

"Dana, I'm fine. It wasn't much to it. The second gun shot was no worse than the first."

"Second! Good Lord, what are you, a bullet magnet?"

"Really! It wasn't nothing and I'm all right."

"Good, then come on, hold my hand and walk me to the café."

Webb turned, signed his name on the three x's and then turned back to Dana without even as much as one look at anyone else.

"I'll have him at the café, Mr. Wakefield."

"Thank you, Dana. I'll be along," Andy said. Before the door closed, everyone laughed loud enough for Webb to hear.

Ed looked at Andy and said, "He could be in trouble if he don't watch it. I do believe she is looking to be hitched up."

"I tell you boys just between us, her sister, Wendy, said she loves Webb like a brother and loves bossing him around. That's as far as it goes, but I ain't telling Webb that. I figure it's too much fun watching him squirm." They all agreed.

The years passed as the men continued their work towards the growth of the ranch. Over the years, more land was bought and with more land, of course, came more cattle and more horses. Friends had been lost during the war, and a toll had been taken on the lives of most. Then, just as soon and fast as it had begun, the war was over.

Chapter Twenty-Four

1866

The war was over, and boys were slowly making their way home. Some were passing through, some headed to Louisiana, some to Texas, some just drifting to anywhere.

Webb was standing in the yard talking to Andy when four men come into view. As they got closer, Webb and Andy both smiled. They recognized three of the four faces.

"Boys, when we left, he was a pup. We come back and I do believe it looks like he is still suckling," Josh Butler said. Josh, Baccor and Clifton were all smiles.

"You come on down out of the saddle, and I'll show you pup," Webb said, smiling.

"Boys, get down," said Andy. "I'm so glad you all made it home. We never heard anything either way, so I have always wondered."

The men climbed down, and Josh introduced the man to them. "Mr. Wakefield, this is my pa, James D. Butler." Mr. Butler was a few inches over six feet, barrel chested with lean hips. He had a beard that matched the brown hair under his hat.

Andy and James shook hands.

"Glad to meet you, Mr. Wakefield. The boys have told me enough about you. I feel I already know you."

"It's Andy, please."

"Fine and I'm James."

"You boys come on inside and let's have a cool drink."

They all went into the house and enjoyed some cool lemonade or coffee of their choice.

"You boys looking for your jobs back? You know you can have 'em. I'll even raise your pay some. Well, everybody but Baccor. I figure he won't be worth a raise."

James laughed and said, "Ain't that the truth. I swear it's like you read my mind."

"You boys just don't know a good hand when you see him," said Baccor.

"That's 'cause there ain't much to see when they're looking at you," Clifton put in.

Josh said, "No sir. We are just here to say hi and let you know we are among the living. Pa is a surveyor, and the railroad is sending him west, so we figure to do some surveying."

"I figure you boys will make a little more surveying than you will with me, so I reckon you're making the right choice. James, I can tell you from experience, if you can wade through all the bull these three put out, then you can make it through anything."

"I've only had 'em with me for a week, and I've already fired each of 'em four times. So, believe me, I know."

The four stayed around for lunch and said hello to all the hands and caught up on insults and told lies about women. The highlight was when Dwayne made Webb tell about his Boggy Creek Monster. Josh looked at Andy and said, "I leave for a few years, and you let him fall in the jug, huh?" Everyone laughed as Webb got up and walked out.

After a good afternoon of catching up with his old hands, goodbyes were said, and they made promises to meet up down the trail someday.

A few days later, Andy was in the barn with Caesar when a voice turned him around. "Excuse me, sir." Andy turned to see a man standing in the doorway. He told Caesar to finish up. He walked out into the sunlight.

When he exited the barn, he found two men in worn clothes, both carrying small cloth bags and both black. "Hello, men. Can I help you?"

"Well, sir, we was hoping you might have a bit of work for us to do to swap for some food and maybe some small pay."

"I sure might, but first, where did you come from?"

"We come from down in Louisiana, sir."

"Louisiana, huh? That's a far piece. No work there I guess?"

"Well, sir, little work here and there, but not for us, sir."

"What's your names?"

"I'm George Ty Turney, sir, and this here is my friend, John T. Walker."

"Well boys, I tell you I am in the need of some hands. I have a few, but with the war, I lost some to it, so let me ask you, do you know anything about horses, George Ty?"

"I know some, sir."

"John T., how about you?"

'Bout the same, sir."

"George Ty, you ever break any horses?"

"No sir, but I had a few 'bout break me," he said, smiling.

"John T.?"

'Bout the same, sir."

"We run horses and cattle here, and we have a few hogs and chickens. We got a nice garden for ourselves, and we do most of our own repairs. Do you boys think you can handle that?"

"Yes sir, I'm sure we can," said George.

"I pay thirty a month and found. Sound like enough for you to stay on?"

They both looked at each other, kind of unsure of their own answer.

"Well, sir, thirty sure sounds fair, but do you think it's too much?" asked George.

"Too much? I ain't never been turned down for paying too much, George Ty."

"Sir, it's just, do you think it will cause problems with the other men, sir?"

"Why would it bother the other men, George Ty?"

"You know, us being paid the same as them."

"I don't know, George Ty. Is there a reason it should bother the others?"

"Well, sir, most folks won't take too kindly to a niggra man making the same pay as a white man."

"So, you two are niggras, you say?" Andy asked with a smile. "I thought the two of you had just been working in the sun so long you were just real dark," he said, smiling.

George Ty and John T both grinned real big and George said, "No sir, we stay about this here color all the time sun or no sun."

"Let me ask you something, George Ty. You plan on working hard doing what I say and doing the best you can at it?"

"Yes sir, I do."

"John T, how about you?"

"Yes sir, I do too."

"Then, boys, I promise you are gonna earn your money. You are gonna find out real quick that we do things different around here. We do things my way. Can you handle that, George Ty?"

"Yes sir."

"John T?"

"Yes sir, sure can."

"Well then, it sounds like you two now work for the T2W."

Andy stuck out his hand, and they both shook it. He pointed and said, "You see that building?"

"Yes sir."

"That's the bunkhouse. You go in, find you two empty bunks, put your stuff away and tell the cook I said to fix you up some grub. Now, before you go, I got to ask you boys if you have a problem with living in the bunkhouse. Because there are some white men, some Mexicans and a Laotian who lives in there as well."

"No sir, I don't reckon we mind at all. But what's a lotion?"

Andy smiled and said, "Not lotion, he is a Laotian. He is kind of like a Chinaman, and he is our cook. His name is Meko."

"No sir, we don't have no problems sleeping in the bunkhouse."

"Good! Now you boys eat and get settled in and walk around and look the place over. The hands will be in soon. First thing in the morning, you boys get fed, then I want that blue roan there saddled for me. You have Caesar there pick you both out a horse, and they need to be saddled with the roan. We will go into town and outfit you from the skin out. You boys work for the T2W now, so you got to look like it."

"Sir, we ain't got no money."

"George Ty, didn't I just tell you we do things a little different around here?"

"Yes sir, you did."

"Ok, then, that's straight. Now one more thing. You men work for me now and if anyone on this ranch or off it has a problem with that, then you send them my way. Understand?" They both shook their heads yes and turned and walked toward the bunkhouse.

The months had passed since the war and, like everywhere across the south, Hell's Valley was suffering from the hands of the north and the carpetbaggers.

The town could keep the Sheriff and deputies the same, but a new judge was appointed, and the town also had a new northern lawyer. Jess Steele was removed from the bench but was still allowed to practice law under the eyes of the south's new overseers. The new judge, Tim Kaper, was enjoying his new position while looking down on the citizens of the town. The new lawyer was Cal Smythe. He was a short, fat, beady eyed man, who followed Kaper around like a whipped dog.

Jess was doing all that could be done to help folks, but the newcomers were doing things their own way. Their way wasn't what most folks thought was right, or even in their best interest.

Since the war had ended, the town had drifters and outlaws in and out of town. Some stayed, some moved on. One of the hanger-on's was a man named Chester. No one knew if it was his first or last name, and most didn't care. He always had a group of four men with him who were rumored to be thieves and murderers. Every single time they were arrested, for some reason, Judge Kaper would find a reason to drop the charges. No one could understand it, but there was nothing anyone could do. So, things just went on that way and they kind of became the normal.

That next morning, Andy, George, and John went into town for some supplies and to get the two new hands outfitted as Andy said, "from the skin out."

"Joe Buck, how is business?" asked Andy.

"Can't complain none, Andy. How is the cattle business?"

"When I rode off this morning, their heads were down, so that means they are gaining weight and working hard for me."

"That's good to hear. Who do you got with you today, Andy?"

"These are my two new hands. This here is George Ty and John T."

Joe Buck stuck out his hand and said, "Welcome to Hell's Valley, men." Both men took the proffered hand and gave a firm shake. "What can I do for you today, Andy?"

"I need to get these two outfitted, and I need everything, top to bottom, from the inside out, and I need hardware for them too." The two new hands looked surprised, and Andy asked, "I assume you two know how to shoot a gun?"

George told Andy, "Never shot a pistol, but we have both used shotguns before, hunting for food back in Louisiana, but even that wasn't very often."

"Fair enough. Joe Buck, give them both 45s, and give them both four boxes of shells, so they have plenty to practice with."

"Yes sir, I will fix them up."

The supplies were bought, and the new men were fixed up and ready to start work. They made small talk on the road home. When they got back on home range, the men hit the ground running. Every day after work, one of the hands would take some time with George and John and give them some pointers on shooting their pistols. George was good and listened and learned pretty fast. John T. was a natural. He could draw smooth and fast and hit everything he shot at.

One evening, George and John were out on the farthest ranges and topped a hill to find Chester and his men driving off about forty head of cattle. George raised his pistol, fired three shots in the air and took an angle to cut the group off. Not far away, Andy and Caesar were hazing some cattle closer to home when they heard the shots. Three shots meant trouble.

"Let's go," said Andy.

As they rounded a corner of a draw, they spotted a group of riders on top of a rise. They rode to the top to find George and John facing Chester and five others. "Hello, Mr. Wakefield. Glad you showed up," Chester said, "We caught your hired darkies trying to steal your cattle."

"I doubt that, Chester. George Ty and John T. are loyal hands, and I doubt they were stealing. They were just driving them home." Andy already knew George and John had caught Chester and the group stealing. He could see it on their faces.

"No sir, they was stealing. Me and my boys are gonna string them up for it."

"No sir, you're not." Andy said it with his mouth, but also with his eyes and body.

"Let me take him, Chester," said a rotten-toothed man next to Chester. Andy knew if it started, he needed to shoot that one first.

"We can't have rustling around here, Wakefield. So, you can stand aside or join them. Now, if you ain't turned and riding by the count of three, you better fill your hand with a pistol 'cause I plan to kill you." At the count of one, Andy was drawing his pistol and firing at rotten teeth. Andy's first shot caught him in the top lip and came out the top of his head. He still had his hand on his pistol when he hit the ground. Andy's next shot was directed at Chester, who was firing his own pistol. The shot hit Chester's horse in the head and caused him to drop sideways, throwing off Chester's shot. It caught Andy in the shoulder, which caused him to fall off his horse. As he hit the ground, his horse kicked him in the head, knocking him out. Caesar emptied two saddles before Chester shot him through the heart. Chester was grabbing a dead man's horse as George shot and killed one outlaw and John shot the last. Chester was gone in a flash and George was on the ground, checking on Andy and Caesar. George was six two, two hundred pounds and all muscle. He tied Caesar across his horse. He got Andy on his own horse and rode behind him while holding him in the saddle. John had taken off in pursuit of Chester, only to give up and fall back to George.

They made it to the house where George told what happened. They got the blood stopped and Webb said, "John T., ride to town and fetch Doc

Peebles." John was in the saddle and gone. By the time John and Doc made it back to the ranch, Andy was awake but wide eyed. He couldn't remember anything. He said he remembered he and Caesar were pushing cattle and then nothing. Doc told him the kick to the head was the cause, but he would be fine. He fixed up the shoulder where the bullet had gone straight through. Doc left instructions to keep it clean and change the bandage and call him if it got infected.

Dane sent out John T., George Ty, Jose, and JD to fetch the bodies. They were kept in the barn until morning and then were taken to town. They went straight to the sheriff's office to inform him about what had happened and told him Andy was in bed at the house. George Ty and John confirmed everything. The sheriff said he would ride out to talk to Andy, but that a warrant would be sworn out on Chester for the murder of Caesar. The bodies were dropped at the undertaker's and Webb paid for them for the simple fact it was a pleasure to be rid of them. As he walked out, he looked up the street and could have sworn he just saw Chester and Cal Smythe walk into the judge's office. He shook off the idea and rode home. The sheriff showed up as promised and took Andy's, John's and George's statements and left to go have the judge sign the warrant.

Two days later, the sheriff was back with the news. "Kaper says Andy's statement is no good because he only knows what George and John told him and he won't take John and George's statement over Chester's. He says he has a good mind to swear out a warrant for George and John but figured it was best for all involved if it was all just dropped. Plus, he said the T2W killed five white men on the word of two niggras, and all your ranch lost was a Mexican."

"There is more to this, and you all know it, and I'm gonna find out what," said Webb.

"Anytime Chester is involved, it's just like this, but what can you do? He's the judge. Who can buck him?"

"We can buck him. Raise enough hell and somebody has got to listen."

"You would think so, but the ones above him are no different. So, we're kinda just stuck," said the Sheriff.

"Well, I ain't taking this lying down. I'm gonna figure it out and scream it to the heavens when I do," said Webb.

"You just be careful because he holds all the cards."

The Sheriff left, and Webb rode to town with him. Webb went to the saloon and had his one beer. While there, Chester came in and was carrying on about folks hiring freed slaves and cattle thieves over white men. Webb stayed quiet. When a group of cowboys moved, Webb could see Judge Kaper sitting at a table by himself. Webb was watching in the reflection of the mirror. The judge took out a piece of paper and wrote something down. He placed the paper under his empty glass and got Chester's attention. "Here, young man, you can have my table. I'm leaving," the judge said to Chester and nodded towards the note. Chester sat down, read the note, and got up. As he walked towards the door, he threw the wadded-up paper in the ash bucket. Webb got up, got the note, and read it. "My office 9pm tonight." He put the note in his pocket, walked back to the bar, finished his beer, and put his plan together.

At 9pm that night, Webb was in a dark alley across from the judge's office, watching the curtain blow in the breeze. The judge had his window open, and it couldn't have made his plan more perfect. Right then, Chester stepped up and walked in the front door. Webb came from the shadows and followed on cat's feet. He knew the rest of the plan would start when he entered the door, and he stepped in. The front entrance was empty and dark. He eased his way to the office door, where light spilled into the darkness. "I told you, Chester. For a little money, I can make anything go away," said the judge.

"I don't call five hundred a little money, Judge."

"Three for me and two for Mr. Smythe here for always being our middleman seems fair, or you can always be hung or go to prison."

"No, I figure I like our little deal, Judge."

"Good, very good. I'm sure you can make it up on your next rustle job. Just be more careful next time. These country folks can't do anything about my decisions, but the less noise, the better."

Webb had heard enough. He stepped out of the dark and his eyes met Kaper's. By Kaper's expression, Chester and Smythe knew someone was there. "Hello, young man. I would like to help you, but as you can see, I'm busy," said Kaper.

"Oh, I heard how busy you are, Judge, and now that I know how Chester keeps getting out of everything, I plan on telling everybody."

"And what do you think people will do? They will do what they can, which is nothing. I make the final decision, and right, wrong, or indifferent, no one can do or say anything about it. And how can you prove it anyway, son?"

"There's always a trail, Judge. Always."

Just then, the Judge's hand came up with a pistol pointed to Webb. "Too bad you broke in here trying to kill us over my judgement. I sure hated to have to kill you, but you were just so crazed, I had no choice."

At that moment, a rifle barrel filled the window and the clicking hammer was like a cannon sounding. The judge froze as he dropped his pistol on his desk. Four men came from the shadows behind Webb, all with guns drawn. "You're not the only one who can use the dark, Judge," Webb said, smiling. "First thing we're gonna do is put Jess Steele back on the bench, and then we're gonna hang Chester." Chester jumped up and went for his gun, but Webb was ready. He shot Chester in the throat. Chester fell on Cal Smythe, who squealed like a scared child and tried to move. "Now, as for you two, you're leaving town and you're not coming back, but first, I want your money. Empty your pockets."

"You can't do this. It's robbery," said Kaper.

"I'm not robbing you, Judge. You and this sorry piece of no-good trash are donating the money to Caesar Monarrez's family." They emptied their pockets and there was more than seven hundred dollars between the two. "Now open your safe."

"You'll pay for this, Boy," said Kaper.

"Yes, but it won't be money and it won't be you I pay it to." The judge had over three thousand dollars in his safe. All blood money in one way or another, Webb figured. "Now strip, both of you."

"You can kill me, but I won't strip," Smythe said. Webb cocked the hammer, and they both got naked. Next, the men from town brought out buckets of tar and sacks of feathers. The two men's screams were enjoyed by all involved. When the job was done, Webb stepped to the judge and knocked two teeth out and busted his nose with one punch. The red liquid painted the white feathers as it dripped down his chin to his chest and stomach. Webb walked to Smythe, who covered his mouth.

Webb smiled and kicked him where the feathers don't grow. "Now get your pup and get! If you ever come anywhere close to our town again, I'll kill you," said Webb.

All men in attendance followed Kaper and Smythe outside and watched them limp away into the night. Webb thanked all the men for the help and said, "Jess Steele will be pleased."

"So will the rest of the town, now that we know for sure what those three were doing," said William Turley.

"William and D.A. Hutchinson had gone in together to open the hotel and, as D.A. said, there was never a dull moment when William Turley was around."

William looked at Webb and said, "Son, I am sure proud of you, and I'm sure I speak for everyone when I tell you thank you. Your plan worked perfect and because of it, our town can get back to business and doing things the right way and the way the good Lord intended." Everyone chimed in with their agreement and they called it a night.

The town continued to thrive, and northern control was short-lived all across the south.

Chapter Twenty-Five

1870 Hell's Valley

Andy asked Dane and Webb. "What do you two think about making another drive from Texas?"

"We got plenty of horses, and cattle too, I figure," answered Dane.

"Yeah, but here lately we have had a bunch of folks wanting to buy cattle for their own places. We are already supplying most of the town in beef with the sale of our yearly steer crop. Big John is in need of a few hundred head of heifers. So, I'm thinking if we could go down and make a drive of another 1500 heifers, it would put us back to good numbers."

"Do you think it's necessary?" Webb asked.

"I do. We lost so much during the war; I think this could fix our problem. The herd is building back, but not fast enough for the growth of the area."

"If you think it's what we need, then I reckon we should do it."

"Good. I'm gonna send you down about three weeks ahead of the rest. That will give you time to find us what we need. I figure Texas is growing as fast or faster than we are, so you may have to go a little farther than last time. But I figure you will have plenty of time to do what's needed and make it back to Austin, and we can see ol' Chuck Davis and the boys again."

"I don't reckon there's any reason to wait then. I can leave in a couple days."

"Then we will leave in three weeks and two days."

"What about hands for the drive? We can't take all the hands from here and we can't take Meko either. He has to stay and make sure everyone's fed."

"I will send Jose, JD, and that new hand, the Womack boy. He is handy with a gun, so I figure he would be a good one to go. Those three, plus you and Dane, is five, and I figure you can hire two or three more when you get there."

"Ok, but what about a cook?"

"Figure it out when you get there. The boys can eat their own cooking on the way down."

"So, you're staying here?" asked Dane.

"I figure I got to see Texas the first drive. It's your turn."

"Webb, I'm feeling like you and me got the short end of the stick."

"Wait until you get some of that Texas heat. You'll think you got more than the short end."

Two days later, Webb rode off towards Texas, the cattle, Comanches and the heat of the Llano Estacado. He made good time, and the trip was uneventful. As usual, when he rode into town, he stopped at the livery. Just as he had been the last time, Jason Reed was hard at it, but not at work. He was still hard at checkers. "Well, look what the cat dragged in," Reed said when he looked up and saw Webb.

"Mr. Reed, I see you're in the same place you was in '55 and '62 when I was here."

"Yeah, but unlike that Chinaman of yours, I can beat this one." He pointed to the man across from him. "This here is Alan Beene. Beener, this is Webb Wakefield." The men shook hands. "I guess if I got it figured right, you're showing up 'bout ever' seven or eight years. So, what are you looking for now?"

"Cattle."

"Texas is full of 'em so you should find plenty."

"How about hands?"

"Texas is full of cowboys too, so I figure you'll get all you need."

"Where are you taking the cattle, Webb?" asked Beene.

"Arkansas."

"I'll tell you what. I got family on the border of Arkansas and the nation. If all you need is hands for the drive, then I'll throw my hat in the ring."

"You're hired. The rest of the boys will be about three weeks behind me. Can you wait that long?"

"Sure can. I'm helping out here and down at the store for Mr. Davis, so I will be here."

"Good. I got some things to do in town, but tomorrow I'm hitting the herds, finding cattle to buy. Then I'll be back in time to meet the hands from Arkansas."

"Sounds good. Are you leaving your gray?"

"Yeah, and feed him plenty of grain. He earned it."

"I'll love him like he was my own."

Webb walked down to Davis Feed to talk to Chuck. When he arrived, he found Chuck talking with a few men, all of who turned to look when Webb walked in. "I wondered if I would ever see you again, Son. Come on in."

Webb walked over, took the hand offered by Chuck and said, "It's all the good cool air Texas offers in summer that draws me in."

All the men laughed. "Do I even have to ask?"

"No sir, I guess not. Cattle and a few hands."

"I can point you in the direction of cattle, but Chas and the boys are all working full time cowboying."

"I just hired Alan Beene when I rode into town."

"He is a worker; he has been wanting to head your way. Said he has family there."

"Yeah, that's what he told me. How about a cook? Do you know anyone interested in makin' the trip?" Chuck nodded his head yes and pointed at the man across from him. "This here is my friend, Ron House, and he has been known to cook a bit."

"Mr. House, how 'bout it? You feel like making the quick trip to Arkansas?"

"I figure I might. I've got my own chuck wagon, so would you pay me for my time, my wagon, and my return trip?"

"Reckon I can. Seems it would save me money in the long run."

"Then you got yourself a cook. When are you wanting to leave?"

"My hands will be three weeks behind me. Can you be ready?"

"Of course. Where do I need to be?"

"Right here. I'm meeting my people here in three weeks."

"I'll be ready."

"Now, Chuck, how about some cattle?"

"I figure you could go back to where you went all those years ago, but there's a man 'bout seventy-five miles out named Warren J. Anderson. He has one of the biggest spreads around. Maybe you could get all you need there. I know he has already sent one herd north, but is planning another."

"Warren Anderson?"

"Yep. Calls it Tump Ranch."

"How about Red Wolf? Is he still around?"

"Sure is. Lives in the same spot."

"Well, I got a few things to do, so I'm gonna leave it with you gentlemen. Mr. House, I'll see you in three weeks or less." Webb took his leave and went to get him a room at the hotel and a bite to eat. He was up in the saddle and gone with the sun rising. He was riding into Red Wolf's yard when the sun was still new. As always, the Indian was standing in the doorway.

"Light and set," said Wolf.

"Believe I will." Webb got down and took up a seat on a bench after shaking Wolf's hand.

"Heard about Caesar."

"Yeah, it was a bad deal, but we got everyone who was responsible."

"Good. His people sure think mighty high of you too."

"Why is that?"

"Sending all that money the way you did, I guess surprised them."

"He deserved it. It was all the money taken from the men responsible."

"What brings you back? Cattle, or horses, or just a friendly visit?"

"Cattle and hands."

"I ain't real busy right now and I may make you a hand if it's just for the trip there. I don't figure to stay on."

"Then you're hired. As of right now, you're riding for the T2W. Can you be ready to go in three weeks when the other hands get here?"

"Sure. What are you doing until then?"

"Buying cattle. I'm on my way to the Anderson place. You know where it is?"

"Tump Ranch? Yeah, I know it."

"Climb in your saddle and let's ride."

"I can ride, but I have to be back here in four days to tell my woman where I'm going. She is down on the border with family."

"Woman?"

"Yeah. The wolf can't stay lobo forever."

"I reckon not. Ok. You can get me there, and then you can head back."

The two men made it to the Tump Ranch before noon the next day. When they rode up to the house, a man with sandy hair came out onto the porch. "Step down, men. Have some water."

"Thank you, sir. Would you be Mr. Anderson?"

"Warren J. That's me."

"Mr. Anderson, I'm Webb Wakefield, and this is my friend, Red Wolf."

"I know the wolf... good man. How are you, Wolf?"

"Dang good, sir. Thank you."

"Well, you boys come on in."

After the men were inside, they got down to business. Webb told him he was looking for 1500 heifers and hoping to find a few hands.

"I can do the 1500, plus I've got some hands I could loan to you, and I've got two part time hands looking to travel."

"Well then, I guess when my hands get here in three weeks, I'll be ready."

"We can have the cattle gathered when your boys get here, and it should go pretty easy for you. I will call the hands in, so you can meet them now if you'd like."

"Sounds good to me."

Anderson fed the men lunch and then Wolf left for home. Webb stayed the night and was introduced to the hands.

"These are the three hands I will send with you for a loan. This is Paul David East, Brian Buck, and Beav."

"Beav?"

"Name's Tim Garner, but I growed up with buck teeth, so Beaver got attached and then just shortened to Beav."

Beav was five foot ten, slim, and easy moving. Paul David had a red tint to his beard but was bald under his hat. Brian Buck was brown headed with the same color beard.

"You boys interested in making a short drive up to Arkansas?" asked Webb.

"We was planning on farther north, but Arkansas will be a welcome trip instead," said Brian.

"Yeah, staring at a cow's south end is bad enough day in and day out, so if you can shorten the days of doing that, then I'm game," said Paul David.

"Good, then I guess since I'm doing you boys such a big favor, you will make the trip for less money," said Webb.

Paul David looked at Brian. They both looked at Beav, and Paul said, "Beav, looks like you're gonna be lonely on this trip."

Webb chuckled, "You boys will fit right in."

Two more hands rode up then. "There are the two who are looking to make a drive and move on. Billy Abney and Mark Reese."

"You boys looking to drift a little?"

"Yes sir. We was hiring on for a drive, then who knows?" said Billy.

"How about a drive to Arkansas? Then if you are both wanting to stay on, fine, or if you want to drift, that's fine too."

"Sounds like you got two new hands," said Mark.

The next day, Webb rode out with plans to be back in two and a half to three weeks. Warren had pointed him towards Kerrville. Webb was in no hurry, so he was enjoying looking at Texas since he had the time. Before he rode out, Warren told him to keep a sharp eye out. The Comanche were raising cane and looking for hair. Webb made a cold camp that night and got an early start the next day.

Chapter Twenty-Six

Wagon Train, 1870 Texas

Webb was taking his time, letting the horse have his head and pick his own path. The big grulla was just about feeling the same way as Webb, so he was taking his time enjoying the slowness of the trail.

"I could sure get used to this easy pace, ol' son. It seems like I've been in a race for so long I ain't sure how to take this easy livin'," Webb said to the big gray.

The horse never changed his pace or took his eyes off what was ahead, but Webb knew the horse understood and felt the same way. Another day, maybe a day and a half, and they would be back in town with people all around and enjoying a few days in a soft bed. Webb loved the trail and had been enjoying nights under the stars since he was ten years old. While he enjoyed his life in the wild and freedom to roam, he still enjoyed a nice comfortable bed now and then.

Something in the distance got his attention. "I think that was gunshots." Webb said to himself and the gray. The gray had his head up looking and ears searching for sound. Just barely audible, he heard it again. It was definitely gunshots. He urged his horse into a little faster trot. He would never go in full speed since he didn't know what he was riding into. So, he was careful and stopped every couple hundred yards to give a listen. He never heard any more shots, but he did see smoke. It wasn't much, but enough to know someone was in trouble.

Another half mile and he came over a small rise. There on the other side of the creek was a small group of wagons with people putting out a fire in one wagon. The fire wasn't the only thing that got his attention.

What caught his eye next were the dead bodies being pulled closer to the wagons. Webb rode down the hill toward the wagon with his hands in sight and going in easy. One woman saw him, gave a startle, and tried to raise a rifle.

The man next to her put his hand on the gun and told her, "It's a white man, Martha. Hold on."

The woman didn't try to fight or argue. She just lowered the gun.

Webb could see the arrows, so he didn't have to ask. "They come out of nowhere and were all around us, plus amongst us, before we knew it." The man said. "We got Mrs. Heidi back here trying to get an arrow out of her. The rest, as you can see, died right off."

"I know something about doctoring gun shots and arrows if you want me to take a look."

"We may need to ask her husband, Steven. The arrow took her in a private spot," replied the man.

"That's nonsense, Mr. Moore. It's my shoulder and I'm sure he has seen a shoulder before. Now all of you get out of the way and let the man through. The rest of you are gonna kill me with worry or let me die from decency," said Mrs. Heidi.

As they stood apart, he could see the lady lying in the wagon with a human mountain leaning over her. "My name's Steven Heidi. This is my wife, Dana. Please, if you can help, do it because, as you can see, we don't know much about arrows and such."

"Don't know much, my foot," replied Dana. "We don't know nothing at all," she said.

"Umm, as you can see, my wife kinda speaks her mind," Steve said with a smile.

Webb just grinned and said, "That's the best ones. At least you know where you stand because they're always honest with you."

"Are you two idgits gonna stand there and talk while I die, or are you gonna let the man do what he said he could do?" asked Dana.

"Yes dear."

Webb climbed up in the wagon and looked into honest eyes surrounded by a sweat filled face. When her eyes caught Webb's face, she said, "Well, you ain't much more than a boy."

"No ma'am. Not much more, but more," Webb said with a grin.

She tried to smile and said, "We are gonna get along just fine. Now give the boy some room to work. I'm dying, can't you see?"

Webb gave a chuckle and said, "No ma'am. You ain't dying. It just feels like it, but you will die if we don't get that arrow out and get you cleaned up."

"Well, what are you waiting for?" she exclaimed.

"Yes ma'am. First thing we gotta do is get you off your side and set you up, so's I can work on you. Now this is gonna hurt some."

"You just do your doings. I'm tougher than you think." She looked and pointed to Steve and said, "I married this big man for the challenge. I needed someone who could keep up with me, and there are days he wants to give in."

"I believe you one hundred percent, ma'am," Webb said with a laugh. "On the count of three, I'm gonna break the shaft of the arrow." He had scored it with his knife to make the break easier. He started to count, "One" and then he snapped the shaft.

"You durned idgit! You said three. I wasn't ready!"

"No ma'am, you weren't. That's the whole point. You ain't expecting the pain, so your body doesn't tense up, and it doesn't resist as bad."

"That's a pretty good trick, Mr., I don't believe you ever told us your name," said Steve.

"My name is Webb."

"Pretty good trick, Mr. Webb," said Steve, again.

"Pretty good trick, my bee-hind. Don't you go getting no ideas, Steven Heidi, or I'll deal with you later."

"Yes, dear."

"Now get on with it and no more tricks."

"Yes ma'am. I'm gonna pull the arrow out the back now and this is really going to hurt. Give her something to bite down on." Steve took off his belt and folded it up.

"Mrs. Heidi, this…"

"My name's Dana, Webb, and I know it's gonna hurt. Let's just do it."

"Yes ma'am, Dana. Ok. On the count of three." Webb grabbed the tip of the arrow and Dana put the belt in her mouth. "On three," Webb said. She gave a nod of her head. "One" again, he did not go farther. He pulled the arrow out and she let out a yell.

"Owwww, you durned pole cat, you! I said no more tricks."

"Yes ma'am. No more," said Webb. "Now, we will clean it with warm water and put a nice poultice on it. Keep the bandages changed and clean it every few hours. You got real lucky it wasn't in deep, or we would have had to go the other way and then we would have had to cut you to get the arrow out the back. We got away easy this time."

"Easy for you to say. It wasn't you being jerked on, you darn fool! Now let's see about getting Hope," said Dana.

"You ain't seeing to nothing, woman. You lay down and rest. We'll worry about Hope and that's final," said Steve.

"You better be glad I'm on death's door, you big idgit, or I'd wallop you with a frying pan."

"Well, thank the good Lord for death's door," he said with a smile.

"Who's Hope?" asked Webb.

"She is Nick and Stephanie's daughter. The Injuns took her," replied Mr. Moore.

"Where are Nick and Stephanie?"

"They were both killed. That's them lying there. That is their boy, Jerry, right there sitting with the other children." Mr. Moore pointed to a little light-headed boy sitting quietly with the other children.

"Hope and my son, Austin, were playing, standing in the edge of the creek, when an arrow hit my boy in the throat. Then all hell broke loose. They was arrows coming from every direction. They got the back wagon, and we were firing in every direction."

"Nick went down at the start. Stephanie seen 'em come in and grab Hope and started to run towards her. That's when an arrow got her too."

"Mr. Hooks there, was next to go. He was our man of faith for the trip. He also knew about doctoring. So, as you can see, we are now in sad shape, Mr. Webb."

"It's just Webb. No, Mister."

"Well, I'm Dustin. Not Mr. Moore. Mr. Moore is my father, and me when I get old, if I make it. My boy sure didn't."

"You'll make it. Ok. What I need is two horses, so's I can run hard, and swap as needed. That's how I'll catch 'em."

"Anything you need, you got," said Dustin.

Webb was gathering up the big gray when Dustin and another man, who introduced himself as Tim Davis, showed up with two horses. One was a big red roan and the other a buckskin.

"These are the best two horses we got. They got staying power, and they're both strong," said Davis.

"Thank you, Mr. Davis. I promise to do everything I can to get these animals back to you safe."

"Call me T.D., everybody does, and we ain't worried about those horses. You get that little girl back to us."

"I am gonna do my best. You men get your dead buried. Get the wagons that can travel to traveling. Get back to San Antonio and I'll be there when I can. If I ain't there in a week, she and I are both dead."

"That's where we came from, so we know the way. Webb, you want help? I can ride and shoot," said Steve.

"No sir, you take care of Mrs. Dana, and help T.D. and Dustin get these women and kids back to town safe. It's three days back in wagons, pushing the teams or not. So go easy and stay alert. I don't reckon they will hit you again, but there could always be another raiding party around."

"Yes sir, we'll keep out guards at night, and I thank you for what you did and are doing for us."

"Don't mention it. I'll see y'all in a week or less."

Martha Moore walked up with two sacks full of food. "Take this, Mr. Webb. There's plenty to last a couple of days. Plus, I put in coffee if you have the time to make it."

"Thank you, ma'am, but I never drink the stuff. The food will come in handy. I can eat from the saddle. Remember. One week."

Chapter Twenty-Seven

The trail to follow was plain as the nose on his face, so he didn't have to search or take his time. He only stopped to swap the saddle from horse to horse.

About two hours before dark, he spotted their dust. He slowed his pace. They were on the edge of the Palo Duro Canyon. The Palo was second only to the Grand Canyon in size. Its mazes were torturous to any who tried to find their way. The Comanche knew every nook and cranny of them, so he had to stay alert.

An hour before dark, he spotted a small drift of smoke coming from a draw behind some rocks. Webb left his horses and approached on foot the last mile. The Indians figured they were so far away and so far ahead that they had no worries. Webb could think of only one reason they would stop in broad daylight. They were planning to abuse the girl. So instead of waiting for dark, he decided to work his way closer to have a look.

After thirty minutes of careful work, he climbed up in the rocks to look down at the scene on the other side. There, in her homespun blue dress was little Hope.

Martha said Hope was Hope Ashlee. She was twelve years old and full of life. Webb knew if he didn't get her out of there now, her life would not be full of anything but hurt, pain, and torture.

The Indians were sitting around a small fire and were not paying any attention to Hope, who was tied by her hands and feet. She was terrified, and she had every reason to be.

The Indians were eating roasted meat and roasting another big haunch. One Indian stood and ran to the other side of the rise and then turned and said something to the rest. That's when Webb heard them.

Another group of horses were coming in. The first rider jumped down from a big black with a blaze on his face. He looked around and said something, then pointed at the girl. Another Indian stood and pointed to himself, then the girl.

The Indian on the black horse was very tall. Bigger than your average Indian. He was all muscle and sinew.

Webb was looking for a way down. There was a fifteen-foot drop where he was. If he could work his way to get behind the girl, there was a nice slope to her that was hidden by brush.

He thought he had counted eight Indians in the beginning. Eight plus the seven that just arrived was fifteen, but now, he only counted fourteen.

Just then, he heard something brush a rock behind him. As he turned, an arrow let loose from its string and found its way into Webb's left thigh. When the arrow flew from its home, the Indian was following fast behind it. He let out a war cry and charged Webb who was trying to stand with an arrow sticking out of his leg.

The Indian had a big war club in his right hand and was swinging it at Webb's head. Webb fell back on the rock that had been keeping him hidden, or so he thought. The club didn't strike home, but landed enough to do its job. The Indian's force from the run was enough to send him flying over Webb's head. He fell fifteen feet below to land on his back with a thud that drove out his breath.

Webb knew only one thing. He was not gonna make it to rescue the girl because he was sinking in a pool of black. As the darkness settled in to take him, he looked up to see one of the fiercest faces of a warrior he had ever seen. The face was fierce and proud but the eyes... he thought he had seen those eyes before, and then, the face spoke just before the dark claimed him and said, "UAV."

In the darkness, he could hear voices. They were voices yelling in words he knew and some he did not. He had pain in his leg and head, but could do nothing about any of it. Just when he thought he would reemerge to the light, the dark would take him again. Then he heard a voice telling him that everything was gonna be fine, and a coldness was on his head.

"I need you, mister, so please wake up soon."

Then he was gone again. The next thing he knew, the sun was on his face and a cool cloth was on his forehead. He opened his eyes, and there was a face looking down at him. Long brown hair, big brown eyes and cute as a spring flower was Hope Ashlee.

"Mister, I'm so glad you are awake. I'm so scared."

Webb looked around. There were only eight Indians, he counted. His voice was weak, but he asked, "Where are all the others?"

She pointed. "That big one made all of them leave. They all left except him." She pointed to the one who the big Indian had argued with before.

Wait, the big Indian had called him UAV. Then everything came back to him. He had been hit in the head and shot in the leg. His head hurt, his leg hurt worse, and then the big Indian came towards him.

The Indian squatted down and said, "UAV."

Webb nodded his head and said, "Yes, UAV." Then he looked at the Indian and said, "Quanah and UAV friend."

The Indian smiled and repeated, "UAV and Quanah, friend."

Hope said, "Mister, I think he knows you, and that's the only reason he untied me."

"Yeah, he knows me. It's been a long time, but he knows me."

Webb knew some words in the Comanche language but could sign as good as any. Webb asked where everyone went, and Quanah told him that he had sent them back to the village. He had sent them all away except Little Bear. Little Bear was the owner of the young girl, apparently, so he was allowed to stay to make a deal with the white man who had come for her.

Webb sat up and tried to stand, but his head was still making him dizzy. So he stayed in the sitting position for a while. Little Bear approached and said he would sell the girl for ten horses. Webb told him all he had was two because he needed one to get them back. Little Bear said no. He must have at least five horses.

Webb said, "Help me up so's I can get to my horses."

Quanah looked and signed, "Where do you go?"

"I need to get to my horses." Quanah pointed, and there were all three mounts chomping grass with the Indian ponies. He also pointed to his saddle, his saddlebags, and the sack of food Martha had packed.

Webb told Hope, "Fetch my saddlebags and that bag of food." She returned and handed Webb both things.

He pulled out the big bag of coffee Martha had packed. Then he pulled out three big pouches of tobacco from his saddlebag, plus a big Arkansas toothpick. He got up with Hope's help, limped over to Little Bear, and gave him the coffee, tobacco, and a knife. He pointed to the two horses T.D. had given him and said, "It's all I have. If Little Bear will trust me, I will bring four more ponies, more coffee, and tobacco to Little Bear's Lodge within ten risings of the sun." Little Bear looked at Quanah and Quanah nodded. Little Bear signed five ponies and Webb agreed. Little Bear took his payment, mounted his horse, and left.

"Does that mean we are safe now, mister?"

"It does indeed, Hope Ashlee. It does indeed."

Webb explained to her who he was and what he was doing there. He also signed for Quanah. When he was done, Quanah told him to rest one more day, then they could be on their way.

He and his band, who Webb found out were called the Quahadi, told him of the Comanche's struggles and life on the plains. He also told him where they would be in ten days so Webb could honor Little Bear with his payment.

The next day, Webb's leg was wrapped with a new poultice from Quanah. They said their goodbyes with a promise from Webb to see him in ten days.

Quanah said again, "UAV friend."

Webb nodded his head. "Yes, Quanah and UAV friend." Quanah smiled and turned and rode away.

For the next three days, Webb and his new companion took their time, letting the big gray rest often because of his double burden.

Webb had found out the wagon had been headed to California and after telling her about her parents, he had been her comfort. She told him that her grandparents, Frank and Jinn Norman, would surely be waiting for her once they arrived in San Antonio. Hope was a talker, but Webb enjoyed it after so long with only a horse and the stars to talk to.

CHAPTER TWENTY-EIGHT

The third and final day, they arrived in town just at dark. Webb went straight to the hotel where he found everyone except Jerry, who was at the Normans' place, but someone went to fetch him. All parties assured Webb they never expected to see him alive again. Everyone but Dana.

"I told 'em all I could see it in your eyes. You were too mean to kill and too young to die hard."

"So, after all that gentleness I gave you, you say I'm mean?" Webb said with a smile.

"Yes, but not in a bad way. Those eyes say a lot without talking and they told me you would be back, guaranteed," she said.

Webb told the story of getting Hope back and said he was sorry for the horses. T.D. and Dustin assured him it was fine.

Just then, Jerry ran through the door, followed by an older couple. Frank was three or four inches over six feet tall and a strong-looking man. Jinn was a woman of beauty. You could tell she had been beautiful her entire life and refined.

They all hugged and fussed over Hope until she broke loose and said, "If it weren't for Webb here, I would be dead or worse."

Frank came to Webb and gave him a firm handshake and said, "Anything you want, it's yours. All you have to do is ask."

He looked at the man behind the hotel counter and said, "Mr. Brown, give Mr. Webb here the best room you have for as long as he wants, and see that his meals are charged to the room. When he leaves, you and I can settle up."

"Yes sir, Mr. Norman. Right away, sir."

"Papaw, it's not Mr. Webb. It's just Webb," said Hope.

"It's actually Webb Wakefield, Mr. Norman, but I go by Webb."

"Well, Webb, we can't thank you enough for everything. Losing our daughter and son-in-law is enough, but if we had lost these two or either of them, it would have been too much."

"I'm glad I could help. Right now, though, if you don't mind, I'd like to find the Doc and have my leg looked at and then maybe get a bite to eat."

"Certainly," said Mr. Norman. "You come with me and I'll get you there."

As they turned to leave, Hope got up and said, "Wait." She walked over to Webb, gave him a big hug, looked at him with those big brown eyes and said, "Someday, I'm gonna marry you, Webb Wakefield."

Webb smiled and said, "Now, I don't wish you to have that burden, young lady, but we will sure see." Everyone smiled, thinking what a nice ending and how cute and sweet.

Everyone but Hope. She told herself, "I will be Mrs. Hope Wakefield. Mrs. Webb Wakefield." She liked the sound of it, and she started planning her wedding right then, along with the last thought, "I love you, Webb Wakefield and someday"

On the way to the doctor's office, Frank asked Webb, "How old are you, son?"

"I just turned twenty-five on February eleventh of this year."

"Twenty-five!" said Frank with shock. "You don't look a day over eighteen."

Webb smiled and said, "I guess it's all this clean living I been doing."

"I would say you're right. After we leave the Doc, maybe we can go down to Tuffy's Saloon and have a drink."

"Well, like I said, I live clean, so it will have to be one beer. I don't drink more than that and never whiskey."

"Boy, you do live a clean life. I guess next you'll be saying you don't chew tobacco or smoke."

"Well, as a matter of fact, I don't. I tried some chewing tobacco when I was a youngster, and it made me sick. Although I do always carry a few packets of tobacco and the makings, I don't touch the stuff unless offered in a peace pipe to be social."

"That is what I call extra clean living, son. I will say, when you don't spend your money on things like whiskey and tobacco, then you have plenty for other things."

"Yes sir. I have a place back in Arkansas, where I'm from. It's a family business, so I put my money there when I can because I always get it back."

"Sounds like a real good decision."

"I like to think I do one or two things right."

"I guess we can just have a bite to eat and coffee since you live so clean."

"Well, Mr. Norman, that sounds real nice, but I don't drink coffee either."

"Good Lord, son. How do you not drink coffee?"

"Just never acquired a taste for it, I guess. It's just too bitter for me."

"What do you drink besides one beer?"

"I love God's life sustaining liquid. Clean, clear, cold water."

"I like good cold water myself, but on those cold nights, you need something warm."

"On those nights, I simply heat up the water and drop a few pine needles in for flavor. If I don't have any pine handy, well then, I just enjoy warm water. You'd be surprised."

"I guess I would be." Just then, they stepped up on the walkway and knocked on the door. Light filled the room from a lantern carried by a man in a white shirt with a black string tie. The name on the shield said, Dr. J.E. Brewer.

The door opened, and the Doc said, "Well, Frank, come on in. You and your friend have a seat."

"Thank you kindly, Doc. This is Webb Wakefield, the young man who went after our Hope."

"Hello, young man. I am guessing since you're back so soon, it all went well."

"Yes, I guess it went as well as we all hoped, except I ended up with an arrow through my leg."

"Well, drop your drawers and hop up here so we can have a look." Webb did as he was told, and the doc unwrapped his bandage.

"I'll say this. Whoever fixed you up did a real fine job."

"It was one of the Indians of the group that took Hope." Doc looked shocked.

"You mean they stole Hope, killed her parents, shot you, and then fixed you up?"

"That just about sums it up." Webb told the story and of his previous meeting with Quanah.

"That has got to be a story for the books. They say that Quanah is one tough cookie. He is supposed to be twice the size of a regular Indian. Plus, he's big medicine with his group of Quahadis."

"I'll admit, he is a striking figure. Not twice as big as any other Indian, but bigger than most, and yes, he is the chief of the Quahadis band. If you ever seen him up close, you would have to ask where he got his eyes. They are just like looking into my own. Ice blue."

"Well now, don't that beat all?" said Frank.

"I'll say. I've never heard that," replied Doc.

"That's probably because the only white man to be close enough to look into those eyes and live to tell is Webb here," said Frank.

"You may be right," said Dr. Brewer. "Well, I guess that's about as good as I can do. Just come see me every day, once a day, before you go, and I will change the bandage."

"How much do we owe you, Doc?"

"I'd say two dollars will do."

"We were just going to Tuffy's for a drink and a bite. Want to join us?"

"Don't mind if I do. Let me get my coat." They enjoyed small talk on the way to Tuffy's. As they sat down in the saloon, a short man with a potbelly and a gap tooth grin walked over.

"Dr. Brewer, Frank, young man. How can I help y'all tonight?" asked the man.

"Tuffy, I would like for you to meet Webb Wakefield. He is the man that went after our granddaughter, Hope."

"I've already heard he found her and brought her home. It's the talk of the town by now. How are you, young man? And it's good to meet you," Tuffy said, as he held out his hand.

"I'm fine, sir, and it's a pleasure. Boy, news travels fast."

"Good news always travels fast here, son," said Doc.

Tuffy replied, "And bad new travels faster." They all laughed. "What can I get you?"

"Whatever you have for a meal, and if you have any milk, I'd like a glass," said Webb.

Tuffy looked hurt. "Did you say milk?"

Webb looked at him without blinking. "I did. Is something wrong with that?"

Tuffy raised his hands. "No sir. Not one bit. It's just the only two people I ever seen drink milk in a saloon is yours truly and the man sitting to your left." He said as he indicated Frank.

Webb looked at Frank and said, "Good clean living, huh?"

"Now, I do drink milk with my meals, but then I drink a beer as fast as I can afterwards," Frank said with a grin. "Which reminds me, you can bring a beer right now for me and Doc, then once Webb is done with his meal, you can bring him one too."

"Coming right up. I'll get my baby boy to fix your drinks while I get your food ready." Tuffy turned and walked towards the bar while motioning for a walking red oak to come with him.

"Who is that tree trunk following Tuffy?" Webb asked.

"That is Tuffy's baby boy, Jeremy. Folks call him Bull Head." Webb looked again at Jeremy. He was six feet two and weighed a good three hundred pounds.

"If that's the baby, I would hate to see the others."

"He is baby only in birth. He is the biggest of the brood. If you look there at the card table, you will see an older brother that I believe is Brady. Then look upstairs on the balcony, and you'll see his twin, Bradley." Frank said with a motion. "It's Bradley who runs the girls. Brady runs the gambling, but it's also said since you can't tell them apart, they swap out regularly. They look so much alike, even Tuffy can't tell 'em apart. He just calls 'em Twin."

Webb said, "It sounds like Tuffy has a nice family business going on with his three boys."

"Oh, it ain't just three boys. As you see, Jeremy takes care of the knuckleheads who cause a ruckus. The twins have their jobs, and you see that tall, slim drink of water with the easy white smile sitting there in the corner?"

"You mean the one with the tied down gun?" asked Webb.

"That's the one. As you can tell by the gun, he handles all the gun play if needed. Goes by the name of Stacy. Easy as Sunday morning, but don't get him riled."

Webb whistles, "Four sons and all in business. Sounds pretty smart."

"He has five sons. Stacy is a nephew and there's plenty more where he came from," said Frank.

"Yeah, but you ain't told him who the real boss is, Frank."

"No, I guess I skipped that part."

Webb asked, "And what part is that?" Right then, a short woman with dark hair, dark eyes, wide hips, and everything else a woman needs came down the stairs in a maroon dress that clung to every part of her body.

"That," said Frank, "is the boss, Miss Vicki Lynn." The woman came down the steps and came directly to their table.

"Hello, Doc Brewer, Frank, and I hear this is Mr. Webb Wakefield, the man of the hour, if I hear right."

"You heard right," said Doc, as all three men stood until she was seated.

"Mr. Wakefield, how come I have never seen you in here?"

"Just Webb, ma'am and, well, the only time I come to town, which has only been one other time, I only went to the general store."

"Well, I guess I need to be hanging out at the store more often," she said with a grin. "So where are you from, Webb?"

"From Arkansas, ma'am."

"You know, I have been telling Tuffy that Arkansas is where we need to head. We have made a ton of money here, and I am tired of this dust and heat."

"You would love Arkansas, ma'am, and I know it would love you."

"Well, I guess that just about settles that."

Just then, Tuffy showed up with a plate of food and a glass of milk. "Here you go, Webb. Two nice thick slices of ham, corn on the cob, mashed potatoes, gravy and a little something special, fresh asparagus cooked in butter sauce, salt, and pepper."

"Tuffy, this looks mighty fine, sir. Thank you."

"You're welcome, son, and enjoy."

Frank said, "Tuffy, now where did you find fresh asparagus?"

"Frank, you writing one of them dime store novels?"

"Well, I might be."

"If so, then you just leave that page out," said Tuff, and they all laughed.

While Webb ate, Vicki talked to Tuffy about Arkansas, and his reply was, "Whatever you want, dear." After the meal, Vicki excused herself and went to check on other customers.

Webb said, "She doesn't seem like the type to be a soiled dove."

"That's because she ain't. She runs this show and may wear a dress that shows a little much, but she is a far cry from a soiled dove," said Doc.

"That's good to know, I reckon," he replied. "So, Doc, what does J.E. stand for?" asked Webb.

"James Edward, but I like the short version, Jim Ed."

Frank said, "I like it even shorter, Doc."

Doc grinned. "Yes, Doc will do as well." He added, "You know, I have thought about going back east a little myself. I would not mind checking out Arkansas."

"It's a nice place, Doc. Lots of good, hardworking, honest people. I am from the Southwest corner, just about forty miles north of the Red River, where Louisiana, Texas, and the Nations meet Arkansas."

"Sounds like it might be a good central location," said Frank.

"Real good and lots of room to grow," said Webb.

Frank and Doc agreed, "Might be something to keep in mind."

Webb finished his one beer and announced that he was ready for a nice, soft bed. Frank paid for the drinks and food, and they all said goodbye to Tuffy and Vicki.

Once back at the hotel, Doc and Frank said their farewells to Webb. They gave Webb the key to his room and no sooner than he hit the pillow he was out like a light.

CHAPTER TWENTY-NINE

Webb slept soundly and didn't wake until after sunrise when he heard a knock on his door. He cracked the door and standing there smiling was Hope Ashlee.

"Morning, Webb."

"Morning, Hope. What can I do for you?"

"Well, Papaw said it would be ok if I came to see if you've had breakfast, and since you're still in your room, I take it as a no."

"You caught me. I seem to have been pretty tired and just now woke up."

"Good. Then I'll wait for you in the hotel restaurant."

Webb washed up, got dressed, and headed downstairs to see a cheery Hope. "I see someone is happy this morning."

"Well, I have every right to be. I'm alive, I ain't living as some Injun's squaw, and I'm about to eat breakfast with my future husband."

Webb almost choked. "Future husband, huh? Don't you think you need to wait a few years?"

"I do, and so do Mamaw and Papaw. They said not until I'm eighteen."

"Sound like smart people."

She just smiled with those big brown eyes. "Tell you what. I'll make my way back here in six years when I'm thirty-one and you're eighteen. If you're still not up and married, then we will think about it." He figured that would settle it all and what would it hurt? In six years, she would have found someone else, and he could pretend to hurt but smile inside.

"Deal," she said.

"There you two are," said Frank as he entered.

"Well, Papaw, we have settled it already. We're gonna wait six years until I'm eighteen, like you and Mamaw want. Then we will be married."

Frank smiled and said, "Now that sounds like a winner to me."

"I'm gonna let you two eat while I go tell Mamaw," she said.

"You do that, darling," said Frank.

As she got up, Webb stood until she was gone. As she left, she gave him a look with those doe eyes and simply said, "Bye, Webb!"

"Bye, Miss Hope."

When she left, Webb said, "Sorry about that, Mr. Norman."

Frank waved him away and said, "She has been going on and on all night, last night and all morning. I'm glad you agreed. She will forget about it in a few weeks and in six years, I'm sure you will be safe." They both chuckled and Webb ordered breakfast.

After breakfast, they talked some more about Arkansas and cattle and horses. "Speaking of horses," said Frank, "I had one of my hands bring in five horses. All good horseflesh. Plus, I had Howard over at the store to box up twenty pounds of sugar, twenty pounds of coffee, ten big pouches of tobacco, and some beads and cloth for the womenfolk. I figure to make you a man of your word and then some."

"Well, that will sure do it. I thought the knife, tobacco, and coffee I gave was plenty, plus the horses to come."

"That reminds me, there are five top shelf knives too. You replace yours and then hand out the other four."

"Frank, this may give them the idea it pays to take white women."

"Yeah, I guess you're right. I didn't think of that. I was just so happy to have her back. You think I ought to cancel the order?"

"No. I'll make sure Quanah knows taking women should not be allowed. I have a feeling he already knows. I figure that's why he was arguing with Little Bear that first night." Webb was right. Quanah never took a white captive, nor did he allow it when he rode in the party.

Webb left that afternoon but promised to return in time for the big race. There was an upcoming foot race and horse race. The talk had been about nothing but one horse owned by a local man named Mark Smith. Smith put on a couple of these big races every year. People came from as far as three hundred miles out to be a part of it. The horse race paid $500 to the winner. It only costs $25 to enter your horse and rider. A chance at $500 had everybody wanting in on it.

With his big gray ready and all the supplies loaded, Webb set out for Quanah, Little Bear, and the Palo Duro Canyon. If he timed it right, he would arrive with two days to spare. He wanted to be there early to show he was a man to be trusted.

So many white men had told lie after lie to the Indians and swindled them out of their land. It was no wonder they hated the white man and didn't trust them. They had pushed the tribes from the Atlantic all the way to the plains.

Now, the plains Indians were pushing back and had been doing so, hard, for twenty-plus years as whites tried to push harder and farther west.

The white man was slaughtering hundreds of thousands of buffalo at the order of the White House and the government. Their solution was that if we can't force them out, we'll starve them out, and make them come to us for food and anything else they need. When that happens, they are then at the mercy of the white man.

For most tribes, it worked. But the plains Indians were a different breed. Their horsemanship was unrivaled. Their warriors could hang off one side of a horse with only one foot over a horse's back while shooting a bow from under the horse's neck at a dead run. Plus, they hit their target. Their horse herds were in the thousands. They could fight on the run because they would survive on anything they could. Comanche warriors could survive in the harshest of deserts by killing one horse and drinking the liquid in its stomach. They would wrap intestines around their necks to take along for the ride. They were always with two or more horses, so they could ride nonstop for days if needed.

There will never be a more beautiful, proud, or resilient people than the tribes of the plains.

Webb knew he was close when he saw the first Indian, but when a group of twenty warriors appeared, he almost got nervous. He kept his hands in view and made no sudden movements. They approached with bows and lances held high. They were screaming war cries and riding circles as they surrounded him and rode with him until he reached the edge of the camp.

From there, the string went single file as it wound down to the bottom of a small part of the canyon hidden from view everywhere above.

When he reached the bottom, Quanah was there, waiting with Little Bear. The look on Little Bear's face was of stone as he waited for his payment.

Five horses were paid. Webb unloaded the rest and told Quanah he had gifts for the entire village. Quanah made the announcement and the entire village let out a huge cry of excitement.

Everyone, from old women, young warriors, to children and old chiefs, made their way to touch him and say, "UAV!"

Once it was all over, Quanah called for Webb to join him in his lodge to smoke the peace pipe. During the smoking of the pipe, different warriors told of battles past with other tribes and whites. Webb listened with enthusiasm.

Webb told of his very first meeting with a then young Quanah. When he was done, Quanah told his version and added, "Quanah and UAV friends."

The women had prepared a feast fit for a king. To be with one of the most feared groups of people in the world, Webb never felt safer.

Honor, and someone who was fearless, meant much to these people. To be trusted was, above all and no different than honor. For them, it was one and the same. The fact that he kept his word and came back alone and unafraid was big medicine for Webb. He had also saved Quanah as a young brave. That carried a lot of weight.

Webb sat in their center circle and was included in more stories of previous battles. After their feast, they invited him to dance and sing. All the kids ran around him smiling and yelling, "UAV!" It was one of the best nights of his life.

Before the night was over, Webb pulled out the last gift, the four knives. He gave one to Quanah and told him to pick his top three warriors for the others.

Webb was invited to sleep in Quanah's lodge and the next morning, they took him on a hunt. Quanah and his Quahadi took him through some of the most beautiful landscapes he had ever set eyes on.

Quanah told him, "My lodge, my village, is also lodge and village of UAV."

Webb promised anytime he could find the village, he would bring food, and tobacco to smoke. Quanah smiled and nodded his head in approval.

He stayed two more days and left on the morning of the fourth day.

Webb was back in San Antonio within a couple of days and in plenty of time for the race. When he rode in that first afternoon, he saw Mrs. Jinn and Hope. Of course, Hope was all smiles and eyes.

"Afternoon, ladies. How are the two most beautiful ladies in Texas doing today?"

"I tell you, Mr. Wakefield, you know how to make an old woman feel good."

"I speak only the truth, Mrs. Jinn." He tipped his hat and rode on towards the café.

The Horned Toad Café was the spot for good cooking. It was said to be the best in town, although Tuffy's Saloon was dang good, especially for a saloon. The owners of the Horned Toad were Hugh Taylor, also known as Boo Boo, and his wife, Sheryl. Boo Boo did the talking, and Sheryl did the cooking.

"Come in, sir. Come right on in and have a seat wherever you can find one."

Webb spotted Doc and joined him. "Hello, Doc. Do you mind?"

"Not at all, young man. Please, sit. I'm glad to see you're back. I take it there was no trouble?"

"None whatsoever. In fact, I had the best time of my life and look forward to another visit."

"That good, huh?"

"Yes sir."

"Doc, who is your friend here?" asked Boo.

"Boo Boo, this is Webb Wakefield."

"Oh, you're the young man who saved Hope from the Comanche."

"Yes sir, I guess I am."

"Well, God bless you, son, and welcome to the Horned Toad. Can I get you some coffee?"

"No sir. I don't drink it, but I will take some milk, or water, and today's special."

"Yes sir. Coming right up. Sheryl, one toad special and a cup of fat!" yelled Boo.

"Hugh, you do know I'm five feet away? You don't have to yell," said Sheryl.

"Well, if I don't yell, you claim you don't hear me."

"It's not that I don't hear you. I'm just choosing to ignore you."

Boo smiled and looked at Doc and Webb. "Would you believe she was the best one of the bunch I had to pick from?"

"Who are you lying to? You know I picked you," she said with a wink.

During lunch, the two talked of travel and southwest Arkansas. Doc said he was enjoying Texas and the western expansion, but another few years, and he could see himself settling some place like Arkansas for good. He said his pa had had a few cows and some farmland when he was growing up. He always had a horse and he and his little sister explored the countryside all around their place.

"Good memories, Webb. I tell you, cherish this time because in the years to come, places like this and people like you who helped settle it will be in the history books."

"People and places maybe, Doc, but I hardly doubt Webb Wakefield's name would ever be in a book."

"Young man, mark my words. It will be. You saving young Hope from the Comanche is just the sort of thing to write about because people everywhere want to hear about it.

You take Quanah, one of the fiercest warriors of his time. Even though Quanah is still a young man, he is already known as a warrior and leader. Then, you take someone who rode into their camp, all alone, to rescue a young girl. You just can't make that stuff up, son, and people will want to hear about it. How big do you think the name Quanah will be in the years to come?"

"I don't know, but I would bet it will be pretty big, or at least very well known."

"It's already well known throughout the west, so it can only grow, and believe me, men like you right along with it," stated Doc.

"Maybe you're right, Doc, but I'd have to see it with my own eyes."

"Just think how famous the names of the old Mountain men are, like Kit Carson, Bridger, Glass, and Johnson. Those are big names already. You may not believe it, but just because you're not climbing the Rockies or finding a path to the Pacific, you're doing things just as important. You're settling something wild and that says a lot."

"Then I promise when I'm traveling the world giving speeches, I'll be sure to mention my good friend, Dr. Jim Ed Brewer," said Webb with a big old grin.

"How's everything here, men?" asked Boo as he came to the table.

"I tell you. I could use one more glass of milk if you got it," said Webb.

"I got it, and you will too, as soon as your apple pie comes out."

"Wow. Now I don't know if I can take a piece of pie."

"You're just gonna have to make room 'cause it comes with the special," said Boo.

"Since when has the pie come with the meal?" asked Doc.

"Since my wife said he earned it by riding into that Injun camp and bringing little Hope Ashlee home safe to Frank and Jinn."

"I can't argue with that then, can I?" said Doc.

"Plus, she said he had a set of eyes worthy enough of any pie she made."

"A hero with nice eyes, huh? Well, I guess I got in the wrong profession, Boo," replied Doc.

"Me and you both, Doc. Me and you both," Boo said, grinning. Webb finished his pie and milk, paid for his food, and took his leave.

Webb went to the store to speak to Howard, where he ran into Frank.

"I just got word from my wife and the future Mrs. Webb Wakefield you were back," said Frank with a big smile.

Webb blushed and said, "Yeah, I spoke to them as soon as I got back. I guess the week and a half I've been gone didn't clear Hope's head."

Howard let out a big laughing roar and said, "Are you kidding, son? She's already been in here twice this week looking at cloth for her future wedding dress."

Frank grinned and said, "She's just a child with her head set on something right now. I'm sure once you're gone from town, she'll move on, but I will say it's nice to see you squirm, son."

Howard agreed with a nod and another laugh. "Webb, tell me about southwest Arkansas."

"I tell you, Howard, she's beautiful. Rivers every ten miles in any direction. Clear flowing creeks everywhere you turn. Huge timber like pine, white oak, red oak, pin oak, gum, cypress, green grass, and rolling hills. There is nothing like it. You can be in the valley between the Red and Little River in the morning and on top of a rocky cliff staring down at the cold, clear waters of the Little Missouri that afternoon. Louisiana, Texas, and the Nations are within a half day's ride. You won't find better people this side of heaven."

"Frank, the boy seems to like it."

"I'm beginning to think that myself," said Frank.

"I do like it. Love it, to be honest. As a young man, I've been like so many others who want to see what's over the next hill or just simply leave home behind. Then you wake up and want to be back home and can't wait until you are. I love my travels and the people I've met, the things I've seen, but there's truth to the old saying, 'there's no place like home'. Especially when it's southwest Arkansas."

"You know, I've been thinking about selling this place in another few years and heading back east a ways. You make it sound so good. I may have to see for myself. Maybe open my own place there. I can see it now, Howard Stinnet's Hardware."

"I promise, Howard, if you come, you won't leave. You'll grow to love it as I do."

"Well, gents, I believe I'm gonna head out. I gotta keep an eye on the home front. You know how it is. I gotta make sure Jinn and Hope ain't planning too big a wedding at my expense," said Frank, smiling.

Howard laughed again while Webb just shook his head and blushed. "Webb, come out to the house tonight for supper. We talked about Arkansas for so long, I didn't get to hear how your trip went."

"I don't know, Frank. I mean, I'm already due to be hitched to your granddaughter. Another visit to your place, and I'm liable to take over your entire operation," said Webb with a smile.

"Son, I figure in six years, I may be ready to sit on the porch and watch the sun rise and set, so that sounds real good to me."

Howard grinned and said, "Backfired on you, huh?" Webb just shook his head and watched Frank walk away.

As Webb walked out, there were a couple of young boys with tacks, hammers, and flyers going from store to store asking to hang up signs.

"What do you got there, young man?"

"Posters about the race this Saturday, mister."

"Yeah, $500 to the winner of the horse race, and $100 to the fastest on foot."

"Which one of you is gonna win the foot race?"

"Neither," came a voice from behind Webb.

Webb turned to see a man standing there. He was a big man, six one, broad shoulders, black hair with gray at the temples. "Maybe in a couple more years one of them might, but not this year, or the next. Will you, boys?"

"No sir, Mr. Smith," they said in unison, and they turned and went into the store.

"You sound pretty sure about the winner of the foot race," said Webb.

"The foot race and the horse race. It's gonna be the same as it has for the last three years for the horse race and five years for the foot race."

"I'll have to admit, I have heard the same horse has won it the last few years running. Maybe you can let me in on the foot race secret so I will know who to put my money on."

"I can tell you, but you won't find any takers to bet 'cause it ain't no secret, and everybody's money will be on him."

"Who's him?"

"Paul Wayne Ray. The fastest thing you'll ever lay eyes on."

"Fast, huh?"

"He's more than fast."

"Just how fast are we talking?"

"You ever heard of greased lightning?"

"I have."

"That's too slow, son. This boy could draw from the hip, shoot his Colt, holster it, run 50 feet, hold up a pie plate, and let the bullet hit dead center." Webb just looked at him, and the man never changed expression.

Web smiled and said, "He sure sounds fast alright, but are you sure he would hit dead center on the shot?"

"Dead center." They both gave a chuckle.

"I'm looking at you, and I don't think you're one of Tuffy's boys, but with so many, who can keep track?"

"No sir, I'm not. I'm Webb Wakefield," said Webb as he stuck out his hand.

"Nice to meet you, Mr. Wakefield. I don't mind saying I'm glad you ain't another one of Tuffy's. They's already enough of 'em to choke a Missouri mule."

"It's just Webb. Mr. Smith."

It is Mr. Smith, right?

"Yes sir. Marion L. Smith, but you can call me Tootsie."

"Tootsie?" asked Webb.

"Tootsie," he reaffirmed.

"Now, that's a handle if I ever heard one."

"You bet it is and with a handle like that, you always know when the girls come calling for a dance. You ain't getting mixed up with nobody else."

"I do think you are right."

"No thinking about it, son. Just believe it."

"Seems like I heard the man responsible for this race is named Smith."

"My son, Mark. He puts on two every year."

"He must do good."

"He's won the horse race for the last three years, but he runs the side bets for the foot race and horse race, so he makes a chunk."

"Plus, the $500 for winning?"

"Plus, the $500!"

"Boy, I guess he does well for a day's work."

"Oh, it ain't just one day. He works his horse every day and travels as far as five hundred miles to run his horse in other races. He has these posters printed, so they go out a month in advance to towns around us for two hundred or three hundred miles. It's a nice bit of work."

"It sounds like it."

"Traveling to towns for other races is where the money really is. Better horses, bigger pots, and not everyone knows your horse. All they have to go on is rumor. So, it's usually on an even playing field."

"Is it true the horse doesn't have a name, just a number?"

"Number three."

"That's odd, I'd say."

"He lives by that number. Every horse he has ever owned was called three. He even named his son Trey."

"Sounds like dedication to me," said Webb.

Tootsie smiled and said, "Sounds like something alright. I just don't know about dedication,"

"I know who you are now," said Tootsie. "You're the young man saved Hope from the Comanche."

"Yes sir, I'm the one."

"Fine job you did, but I thought you were gone to deliver horses promised for her return."

"I was, just got back."

"I don't know how you pulled it off, but good for you, son."

"Tootsie Smith, what lies are you telling now?" Both men turned to see Tuffy standing there grinning.

"If you must know, I was just telling young Webb here what an upstanding citizen you were, but now that you ruined it, I will admit to you, Webb, it was all a lie, as Tuffy said. He's a no count pole cat!" said Tootsie.

"Pole cat? Why you no good yeller bellied son of a gun. I'm better than the likes of you any day."

"I see you been in your own who-hit-John this morning."

"It's better than that snake head you drink."

Webb tipped his hat and left them there on the walk, slinging insults back and forth.

CHAPTER THIRTY

Webb took a room at the hotel, got cleaned up, and waited for supper.

The conversation that evening was about the trip to the Indian village and some of the stories he had heard.

Hope seemed no worse for wear by the stories, or her time held captive. She seemed to be a strong young woman. Of course, Webb had to endure her big doe eyes and smiles all through supper. No comments were made about marriage, which was pleasant, although she did announce that she helped prepare the meal, and she was gonna take good care of her husband when she turned eighteen. Webb agreed with a smile and changed the subject. After dinner, Webb said his goodbyes and thanked them for a lovely supper.

The next day, Webb helped Frank's hands break a few new horses he had gotten to replace the five he had given to Little Bear.

The following day, he had lunch with the Moores, Heidis, and T.D. at the Horned Toad. Dana was healing nicely and assured Webb she would make it to California or die trying. They announced they were going to wait on the next wagon train and fall in with them. T.D. and Dustin had said that Frank had replaced the two horses they had given for Hope. He was also going to supply them with work until they were able to leave. They parted ways and Webb went to the hotel to write a letter to Andy and let him know how things were going.

The following day was the day before the races, and the town was filling up. Webb stopped in to see Howard when a team of bull whackers rolled into town.

"Right on schedule," said Howard.

"Are you restocking?" asked Webb.

"Yes sir, and none too soon. With all the people in town, I need everything and then some."

They stepped outside and were greeted by a solid built fellow and another driver. The first driver was six feet tall but looked like a stump. He had to weigh two hundred and forty pounds. He had his hat off, knocking the dust from his clothes, and a dark brown head full of curls fell over his face.

When he looked up, he had a friendly smile and said, "Howard, I'm right on time, just like always, and it looks like the race is drawing a good shopping crowd for you." The big man stepped up on the walk and shook Howard's hand.

"Rocky, I want you to meet Webb Wakefield. Webb, this is Rocky Ray." Webb took the offered hand with a nod.

"And if he will quit dilly dallying, I'll introduce my brother." He motioned to the young man behind him. He was shorter than Rocky but with the same build. His hair was blonde, he had a big smile, and he was singing a tune. "Webb, this is my little brother, Stoney."

The two men shook hands and Webb said, "Rocky and Stoney, huh?"

Rocky smiled and said with a grin, "Yep, our little brother Gravel couldn't make it."

"That's enough chitchat. Let's get this stuff unloaded and put away," said Howard.

"Howard, I figure I don't have anything pressing, so if you need help"

"I wouldn't turn down help and when we're done, I usually pay for lunch."

"Sounds like we got a deal," said Webb.

When the wagons were empty, Howard sent Webb and the Ray brothers to eat at the Horned Toad with a note for Boo to charge their meals to him. Over lunch, Webb learned the Rays were cousins to Paul Wayne Ray.

"Yeah, he's fast as greased lightning."

"Tootsie says faster."

"That old rap scallion. Well, if he said it, then that's probably the only thing he ain't stretching into one of his yarns."

"Oh, believe me. He stretched it alright," Webb told of the draw and shoot and pie plate, and they all had a good laugh.

Rocky told him how he had been hauling freight his whole life, and in a few years, he was hoping to slow down and settle somewhere nice and peaceful. Webb told of Arkansas while the other two listened.

"I'm right by the southwest corner. Right down the road from Washington, where Jim Bowie's knife was forged."

"Sounds like a place I could get used to," said Rocky.

"It's a good place. I'm sure you would enjoy it. I sure do. If it weren't for coming back and forth to this area for horses and cattle, I don't think I would ever leave."

Lunch was over, so the men left the cafe. On the walk over to the store, a man walked up.

"Hello, men. J. McCullough is the name and making you well is my fame." He was six two, two twenty-five, dark hair, light blue eyes, and held a bottle of Jerm's Cough Killer.

"You men look like smart men. How about I fix you up with a bottle each of my healing liquid? This cures what ills you. It's one dollar a bottle, and you can't go wrong."

"Well, Mr. McCullough, what if we ain't sick?" asked Rocky.

"Just keep it until you are, my friend. You can't go wrong. I promise."

Stoney said, "I think I'll take a bottle."

Rocky looked at him, shook his head, and said, "You would."

"Gents, I'll be here for three days only."

Rocky said over his shoulder, "Good. Thanks for the warning."

Saturday, the day of the race, finally came, and the town was packed. People were still coming in by the wagon loads. The hotel was full. The Horned Toad was packed, and Tuffy's was jumping. Webb saw a sizeable crowd gathered around, so he decided to see what the fuss was about. In the middle of the crowd was one of the prettiest horses he ever saw. It was so black that it looked blue. His coat was slick and glossy. There was no question this had to be Three.

"What do you think?" said a voice.

Webb turned to see Tootsie, a young couple, and a boy and a girl. "I think he is the finest horse I've ever seen."

"Before the day's over, he will be the fastest," the young man said.

"Webb, this is my son, Mark Smith." The men shook hands.

"It's a pleasure, Webb."

"Indeed it is," replied Webb.

"This is my wife, Amy, and our children, Paige and Trey."

It was said in town that Amy Smith, who was the teacher over at the school, was what you might call high maintenance. I promise you, one look into her eyes and you knew she was worth every single penny.

"Mrs. Smith, it's a pleasure indeed."

"I would like to thank you, Mr. Wakefield."

"Webb, ma'am. Just Webb, and thank me for what?"

"For saving Hope. She is one of my students, and I hated losing her to a move to California, of course. I could have dealt with that, but not murdered, or worse, by Indians."

"I couldn't agree more, ma'am."

"I hate for her and little Jerry to have lost their parents, but Frank and Jinn will do just as good a job in raising them. Plus, we all come together in time of need. I am happy to have them both back in school."

"Yes ma'am. I'm sure you are."

"Webb, who are you putting your money on today?" asked Mark.

"Your father tells me there is only one smart bet, and that's Paul Wayne and Three."

"Then that's proof he hasn't lost his mind yet." Tootsie just looked on with a blank face.

"So do you ride the horse yourself, in the race?"

"No. I usually have a rider, but a man who owns a big horse farm all the way up in Kentucky hired him. So, I had to find someone new."

"How far did you have to go to find someone?"

"Oh, about five feet," said Mark, grinning as he pointed to his son, Trey.

Webb looked shocked. "Son, do you think you can handle that horse?"

"Yes sir. Only I don't think it, I know it."

Webb smiled a big smile and said, "I believe you're right."

Mark said, "He takes after his Grandpa Tootsie." Trey wasn't no bigger than a fly's fart. He had his momma's look with a shock of blonde hair. Paige was her daddy made over with blonde hair and blue eyes. Seeing them together was the perfect family picture.

When it came time for the foot race, people lined the street and sidewalk. The race was right down Main Street for a hundred yards. There were forty men and teenaged boys lined up to run. As the Judge said, "Mark, set..." the crowd was quiet. At the sound of the gun, the crowd roared to life as the runners took off. It wasn't even close. By halfway, Paul Wayne was fifteen feet ahead of the second-place man. By the end, he was thirty feet ahead. Webb watched the race with Rocky and Stoney from Howard's store. When he was done receiving his blue ribbon and $100, Paul Wayne walked to Webb's group. He was six feet, he had light hair, light eyes, and a calm smile.

Rocky said, "If I couldn't run no faster than that, I would have just stayed home."

Paul Wayne smiled and said, "You mean if you could run at all." Stoney and Webb cackled while Rocky muttered under his breath.

They introduced Webb and Paul Wayne, and Paul Wayne said, "I hear you're trying to recruit the family to become citizens of Arkansas."

"I don't know about recruiting, but I've sure put it out there."

"Where one goes, we all go, so you may have to make room."

Webb smiled and said, "Be happy to find you a spot."

People started heading to the outside of town, getting ready for the horse race. The race was three quarters of a mile long. There were some fine-looking horses, but none to compare with Three. As they lined the horses up, it was strange to see all those grown men sitting their saddles and right in the middle was little Trey sitting atop the big black. At the sound of the gun, you didn't know how he stayed on the horse. It was like he was shot out of a cannon. It was a close race for the first quarter, then at the half mile mark, Three was ahead by five lengths. At the finish, he was ten and a half lengths ahead and Trey was all smiles. Congratulations were made and bets paid. Since both races were so lopsided, people were betting big on second and third place. Webb won $100 on the ugliest horse in the race. He was a hairy gray horse with one ear missing.

One guy asked Webb, "How in the world did you know that ugly beast was gonna come in second?"

Webb smiled and said, "Anything that ugly has to be fast, especially if he wants to get to the women first."

The red-headed, freckle faced man next to them laughed and said, "That's a fact. That's how I got my wife. I outran the good-looking guys."

"Brandon Derrick, you are full of it as a Christmas goose."

Brandon smiled and said, "And then some."

That night, there was a dance and bake sale. The bake sale was before the dance began. Webb bought a homemade apple pie made by Sheryl at the Horned Toad, and, of course, a plate full of sugar cookies made by Mrs. Jinn and Hope. He quickly carried them to his hotel room and then headed back to the dance.

As he approached, a voice said, "Well, if it ain't the hero himself."

Webb looked at the group of four young men and said, "I'm sorry. Do I know you?"

"Of course you don't. Why, you're too high and mighty to associate with the likes of us."

"I'm sorry you feel that way, friend. How about we go inside, and I'll fix us some punch?"

"You hear that, boys? He wants to fix us some punch. It's too late for punch, Hero. How about we give you some punches?" He sneered the word punches.

The four toughs started to spread out until a voice said, "Now, Clay Dade, I can't believe you are fixin' to fight a man head on by yourself in a fair fight." The man named Clay turned as did Webb and standing there with the twins and Bull Head was Stacy Day and he was all smiles.

"This don't concern you none, Stacy. It's just a little disagreement between me and the hero."

"Well then, by all means, you and the hero need to settle your differences. We'll just stay here and watch you to make sure it's you alone." Every time he said, 'you', he said it with conviction. Well, folks, Clay didn't like that one bit. He thought him and his friends were gonna teach Webb a lesson. Stacy was right about facing a man in a fair fight. Clay was not one to be man enough to come at you from the front, and he was never alone. He liked the odds in his favor. Now, with a crowd gathering and no way out, he watched Webb take off his gun belt, and he did the same.

"Ok, Hero. I'll give you a chance to walk away right now before"

He couldn't say anything else because four punches, two jabs, one uppercut, and a roundhouse were smashing his lips. He tried to cover his face, which only helped Webb. His fifth punch knocked the air from Clay as it landed square in his gut. Punch number six was a shot to the kidneys. While lucky number seven was an uppercut to the chin that ended all Clay Dade's pain, because he was out like a light.

"Very well done, Webb. Since you seem to just now be warming up, would you like to have a go with one of the other three?" asked Stacy.

Webb looked at the three young men standing there with worry in their eyes and said, "I guess I can. Can any of you fight better than your friend?"

None spoke, so Stacy said, "I guess you have no takers. Boys, the dance is over for you three and your friend laying there sleeping. Get him up and all of you get gone. If I see you again tonight, I will assume you came to fight me... With that last word, there was a pistol in Stacy's hand, cocked and steady. Where it came from, nobody could say, but none of the three toughs were trying to figure it out because they were dragging Clay away.

"You look like you know how to use that thing."

"Well, Uncle Tuffy don't keep me around for my good looks and smile," said Stacy, showing that big white smile.

Webb stuck out his hand and said, "Thanks."

"Think nothing of it. I love a good, even fight, and Clay has never had one, so I thought we'd help him out."

"Let's go, boys, the women are waiting," said one twin. Webb strapped on his guns and they all went inside.

The rest of the night went off without a hitch. Webb tried to dance with several ladies, but Hope had staked her claim. Of course, all the men were sensitive to his discomfort. They only laughed and made comments for half the night.

The next morning, Webb attended Sunday service, where he listened to one of the best sermons he ever heard.

He was shaking hands with the preacher as he walked out when the preacher said, "Son, we are all real proud of you and so thankful you brought little Hope back to us."

"It was a pleasure, and I was glad to help, Brother Riddle."

"How did you like my sermon, Webb?"

"I tell you, Preacher, it was one of the best I ever heard a man give. Even if you are from Texas, I'll remember Reverend Butch Riddle for the rest of my days."

"Well, I guess I have to thank you, even if you are from Arkansas."

After Sunday service, the town was back to normal. The crowds went away, and normal life resumed. Webb said his goodbyes and promised to return. He loaded himself in the saddle and headed for the open sky and a land full of horses. As he rode away, Hope watched him go, but knew in her heart he would one day return.

Back in Arkansas, life was still being lived and nothing much had changed in his absence. The letter he had written to Andy had made it home, so Andy already had an idea of what was going on.

The word of Webb's journey spread through the hands and the town, so Webb retold the story many times to any who asked.

As Webb was preparing to leave the Pearl one day after lunch, a big voice and its Irish brogue greeted him. "Webb, me lad, I hear we almost lost you to the Comanche down in Texas. Tell me the tale and let me enjoy some excitement," said Big Irish Bob McGill.

Webb smiled as he heard the voice. "Bob, it's good to see you, and you know if I get you stirred up too much, Mrs. Gail is liable to give us both a knot on the head."

Bob looked at Webb with shock and said, "Bite your tongue, lad! It is I that is the boss, so there will be no knots upon this head."

Webb chuckled and asked, "Does Gail know you are the boss?"

Bob winked and said, "Can't say as she does, but I plan on telling her one day very soon, laddy." They both laughed and shook hands.

Webb told of his latest trip and his rescue of the young Hope Ashlee. They talked of life in Hell's Valley and how Bob and Gail were enjoying their new home. Bob shared the news of their second child, who was on the way and hoping it was a son to call Marcus. Their daughter, Michelle, was growing like a weed. Webb gave Bob a congratulation and told him to pass along his best to Gail.

Wendy walked up to Webb's table as he and Bob parted ways. "Wendy, that was the best meal I have ever had," said Webb.

"I might believe you if you didn't tell me that every single time you eat in here."

As Webb stood up to leave, the front door swung open. "Webb Wakefield, I am sick and tired of having to track you down every single time you come back from one of your trips. I have to hear all the bad news and good news alike from everyone but you. This time, I hear you got shot by a Comanche arrow and almost died on me. Then, I hear you saved some girl, and she wants to marry you. Well, just when did you think you were gonna come tell me your plans?" asked Dana.

"Dana, I was just getting ready to come see you, and it really wasn't anything. It was just one arrow, and it wasn't even deep."

"Well, how about this woman you saved and are planning to marry? I guess I'm just supposed to agree to all of this?"

Webb looked at Wendy for some help, and she said with a smile, "Don't look at me. I'm kind of curious myself."

"I ain't getting married, and the woman I saved was just a girl. She just has a crush on me, and why wouldn't she? I had just saved her life."

"You better not be getting any funny ideas about running off with another woman. Now, take my hand and walk me over to see Momma, and you can tell me all about this other girl."

Webb took Dana's hand, and out the door they went. As they left, William Turley said, "When is she gonna tell him she has been courting a boy from down Mule Shoe?"

Wendy laughed and said, "Not until she absolutely has to."

Over the next few years, Hell's Valley grew and expanded, as did the T2W. Andy bought more land, and the cattle and horses took hold and multiplied, just as God intended. New families moved into the area, and with Andy being the biggest source of beef, they all called on him for their cattle needs. This area in the southwest corner of Arkansas was thriving, and life was good.

Dane had met a strawberry blonde beauty who had him hearing wedding bells. With plans for a wedding, he and his bride to be were thinking of heading back east to Normalville. He had been corresponding with friends during the years of his absence. They assured him, if he returned, he'd be the town's choice for mayor. He had also given the idea of opening a new store some thought. So, with the wedding date approaching, he sat down with Andy to tell him the news.

"I can't thank you enough, old friend, and I won't ever forget the times we have had. Karen and I just think that going back east is what we need to do to start our new life."

"Well, Dane, I will tell you this. I could never have asked for a better partner, and you know if you ever decide to come back this way, you will always be welcome. I'm just happy you found Karen, and I'm glad to know she will keep you in line."

As a wedding gift, Andy paid for the entire wedding and outfitted their trip back to Normalville. As a going away gift to Andy, Dane secretly had Big Eddie make three new brands. The new brand was a WF2. Wakefield Farms times two.

When Dane gave him the new brands, Karen looked at Andy and said, "Now you hold on to the T2W brands. If Dane doesn't act right, I may take a frying pan to his head and send him back to Arkansas."

Andy laughed and said, "No ma'am. It's all over with now, he's your problem. You can beat him over the head and ruin your frying pan if you want, but you're stuck with him in Normalville." Everyone had a good laugh before the wagon pulled away and headed into the sun. The two friends waved goodbye one last time as the wagon crossed Dillard creek and crested a hill it would never again see.

Chapter Thirty-One

1876 Texas

Back in Texas, it seemed to Webb that every time he got home and was about ready to enjoy the good living of Arkansas, his father would send him on another mission. Some for business, others for pleasure. The pleasure was his father's, but Webb had to admit, he always seemed to enjoy the trips.

He had been back to Texas more times than he could even count. Being so close to the tri-state borders and the Nations, he was always just across one state line or the other. In all his trips to Texas, he had not been back to this area in almost four years. If his calculations were right, that was back in '72, when they made their last catch of horses. Two years before that, they had been in the area, and he had helped rescue little Hope Ashlee. He smiled at the memory, as he remembered the little girl and her insistence on marrying him when she was grown. He laughed and wondered what happened to the cute, brown-eyed girl.

"Let's see, Red," he said to his big Roan. "In '70, is when we picked up Billy Abney and Little Mark Reese."

Billy was a round-faced young man with black hair that had a touch of gray too early in life. He hired on with the T2W and made one heck of a hand. He had finally left half a year back and was living down on the Red River where he bought him a nice size spread and was doing fine for himself.

Reese was a top hand too. He was no bigger than five feet five inches and maybe one hundred thirty pounds, but he could stick to the back of a wild Bronc like he was glued to the saddle. Mark was a traveler. He didn't stay long on the ranch. After about a year, he had moved on and was now married, enjoying the family life. They had a small place of a few hundred acres, with a few cattle he had bought from Andy.

Webb knew that, if at all possible, he would try to find his old friend, Quanah.

The army was after him, hard. Quanah and his Quahadi had been kicking the Texas Rangers' hind ends for so long that the Rangers had to give in to the army. For the last several years, the army didn't do any better.

The President was livid and could not understand how one band of outlaw Indians could escape and humiliate the U.S. Army for so long. It was simple. This was another group of people the government was trying to force itself on, to rule and conquer. Just like the War Between the States, the Indian was the new south, and they were defying the high and mighty north. It didn't sit well in Washington and the White House. They pulled out all the stops.

The great buffalo that once roamed the plains in the millions were now decimated to a few thousand. They did this in the name of progress. Kill the buffalo and progressively you kill the Indian. You either kill them literally from starvation or kill their spirit enough to surrender and live under your control.

For a nation that started free to live and worship as free people. Who fought to assure a certain way of life for the people within its boundaries. It didn't take long to change their tune. Now, they kill women, children, and old people who can't run or fight. And why? Because the Indians, like the founding fathers of the United States of America, want to live free. Didn't sound like much progress to Webb.

The Palo Duro was a big place, and the entire U.S. Army couldn't find Quanah. Webb thought, after only four years, he was sure he could sniff out his old friend.

The town was visible, and he could tell it had grown four times since his visit in '70.

"All my old friends may be gone," he said to Red as they rode. He rode on, thinking of the past and hoping to see some familiar faces.

As he rode into town, he could see things had changed. Not for the worse, but things were different. A lot more people were coming and going, and things were moving faster. There was even a big banner hung across the main street announcing the fair and rodeo that was one week away.

His first stop was Tuffy's. He tied up Red at the hitch rail and knocked the dust from his chaps. He stepped in through the batwings as if he was back in time. Not a single thing had changed. The twins were sitting at the poker table and looked to be up, judging from the chips. Stacy was kicked back with his feet in a chair, grinning that easy grin.

"Well, I'll be hog-tied and dipped in honey. If it ain't Webb Wakefield," said Stacy.

"Stacy, Twins. I see ain't nothing changed much but the size of the town."

"Things are changing more than you know. You just can't see the changes yet."

"Oh, and what are the changes?"

"Vicki Lynn finally got Tuffy to sell this place. The new owner will be here within the month."

"You don't say?"

"I do, and it's not just Tuffy and Vicki Lynn. After you left, a seed was planted. You talked up Arkansas so much that now there's a handful of folks going with us."

"Us?" asked Webb.

Stacy grinned and said, "You don't think Tuffy's gonna leave us behind, do you?"

"I reckon not, but who else is making the trip?"

"Well, let's see. You got Howard over at the store. He has already sold out, but is helping the new owner until we leave."

"You got the Ray brothers and their cousin, Paul Wayne and, of course, the rest are following close behind. There's Boo Boo and Mrs. Sheryl too."

"You mean they ain't killed each other yet?" asked Webb.

"Not yet, but not from lack of trying."

"Tootsie and Mrs. Polly are making the trip with all their brood, Mark, Amy and their young'uns."

"You mean to sit here and tell me that all the people you just mentioned are planning to move to Arkansas in the next month because of me?"

Bradley and Brady laughed and said, "Tell him the best part." That cat that ate the canary grin on Stacy's face got even bigger.

"Like I said, you planted the seed, but the Normans have pushed the issue pretty hard the last few months."

"What in the world for? I didn't know Frank had any plans to ever leave Texas."

"Texas is where Mrs. Jinn is from, so he was just a transplant, I guess you'd say. Anyway, you made Arkansas sound so good, and then there is the wedding and all."

"Wedding? What wedding are you talking about?"

"Well, yours, of course," Stacy and the twins howled in laughter.

"I ain't married," said Webb.

"No, you sure ain't, not yet anyway." Webb looked lost.

"Don't tell me you done forgot you was due to get married this year, 'cause Hope sure ain't forgot."

"Are you three telling me that little Hope still has plans and thinks I'm going to show up for a marriage?"

"You're here, ain't you?" said Bradley.

"Yeah, I'm here, but only to check on a bull and some cattle. Not to get married!"

Brady laughed. "I'd like to see you trying to tell Hope that!"

"So, if I hadn't of showed up today, how do you think there would be a wedding?"

"If you hadn't showed up, then she had plans of tracking you down."

"Y'all are crazy as betsy bugs," said Webb.

Stacy chuckled and said, "He says we're crazy, and he just rode seven hundred miles to get married."

"I ain't getting married!"

"You better save all that energy for her 'cause you're gonna need it if you think you're gonna tell her you ain't getting hitched."

"I need a drink." Webb turned and walked towards the bar. Standing there with his arms crossed and grinning was Jeremy.

"I see you think it's funny," said a slightly annoyed Webb.

"Yep."

"Well, it ain't. By the way, what happened to your face?" Jeremy's face was yellowish green with enough black, blue, and purple to tell he had a run in with something.

Tuffy came out from the back just then and said, "Webb, son, how are you?"

"I'm good, Tuffy. How about yourself?"

"Can't complain none. Now that I'm leaving this dry, dusty Texas plain, I'm getting better."

"Stacy and the twins just told me about your departure."

"Is there still room for us, you think?" asked Tuffy.

"I'm sure we can squeeze you in somewhere."

"Good, 'cause in another month, there's a string of us coming."

"Well, I will be gone by then, or I would lead the way."

"You mean you and Hope are leaving that soon?"

"Not you too?"

"What do you mean, not me too?"

"Those three heathens over there have informed me that Hope still thinks we're to be married."

"I figured that's why you're here."

"I'm here for cattle and nothing else. I think everyone has done lost their minds."

"Didn't you tell her you was gonna marry her?"

"Well, technically yes, but that was 6 years ago. She was just a twelve-year-old kid with a crush. I didn't really mean it. I was just trying to be nice."

"Well, she still thinks you're to be married, either here or when she finds you in Arkansas. She sure plans to marry you."

"I can't believe it. You know, I really can't believe it. I was just agreeing with her so I wouldn't hurt her feelings."

"Son, for six years she has thought of nothing but you. She thinks a promise was a promise. What do you think you're gonna do to her heart and feelings now?"

"I can't get married, Tuffy."

"Why not?"

"I just can't. I mean, this is nuts."

"Wait 'till you see her, then come tell me that."

Jeremy giggled and said, "Yea, wait 'till you see her."

Webb said, "Give me a beer. Heck, I may even need a shot of whiskey."

Tuffy gave him a beer and said, "One beer. After that, it's milk for you."

"Now how in the world did you remember that?"

"You're one of my boys, son. How could I forget? Now, what do you think of my baby boy's face there?"

"Yeah, I noticed that. What in the world hit you? A wagon?"

Tuffy said, "Close enough. 'Bout three weeks ago there were some cowboys in here blowing off some steam. One of them got a little too rowdy and started picking fights, so my boy tossed him out on his head. He didn't much like that, so in he comes five minutes later with a two-by-four. He up and calls Jeremy's name and when he turned around, WHAM! Right across the face. He hit him so hard it broke the board. I think it would've killed a normal man."

"You're telling me you got hit in the face with a two-by-four?"

Jeremy nodded, "Yep."

Tuffy chimed back in and said, "That ain't even the best part. After the boy hits him, Jeremy ain't done so much as to rock back on his heels and just look at him. The boy leaned over and looked behind Jeremy. He asked the boy what he was looking for and he said, "I'm trying to see what's holding you up!" Then he dropped what was left of the board, ran off, and we ain't seen him since."

"I can't believe he didn't kill you."

Jeremy just shrugged and said, "Well, it hurt pretty good." Webb just shook his head in wonder.

"Now, son, I'm telling you, when a man gives his word, he has to honor it. If the shoe was on the other foot, and you had plans to marry her, and she up and ran off and married another, what would you do?"

"That's just it. I ain't married to nobody else."

"Well then, what if you had plans, but she decided against it?"

"I guess we would talk it over."

"That's all I'm saying, son. Talk to the child before you decide."

"Yes sir, I guess you're right. I will just have to talk to her." Webb finished his beer and left.

As he walked out, Stacy hollered, "Hurry back, Lover Boy!"

Webb made his way to the Horned Frog, where he was greeted by Boo Boo and Sheryl. They all talked about the upcoming trip and possible locations for good land.

After dinner, he paid for his meal and as he turned to walk out, the most beautiful girl he had ever laid eyes on walked through the café doors. She had gorgeous long brown hair, brown eyes, perfect skin, and small ears. When she smiled at him, he thought he had died and gone to Heaven. He smiled, tipped his hat, and said, "Ma'am."

As he walked by, he felt her stop, and she said, "Webb Wakefield, is that all you have to say to me after six years?"

Right then, it hit him. He turned and looked into those eyes. They were the same big brown doe eyes he had seen six years before. It was Hope Ashlee.

"Hope? Is that you?"

"Of course, it's me, Webb. Have I changed that much?"

"I'll say. Boy, the last time I saw you, you were just a twelve-year-old little girl. Now, well I, uh, you're uh." He was lost for words.

She smiled and said, "And now I am eighteen and a grown woman. You do remember what you said about when I turned eighteen?"

"Well, yes I do, and I guess we better talk."

"Webb, I have waited six years to see you again, and I knew you would come back. I knew in my heart, no matter what happened in life, you would come back to marry me."

"Hope, I don't really know what to say."

"What do you mean?"

"Hope, I'll be honest. I have thought of you on several occasions. I've even told of you to my friends at home but always as that twelve-year-old little girl I rescued. Not as a... I mean, not like a... umm."

"You mean you have never thought of me as your future wife?"

"Well, no."

"Webb, do you believe in fate?"

"I guess I do."

"Then why do you think you came back here?"

"I came back to check on some cattle."

"Then why are you not married after all these years?"

"Well, I don't guess I ever found the right woman."

"No, Webb. You're not married for the same reason you're back here and it's not cattle. It's fate."

Webb just looked at her. "Webb, true love knows no bounds. You can run, try to hide, but it doesn't do any good. Sooner or later, it's right back in front of you. I have had young men callers and admirers, but I always knew I was bound to you. No matter what they said or promised, I knew I could not forsake my heart. I love you, Webb, and whether you think it or believe it, you love me too. That's the real reason you're here."

Webb was lost for words, but more than that, he was lost in her beauty.

"Well, I'll be doggone. Jinn, would you look here." Webb turned to see Frank and Jinn Norman.

"Frank, Mrs. Jinn. Nice to see you again."

"I see you two found each other," Jinn said with a smile.

"Umm, yes ma'am. I was in town to look at some cattle and we just ran into each other."

"Oh posh. Young man, you can't fight fate."

"Yes ma'am. I mean, no ma'am. I'm beginning to wonder about that myself," said Webb.

"Come in and join us for lunch," said Frank.

"I would, sir, but I just finished eating."

"Then how about six o'clock tonight? We'll have dinner at the house, and we can all catch up."

"Yes sir, I'd love to. Thank you."

Hope turned to go into the café but stopped to say, "She's right, you know? You can't fight it." She then walked away.

Webb paused as he turned and started for the store when he looked over at Tuffy's. There, standing in every door and window, was Tuffy, Jeremy, the twins and, of course, Stacy with a big ol' grin as he mouthed the words, "Lover Boy."

Webb's trip to the store was a pleasant trip. He ran into Rocky and talked with him and Howard. Of course, everyone mentioned the fact he and Hope were to be married. He just changed the subject and didn't try to argue. They talked about the upcoming rodeo, and Howard showed him the new rifle that was first prize in the shooting contest. Webb assured them he'd be entering that. After more discussion about locations for their future in Arkansas, Webb said his goodbyes and promised to see them again. He made his way to the livery, stabled his horse, and went to the hotel.

CHAPTER THIRTY-TWO

At six o'clock, Webb found himself nervous and at the front door of the Norman's. All day, he thought of nothing except Hope. Good Lord was she beautiful! During the meal, talk was of the past six years and of locations for the Norman's future in Arkansas.

Webb was told that Jerry turned sixteen and had joined the army. The army loved having him because he knew so much about the area, and right now, they were covering as much of it as possible looking for Quanah. Webb heard the army had orders to do what was necessary to put an end to Quanah and the Comanche nation. Anything necessary meant, of course, killing or rather slaughtering men, women, and children. Webb decided then that he would indeed try to find his old friend, Quanah.

After dinner, Hope asked Webb if he would like to join her on the swing. They had a pleasant conversation about what the other had done for the past six years. Hope then told Webb's that his old friend was his biggest rival.

"Who is my old friend?"

"Clay Dade," she said, smiling.

Webb grinned and said, "You heard about that, huh?"

"Everyone did. He tried everything to assure me you would never return. I, of course, am polite and said I guess we'll see, and now, look, here you are."

"Hope, I know I told you six years ago we would marry, but well, I just don't know."

"Webb, are you a Christian?"

"Yes, I am."

"Then do you believe God has a plan for us all?"

"I do."

"Do you also believe he is the creator of everything? That in his perfect purpose, he has one person chosen for each of us?"

"Yeah, I guess so."

"Then you just said it yourself. That's fate, and it's true love. The good Lord brought you back here." Webb just stared at her.

"I love you, Webb Wakefield, and you and I will marry. If something happens, that should keep us apart in this life, I promise we will be together in the next. I will never stop loving you, nor will I ever give up. If you're not ready now, then I will wait, but no one other than you will ever be mine."

"I think I better go, Hope."

"If you must, but remember, true love is forever."

As he turned to walk away, he said to himself, "Thank God Dwayne ain't here for this."

For the next three days, Webb revisited old friends and enjoyed meeting new people. He decided to wait until after the rodeo to head on to Lampasas to check on the bull and cattle. After that, he hoped to find out something about Quanah.

Those three days he spent every night at the Norman's for supper. After which he and Hope always spent the rest of the evening in the swing, talking about life but never again discussing marriage. He asked if she would accompany him to the dance after the rodeo.

She replied, "Well, it took you long enough to ask."

"I guess it did," he said, smiling and blushing.

On the day of the rodeo, there were people everywhere. Booths were selling cakes, pies, and other desserts, and there were games for the kids and adults.

The first big event was a shoot-out for the new Winchester Model 1876 Centennial. There were so many men entered, they set up 5 groups of 15 to compete. When each group got to one winner, those five shot for the championship. Webb kept seeing a man eyeing him, but could not place him, not until he said,

"It's so good to have you back, hero."

"I thought we got past that hero bit six years ago, Clay?"

"Oh, I'm just having a little fun, hero. Don't get bent out of shape."

Webb smiled and said, "You're right Clay, if I remember correctly the last time I got bent out of shape it didn't end well for you."

Clay turned red. "I've tried to talk some sense into Hope, but I guess you showing up has ruined that."

"Believe me Clay, you may be good enough for a dance or buggy ride, but good girls don't marry guys like you."

"Guys like me? What's that mean?"

"You know, Clay. No account losers."

Clay was burning mad but didn't want it to show so he gave a smile and said, "Well, I guess we'll see who the loser is after today, won't we?"

"Yes sir, we sure will."

In the end, the shoot-out came down to Webb and Clay. With each shot, Clay got madder but covered it with his fake smile. "I tell you what Clay. It looks like we could go on forever like this. How about we strike a match at fifty yards?"

"What do you mean?"

"I mean, one of us shoot for all the marbles. One shot, win or lose. I'll even let you shoot first," Webb said, smiling with confidence.

"So, you're saying if I can light a match with my bullet at fifty yards, I win?"

"Yep, but if you miss, you lose."

"You can't even see a match at fifty yards. No wonder you want me to shoot."

"Ok then, I'll shoot if that's what you want."

Clay grinned. "Sure, I'll go with that. One shot, one match, fifty yards, win or lose."

The match was stuck in the top of a block of wood fifty yards away. Clay was right, you couldn't see it. Webb raised his rifle, took a deep breath, let it out slowly, and squeezed the trigger. The gun jumped with the sound, and just for an instant, there was a flash at the piece of wood. A boy ran the fifty yards, grabbed up the log, and came back. He held up the log for all to see, and there was the match. Instead of a red lucifer, it was now black from the ignition of the flame. The judge declared Webb the winner, and with it came the new 1876 Centennial. Webb accepted the gun and got to present the second-place prize to Clay himself... a free lunch from the Horned Frog, one coupon good for anytime.

As Webb handed the coupon to Clay, he said, "Like I said earlier, Clay, a no-account loser." Clay wadded up the coupon, threw it on the ground, and stormed off.

"Didn't want that trash in my place no way," said Boo Boo.

Webb walked over to the Norman's to show off his new prize and standing with them in an Army blue uniform was young Jerry.

"Hello, Mr. Wakefield," said Jerry, with his hand extended.

Before he even knew what he was saying, Webb said, "Jerry, if we're going to be brothers-in-law, you'll have to call me Webb."

The look on everyone's face was surprise, but none more than Webb. "I mean... um... I guess what I'm saying is... um... if it's alright with you, Frank?"

"Son, I told you six years ago you would make a fine member of this family, and nothing has changed."

"Will you still have me, Hope?"

"Webb Wakefield, like I said, you can't fight fate."

The rest of the day was a blur for Webb. He and Hope danced just about every dance together. The only breaks for Webb were when Stacy or one twin would ask if they could cut in on "Lover Boy".

After the dance, Webb walked home with the Norman's. "Webb, said Jerry, after church service tomorrow, I'd like you to come home and have lunch with us. I have something I want to talk to you about." Webb agreed, and they said their goodbyes.

Before he left, Hope asked, "What made you change your mind?"

"I didn't change my mind, Hope. My heart made that decision for me."

She looked up at him and said, "Tell me you love me."

"I love you, Hope Ashlee, for the rest of my life." He leaned in and kissed her. He knew right then, no matter what, he would never love another.

After Sunday service, Webb went home with the Norman's. As they approached the house, they noticed a man in the same Army blue uniform standing on the porch, waiting for them.

As they walked up to the porch, Jerry said, "I would like to introduce y'all to my Captain, Grant Herndon." The men shook hands all around and the women went in to fix dinner. "Webb, I didn't say this before because I didn't want anyone to hear. I've told Captain Herndon about you and your relationship with Quanah, and he wanted to talk to you in private."

"We are getting ready to put pressure on Quanah, so they gave us some time off. Once we start after him, we have been told we will not stop until every Comanche gives up, dies, or kills us," said Captain Herndon.

"So that's it, huh? The army is just gonna hunt down and kill women and children?"

"I don't like it any more than you. That's why I'm telling you. I know you can find him, and if you find him, maybe he'll listen to you."

"That's if I can find him."

"You can find him. If you can't I'm sure you can get close enough that he can find you."

"He saved my sister just as much as you did, and I know that. I don't want to pay him back with death, especially women and children," said Jerry.

"Do you have any idea where I should start? Palo Duro is a big place."

"As a matter of fact, I do, and it just so happens the Army doesn't." Jerry explained where he thought the band was hidden and Webb just laughed.

"What's so funny?" asked Jerry.

"It just so happens that I think I know where he is." Webb knew the area was the same place he delivered the horses six years ago. It was the perfect hiding place, and you could not see the valley below from above. There was no way possible for the Army or anyone to come at them more than one at a time, because the trail was only wide enough for one horse.

Webb decided he would go to Quanah first. From there, he would check on the cattle. His friend was more important than cattle any day.

"Ok Captain, I'll leave at first light and see if I can find him."

"I'll tell the Army I think he's in a place in the opposite direction to make sure we don't happen to stumble up on you while you're trying to help us," said Captain Herndon.

The women called them for dinner, and they spent the rest of the day with pleasantries.

Webb made plans to leave at first light. He told Hope what he planned and promised to return as fast as possible.

"What if something happens?"

"Were you this worried for the last six years?" Webb said, smiling.

"No. I knew you would be back."

"Then why worry now?"

"Because you don't know how bad it is with the Comanche. You have been gone six years and feelings could have changed between you and them."

"They didn't change with you."

"That's different. With the Comanche, they have killed so many settlers and travelers. We have killed many of their people in return. They are mad and desperate. Just because you say Quanah won't hurt you doesn't mean another warrior won't." He tried to smile and reassure her he would be fine, but her worry continued. "Just please promise you'll come back to me."

"I promise, Hope. I will be back."

"And if not?" She asked with tears in her eyes.

"Then it's like you said that first day I came back. If I don't get to spend this life with you, I'll be waiting for you in the next." With that, he kissed her.

Webb was in the store loading up with things he might need when Stacy came in. "Amigo, you may want to watch your back? Clay ain't real happy with the outcome of the shootin' match. Plus, you took his girl, or who he thought was his girl."

"Well, if he wants me, tell him I'll be back in ten days. We can settle up then."

"Where you off to?"

"I'm going to see an old friend, then I have to check on those cattle."

"So, you're gonna try to talk to Quanah?"

"I am, if I can find him."

"All I can say is, be careful and vaya con dios, amigo."

"Thanks. If I don't return, say hello to Arkansas for me."

"I will."

Stacy turned to walk away, and Webb said, "I'm serious about telling Clay what I said. As soon as I'm back, we can settle this."

"I'll tell him. I'll do it in front of everyone so he can't crawfish out of it."

Webb got his supplies loaded and, instead of waiting for the morning, Webb set out on his journey.

Chapter Thirty-Three

He fried bacon and made biscuits the first night and made enough for the next day so he wouldn't have to stop for lunch or make a fire the second night. He rode hard that next day, stopping only to water his horse. As planned, he made a cold camp, stopping only after dark. When he woke the next morning, he waited until daylight so he could make a small fire and cook some more biscuits and bacon for the day and the next night's supper. After the food was cooked, he was in the saddle and gone again. The next day, he rode cautiously towards the end of the day. He had been riding hard and made good time.

He didn't want to enter the canyon without at least seeing an Indian, because once committed to the path, there was no turning back. If Hope was right about another warrior, then he wanted to be safe rather than sorry. He figured he was about two miles from the canyon entrance, so he stopped, made a fire, and put coffee on, just in case he had a visitor. Night came and nothing. He started thinking he should have gone on to the canyon.

He put out the fire, laid out his blankets, and said, "Red, get ready, 'cause in the morning, we may get in to more than we can handle." He closed his eyes and let sleep welcome him, and his dreams take over.

He suddenly woke to a snort from Red. He looked at Red with his ears pricked, looking at Webb. "What is it, partner? Is there something out there?"

A voice from the darkness said, "UAV."

Webb turned to see only a dark figure and said, "Quanah!"

There were four warriors with Quanah that Webb didn't notice. The fact he didn't notice them wasn't what worried him. It was that they all had their faces painted black as night with slashes of crimson red. He knew they were painted for war.

"Quanah, I was hoping I could find you. I'm worried about my friend and his people."

"I am glad you are here. The blue coats are trying to force us onto the reservation. My people are starving. We are always on the move, so there is no time to hunt and supply meat for the people."

"Is that why you're painted for war? You plan on fighting?"

"It is the only way. We must fight to give our women, our children, and our old elders a chance to flee and survive."

"What will you do when they can no longer run?"

"We will all fight!" proclaimed Quanah.

"If you're killed? Then what happens? What happens to the Comanche nation?"

"The young ones will carry on," said Quanah.

Webb quickly said, "No, not this time, my friend. The blue coats have orders to kill everyone, including the women and children." Quanah stood silently as Webb continued. "The government wants you to be civilized. There will be no more of this," said Webb as he waved his hands out toward the plains. "You are the last great chief of the Comanche. If you decide to give up, then it shows you are greater than the others."

"Why do you say this?" asked Quanah.

"Because they have never caught you. They have never out fought you. You have kept you, your warriors, and your people one step ahead, always. If you agree to live on the reservation, then you not only will have led your people as a nation of warriors, but you will also lead them into a new way of life."

"The reservation is no way for a warrior to live," demanded Quanah.

"You're right, but the days of war are over." replied Webb.

"If it were you, would you give up?" asked Quanah.

Webb said, "No. If it was me, I would fight because it is the way of a warrior. If it was just you and your warriors, I would say fight. But your women, children, and old ones are not warriors. They need a great chief to lead them in the next way of life. If you die and go to the great spirit in the sky, who will lead them? Who will protect them? Already, the Comanche sing songs and tell great stories of battles of their chief, Quanah. All the whites from here to the great father in Washington know about Quanah, the great war chief and leader of his people. Why not go to the reservation free to live and lead your people?"

Quanah stood silent in thought for a moment and said, "You are truthful in what you say, and you speak the truth in that you would fight. That is why I listen to your words. I will council with the old ones and my warriors."

"I think that is why you are wise and why your people look to you as their leader." Said Webb.

"Come, you will go with us," said Quanah.

Webb packed his horse, and they left for the canyon. All the warriors were on foot and clearly Webb was wrong... there were more than five. There were at least twenty more in the dark.

"What took you so long to come to me?" asked Webb.

"It was your horse. You are always on a gray horse. When Little Bear spotted you, he said to me, "I think it is UAV, but he does not have a gray horse." So, we waited for the darkness."

Webb laughed and said, "Well, this is the first horse I've ever owned that wasn't gray. I guess I'll just have to make sure I find another gray before I come again to visit."

Daylight came and with it much counsel. Quanah repeated what Webb said. There was much debate, but in the end, it was ultimately up to Quanah.

"How long can you stay?" asked Quanah.

"I must leave today. I need to look at some cattle while I'm here and then back to Arkansas."

"How long will the blue coats give us to decide?"

"Not long," said Webb.

They talked more as the women prepared food, and they ate.

After their meal, Quanah said, "Come. I have a gift." They walked to a small group of horses where Quanah pointed to a beautiful gray. He had black socks, a black mane, black tail, and a face that was so light gray it almost looked white. It was the best-looking gray Webb had ever seen.

"Thank you, friend," said Webb.

"It is my finest war horse. It is for a true warrior." Webb was grateful. He proudly swapped his saddle from Red to the gray.

"Thank you, Quanah. I hope to see you again my friend, and remember, a true warrior is there to protect his people," said Webb.

Quanah assured him, "I understand." Webb nodded and rode away with Red in tow.

Webb made camp the first night, about thirty miles away from Quanah's village. He had a hat-sized fire lighting his camp where he made biscuits to go with the meat the women in the village gave him. They had so little and were near starving, yet they prepared him a meal and insisted he take food when he left.

If only the world could see them for the generous people they were. Yes, they lived different lives. Yes, they were known for violence. They lived for thousands of years fighting other Indians. It was how they measured the status of their warriors. They raided for horses, and the better horse thief you were, the higher your status within the group. Their lives were so different. It was this that scared the whites as a people.

What did we say about them? We called them murderers, heathens, and red devils. What was our answer for them? Kill them.

These people lived off the land for thousands of years. The same land we were destroying in the short time we were here. Cities in the east were being built where forests once ruled. The population was growing so fast, people had nowhere to go but west. The west was too big and too open for the taking to be stopped by the Indian.

What if they would just stop living as heathens and red devils? Then our opinions would change, we say.

Webb's thoughts went to the Five Civilized Tribes. Did we treat the peaceful Indians so much better? We took their land and wiped out entire tribes. We killed entire civilizations. Tribes that are forever gone. Extinction by our own hands.

The civilized and peaceful Indians were treated so well for not fighting us for their lands that we rewarded them with more death. We marched them halfway across the U.S. When that wasn't enough we blessed them with blankets filled with disease that killed thousands more. Yet we wonder why these last people, these wild heathens of the plains, fight. Maybe because they're smart enough to see a wolf in sheep's clothing. Heathens, Red Devils? Yes, and are we so much better?

Webb slept a restless sleep and woke early the next morning. He was back in the saddle with the gray, burning up the miles, thinking of Quanah and of Hope.

He stopped along a narrow creek to give the horses a needed rest with fresh water and rich grass. With his thoughts now completely focused on Hope, he gave a smile and then a little laugh that broke the silence of the world. Both horses turned and looked at him.

"What? Like you two ain't never seen a man in love." He said to the horses.

A good hour's rest and he was gone again. He slowed the pace, letting the gray mosey along the trail while he thought of Hope and their talks.

He was honest with her when she asked if he had a woman at home or anywhere else. "No. I don't have a steady girl. Never have really." Even though he had been in saloons all across Texas, Louisiana, and Arkansas. He had, of course, known a few bar girls. She assured him that the past was just that. The only thing that mattered was from that day forward because, as she had said, true love knows no bounds. He smiled to himself and said, "Gray, I do believe she is a keeper."

A horse whinnied from somewhere on the rocks. Webb turned in time to see the flame from a gun and hear the shot. In an instant, he was flung from the saddle as the bullet struck his head.

He never felt the pain of the bullet or the shock from his body hitting the ground, nor did he feel the pain of the second shot as it went in his back.

He did not hear Red chomping on grass a few feet away because his life was pouring out of his body from the two bullet holes, one to the head and one to the back.

As Webb lay there dying, he didn't even have thoughts of Hope. There was only darkness and then the gray was gone back west into the setting of the sun.

Printed in the USA
CPSIA information can be obtained
at www.ICGtesting.com
LVHW091746121123
763661LV00066B/2214